MAGE KNIGHT™

Rebel Thunder

Rebel Thunder

BILL McCAY

BALLANTINE BOOKS • NEW YORK

Mage Knight 1: Rebel Thunder is a work of fiction. Names, places, and incidents either are products of the author's imagination or are used fictitiously.

A Del Rey® Book
Published by The Random House Ballantine Publishing Group

www.delreydigital.com
www.wizkidsgames.com

ISBN 0-345-45968-7

Maps by WizKids, LLC

Manufactured in the United States of America

First Edition: May 2003

OPM 10 9 8 7 6 5 4 3 2 1

With thanks to Don Maass, my agent,
and to Janna Silverstein, my editor—
two pillars of reason and patience
during a pretty chaotic time.

And, of course, to Mom.

Hi, Mom!

Historian's Note: This novel takes place in 419 Tz.

Prologue

"KEEPS getting worse." Snow spat a mouthful of smoke-flavored grit as he shifted behind the cracked block of stone he used as a vantage point. Brisk winds lifted sand from the surrounding drylands, mixing it with smoke from the burning city of Caero. Instead of clear desert air, Snow confronted a featureless haze that barely let him see halfway down the hill.

All he could make out was a shifting curtain of dull red some miles off—the conflagration devouring the city.

"Times like this, I could wish for one of those farseeing Magestone trinkets the Imperials use," Snow groused. "Or maybe you could invent something to take care of the job, Sigwold."

A laugh emerged from the quarry mouth behind him, then so did Sigwold Tinker. He was slender for a Dwarf, which meant that his barrel chest was about as burly as Snow's, though he barely came up to the human's breastbone.

"I've been busy with more destructive things." Sigwold cast a dismissive glance to the crossbow he carried. "If you're going to wish, why not ask for a hundred-hand escort armed with black powder weapons guarding the barrels in the cave inside?" He paused, taking in the lurid light show on the plains below. "Or that all the Imperial pigs vanish from the face of the Land?"

"Won't happen," Snow replied. "I've wished that very thing four solid years now." He ran a finger along the ornamented head of the broadaxe he carried. Dwarven work, of a skill and forging that human craftsmen could never match. And that was just a simple weapon. Sigwold's bow was a mechanism of marvelous complexity and strength. Yet the Dwarf considered it a bare toy compared to the arms he'd been working on.

Yes, Sigwold might be considered slim by Dwarven standards, but he had deft hands and an equally adroit brain. He'd won acclaim among his fellow Dwarf smiths and fabricators for his inventions. His contributions had helped them create a whole new order of intricate but powerful nonmagical implements of war. Weapons to make the Atlantean Empire pay for a host of crimes.

Snow looked off toward the shrouded destruction in the distance. "Many human folk outside the boundaries looked on the Empire as the great equalizer. They thought the Imperials' Magestone Technomancy would help us against the more magically gifted races."

So his father had believed, and that belief had been the death of him.

"A nice thought," Sigwold growled. "So long as you don't live near any Magestone."

Snow felt the muscles in his shoulders tighten. Wide shoulders—miner's shoulders. But then, he'd spent his last growth spurt working fourteen-hour shifts in a Magestone mine. Imperial diviners had discovered a major seam of the crystal that powered the magic of the Atlantis Guild in the fields where Snow's people made their living. As it turned out, his home village, Linzfarne, had stood at the confluence of several ley lines. And where the magical currents conjoined, Magestone was often to be found. Very soon after, the Atlantean army had descended on Linzfarne.

"We did, you know," Snow said, half to Sigwold and half to himself. "We lived near Magestone."

"You never mentioned that before," Sigwold said.

Snow looked at the Dwarf. They had nothing to do but wait, so he continued, dulling the anxiety with conversation. "All our fields disappeared into that great hole in the ground." He turned his gaze back to the distant haze, unwilling to betray too much feeling. "It ate my family, and all the farm-folk in the area. People sickened from the raw Magestone they had to dig up. But my father clung to his crazy ideas."

He smashed a fist into the rock in front of him—like trying to get an idea out of his father's thick skull. "And Pa clung to Linzfarne, even after it turned from a human steading into a spot where only Dwarves could live."

Snow glanced at his companion and cleared his throat. "No offense meant."

"None taken," Sigwold replied grimly. "The wild Magestone doesn't kill us; it's nothing but the truth. That's why my folk are valuable to the Empire." He spat. "Of course, whatever the wild Magestone gives off kills every other living thing and turns animals into monsters. And if *they* don't get us, there's always the overwork and the slave-drivers to take care of it."

His clever hands clenched around the crossbow. "My great-grandsire was taken by the Imperial offal, so slavery is all my family has known." The Dwarf stepped over to his fellow guard. "I don't know which is worse, young Snow—to be hunted and used like a thing, or to have your hopes and spirit killed before your body. But now we have the tools to change things."

Snow grinned. A typical Dwarvish response, to think in terms of tools. But his smile dimmed as he was reminded of the mind behind the tools. "Where *is* Sarah?" he said, putting into words the thought that had been nagging them both. "I knew she shouldn't have gone into the city."

"As if you or anyone else could stop her," Sigwold snorted. Snow couldn't argue that. But he could worry. *The problem is, without Sarah Ythlim's leadership, the Rebellion might die with a whimper before it's even born.* He sighed. *Where* is *the woman?*

The roughcast adobe wall scraped against Rikka's side as she crept to the corner. The buildings of Caero were made of nonflammable mud-brick. But the structural elements were made of river reeds, twisted together, dried, and tarred. A touch of flame, and they blazed up like torches, as Rikka and her companion had already discovered.

Plentiful flame was all too available, thanks to the Empire's Incendiary Golems.

The reins in Rikka's hands tightened as the horses she led halted, trembling. In spite of the damp wrappings around their eyes and noses, the animals detected smoke. Making quiet, soothing noises Rikka gentled the horses and brought them closer to the end of the wall. Then she peered around it.

A squad of Imperials patrolled the main thoroughfare a block away. They carried the short spears and crossbows the Atlanteans used in close city fighting. In the midst of the armored soldiers strode a robed figure, firelight gleaming off the Magestone jewel set in his brow. An apprentice wizard, controlling a Golem for the troops—or, perhaps, searching for Rebels . . .

Rikka's lips reflexively skinned back from her gritted teeth. Her right hand went to the hilt of a throwing knife.

But the light touch of a hand on Rikka's shoulder stopped her. The loss of a low-level initiate would scarcely hurt the Atlantis Guild. Rikka had a weightier responsibility—getting Sarah Ythlim out of the city.

A difficult enough task if Sarah were healthy and whole. Instead, she sat half-crouched in her saddle, favoring her right side. That was what had taken the brunt of the force as a warehouse wall had suddenly collapsed in a rush of flaming debris.

Rikka had managed to free Sarah from under tumbled brick before the burning reed-bundles had roasted her. But Sarah had been hurt, slowed. They'd had to get horses. Now they dodged to evade the net that the Imperials were trying to draw around this part of the city.

The larger streets ran thick with Imperial patrols. Still worse were the flame-wielding Golems. As Rikka watched, the Imperial mage summoned one of the Magestone-powered machines. The mage's shaven head barely reached the hulking shoulders of the construct. Indeed, the Golem's own head was lost in the upper-body superstructure, where fuel tanks were built in for the flamecasters in the machine's hands. Metal feet thudded against the hard earth of the street as the Golem moved to face its master. Its bronze body was stained and streaked with soot. It stopped mere feet from the mage, who mouthed something and gestured.

The Golem immediately moved off in the indicated direction, its deliberate gait eating distance quickly, until it disappeared.

Rikka hoped it was a sign. The Golem was moving into the wind, away from the walls of fire. Perhaps the Imperials had finally become aware that their flamecasting was threatening the entire city. If the searchers also had to fight the flames, the Rebels' chances of escape increased.

With renewed energy, Rikka went back to picking a route through the helter-skelter back alleys. She couldn't check her course by the stars—smoke clouds obscured the skies. She could only trust that the wind hadn't shifted as she guided herself and Sarah away from flames and prowling soldiers.

Wherever she could, Rikka refreshed the water on the sacking that enshrouded the faces of their restless horses. After what seemed like an eternity of tramping, the smoke grew thinner—the houses farther apart.

They had escaped Caero, and just in time. Sarah's lopsided riding stance had grown more dramatic, and she clung to her saddle with a death-grip. Rikka swung onto her own horse and brought it close, offering what support she could.

Progress was slow, and Rikka didn't like the sound of Sarah's short, gasping breaths. They had to cast about to find their group's rendezvous point, an abandoned quarry south of the city. The only consolation for Rikka was that they'd be as hard to spot as the shelter they were looking for. Between the trail dust that coated their traveling leathers and the haze in the air, they were practically invisible.

Snow's eyes stung—whether from smoke, wind-borne grit, or simple fatigue, he could not say. None of the group that had gone into the city had returned. They'd had no word about Sarah.

As he maintained his watch, Snow spun fruitless plans. Maybe one of them should go into the city in search of some news.

Brilliant plan, his brain mocked with Sigwold's voice. *The way things are down there, the first thing the Imperials will do with likely lads—or Dwarves—is bundle them off to the mines.*

Even so, Snow began to think the risk preferable to standing and waiting in this nerve-tearing ignorance.

He was about to voice his plan to Sigwold when Rikka suddenly appeared out of the murk downhill. She barely paid attention to where she rode, twisting back to look across her horse's rump.

Then a second horse appeared, the rider precariously canted in the saddle.

Sarah!

"Sigwold!" Snow cried, bolting from behind his boulder to charge down the slope. Halfway down, he braked himself to avoid spooking the horses. From the way Sarah swayed in her saddle, that could be a worse disaster than what they were facing now.

Reaching them, he took the reins from Rikka, then reached up to support Sarah.

Her face was pale, drawn with pain. "I'm afraid the Imperials interrupted our business," she said.

"They nearly surrounded us—we had to scatter." Rikka pointed to Sarah's side. "A burning building collapsed—"

Snow interrupted the flow of information. "Can you get down?" he asked Sarah.

She gave him a dirty look, but when Sarah tried to dismount, she nearly collapsed with pain. Snow caught her around the hips and gently shifted her from the saddle. Then he began carrying her up to the quarry opening. She braced herself against his shoulder, her upper body curled in pain.

Sigwold had taken the lookout post behind the boulder, his crossbow at the ready in case there was pursuit.

"None follow," Rikka called up to him. "But Sarah was hurt as we got away." She looked around. "The others?"

"There are no others," Sigwold said shortly. He all but glared at Snow. "Get her into the cave in the back and start stirring up a fire."

Then to Rikka, "Leave those horses and start searching the supplies. See what simples we've brought along with us."

The Dwarf's clever hands were as adept at medicine as they were with this strange new art of technology. By the time Snow and Rikka had finished their tasks and bedded down the horses, Sigwold had Sarah resting comfortably enough in the cavelike recess in the rear of the quarry.

"The burns are worrisome, but not crippling," he reported. "A little salve took care of them."

His bearded face assumed a grimmer aspect. "Several ribs were broken, however. Our Sarah is lucky she didn't pop a lung."

Sarah responded with a dismissive gesture. "Well, you've greased me and bound me up. If the others haven't rejoined us by daybreak, we'll head off for Atlantis on our own. If needs must, we can recruit along the way—"

"Not so, Lady." Sigwold's contradicting words rode over Sarah's.

Her eyebrows drew together, her face assuming the haughty anger of an aristocrat rebuffed. It was an expression Snow rarely saw on Sarah Ythlim's face—a reminder that her father had been a Trading Ambassador, one of the merchant-princes of Khamsin.

"I *will* bring our cargo to Atlantis!" Sarah's tone brooked no denial.

"Then you *will* be coughing blood before you go four leagues—and be dead long before we reach the Floating City," Sigwold retorted bluntly.

"With a gentle-gaited horse—," Rikka suggested.

Sigwold shook his head but softened his tone. "Sarah, this isn't a case of will defeating pain. It's a question of how long it will take your body to overcome a serious injury."

"I needn't ride," Sarah insisted.

"What are we to do, then?" Sigwold demanded. "Pack you into one of our crates? It would become your coffin soon enough, Sarah—sure as Necromancers love bones."

He spread his Tinker's hands before her. "You know I'm quick enough to repair broken things," he said. "But bones need time and quiet to knit back together. Give over, Sarah."

"Give over all our work and planning? I think not." Sarah began to draw herself up, then gasped, clutching at her side. "Death and spoliation!" she swore. "We can't miss this opportunity."

"Then we won't." Snow knelt beside her. "I pledge that I will be in the proper place at the needed time. You must pledge to wait . . . and heal."

"Karrudan's death is mine by right," Sarah said. "If you think I'll tamely stand aside—"

"I know you will realize what must be done," Snow replied, marshaling his arguments. "You speak of striking down Karrudan when you can't even sit up straight. I'm ready—and I have the best record at using the new weapons."

"In practice," Sarah argued.

"And have you been out aiming in earnest against human enemies?" Snow asked. "As for eagerness to strike the blow, I know that Karrudan connived the wreckage of all you'd built in Prieska, and the death of your father. But we all have scores to settle. Karrudan's Imperials killed my father, too. They stole the freedom and heritage of Sigwold's family. Rikka, too, knew only slavery . . . and she lost her mother in the mines."

His face had grown grim recounting the Empire's crimes. Now a bitter smile crooked his lips. "Better, perhaps, that a low fellow like myself take this mission to the enemy. Your face—and your quest for vengeance—are too well-known to the Imperials."

"The lad talks sense," Sigwold rumbled.

Rikka suddenly spoke up. "There's another thing. While

Sigwold saw to the building of the weapons, you recruited the folk to fight the Imperials. But unlike the Empire, you insisted on many leaders in many places."

Sarah nodded. "So we won't replace one monster with another, plundering the Land and its folk to build new weapons."

Rikka looked down. "Better, then, that Karrudan fall for many folk's justice than for one person's vengeance."

Sarah Ythlim looked for a long moment at the young Rebel. "You make a point," the leader finally said.

She looked at Snow. "Very well, then, you and Sigwold will journey on. Take the best of the packhorses with as many barrels of black powder as you can handle. Rikka and I will stay with the rest, waiting to see if any of the others find their way here."

Sighing, she shook her head. "By tomorrow I should be healed enough to travel. The rest of the munitions will follow you."

Sarah whispered to Rikka, who headed deeper into the cave. "So, it falls to you, Snow. You'll need a token to show our people in Atlantis and Down Town."

She removed a ring from her right hand, demonstrating how the bezel moved on a hinge to reveal the seal of Khamsin. "This will let them know you come on my business."

Rikka reappeared with a cow's horn from their cargo, using her knife to pick out the wax that sealed the end. Sarah reached into the container, removing a pinch of black powder. She placed it within the hollow bezel, closed it, and dropped the ring into Snow's callused, scarred hand.

"Another token," Sarah said. "A sign of what business we're about!"

Chapter 1

Blaize Audrick's son, Altem Guardsman of the Atlantean Empire, squinted in the bright sunlight beating down on the arena. It was hot in the padded practice jerkins he and his squad wore. But the brilliance was worse as it glinted off the raked sand underfoot, the rising ranks of polished marble seats, the huge crystal statues of beasts and warriors. The arena seemed like a vast, shining bowl, concentrating heat and light down upon them.

"A bit easier to take from the stand than the sands," Blaize quipped.

"As though you ever sat in those seats." Utem Guardsman Jacot leaned against his pike, hawked, and spat.

Some Altems would have knocked down a subordinate for talking like that. Blaize merely shrugged. The guardsman wasn't in his usual squad, and it was doubtful that a thrashing would improve Jacot's performance in this practice bout. "I've stood at attention along those steps often enough," he answered mildly.

"Have you ever stood guard . . . ?" Colass, the rawest recruit of the four guardsmen in the arena, nodded in awe toward the Imperial Box.

"Oh, we broil often enough at the edge of the emperor's awning." Jacot's voice sounded even coarser than usual as he laughed.

"The better post is up there." He gestured to an opening inset like a cave in the gleaming marble. "That's where the Prophet-Magus watches the games—when he deigns."

Machau, the other pikeman, joined in the laughter. Blaize

said nothing as he checked his crossbow. But he wondered at the orders that had brought them together—two barely competent Utems, a raw recruit . . . and himself.

The command to appear here—and what weapons to draw—had caught them all at breakfast. It might be a punishment detail. The question was, for whom?

"Looks like you've been demoted down to the level of us Utem Guardsmen, sir." Jacot's joshing tone didn't hide the nasty light of mockery in his eyes. "Guess the Powers hope you'll teach the boy something," he went on, gesturing at the weapons Blaize and Colass held.

"Utem crossbowmen have their parts to play," Blaize replied easily. On the battlefield, the Atlantean army was as powerful a machine as any mage's Technomantic creation. Hollow squares of pikemen provided the basic defensive arm, protecting mage-officers with a wall of human flesh and spears. At each corner of the square, bastions of crossbowmen and specialist troops with Technomantic weapons provided ranged fire. And once the magic blasts, lightning, and mage-fire had broken the enemy's line, the pikemen dropped their polearms, following the Altem Guardsmen to finish the job with their blades.

But an Altem Guardsman was supposed to be able to master any weapon found on the battlefield, so Blaize had practiced with crossbows and everything else available in the guardsmen's armories.

Jacot's strongest weapon, on the other hand, is his mouth. Blaize kept that thought unspoken. It was never wise to argue with squadmates before combat—even practice combat.

The fact was, Jacot and Machau looked like the awkward squad with their twelve-foot pikes. Spears that long weren't handy for guardsmen patrolling the cramped, twisting alleyways of Down Town. Short-hafted darts were better suited either as missiles or close-in weapons. And when reversed, their weighted ends worked well as truncheons on obstreperous Down-Towner heads.

Blaize turned from the wobbling pikeshafts to Colass. At

least the kid seemed to know which end of his crossbow the bolt flew from.

Pikes were best against mounted troops, Blaize knew. So what would they be up against? Cavalry? Captured Orcs?

At the far end of the arena, two sets of ironbound doors swung open, and Blaize got his answer.

Mage Spawn—one tall and stocky, the other crouched and lithe. Both were covered in matted, filthy fur. But they stood on their hind legs in a monstrous parody of humanity as they blinked in the sudden sunlight. *A Werebear and Werewolf,* Blaize thought. *We are in deep Troll scat!*

The Werebear was a nine-foot slab of shaggy muscle. Its snout wrinkled as it snuffled in air, depending more on smell than on its weak eyes. Blaize could see the moment it caught human-scent in the air. The creature roared, raising its forepaws in fists larger than a man's head. The fingers spread out to reveal claws several inches long. The bear-beast's Mage Spawn companion was less demonstrative, curling in on itself while it took in the human quartet. But the Werewolf's eyes blazed like the green fires in Feshku's Pit of Perdition. And a bilious string of slobber dribbled from the corner of its mouth to steam on the hot sands—hunger-drool.

The width of the arena separated the creatures from Blaize's squad—a good hundred paces. But the Altem knew the Mage Spawn could close that distance all too soon.

These need a quick finish, Blaize told himself. *Their bloodlust rises the longer they fight.* Aloud, he said, "Colass, you aim for the wolf. I'll take the bigger one."

Even as he spoke, he triggered his crossbow. His bolt took the Werebear in its muscle-ridged belly. The beast raked claws across its own flesh, trying to dislodge the missile. Blaize caught his bow under one foot, using his stronger leg muscles as a lever to help him recock the weapon. He was up and reloaded as the abomination before him flung back its head and roared its rage.

Blaize's second shot drilled the beast in its throat and disappeared, penetrating flesh and entering the skull from below. That was damage even the Mage Spawn's unnatural vitality couldn't shake off. Master Werebear dropped, twitching.

Through all this, Colass' bow had wavered while he tried to force trembling hands to take aim. His shot wasn't bad—it should have caught the oncoming Werewolf in the chest. But the beast's advance was a twisting, sinuous lope—a tribute to its legendary skills at evasion.

The Mage Spawn's shoulder dipped just as Colass' shot reached him. The crossbow quarrel tore a red stripe across hairy, muscular flesh. Wolflike, the Spawn snapped at the pain. But it kept coming.

This was the moment the two pikes should have come down to threaten the beast's chest, keeping it at bay.

Instead, Jacot revealed himself to be a worse soldier than Blaize had ever expected.

"Tezla's knob," the veteran guardsman croaked. But then the blasphemy was forgotten in the wake of a worse sin. Jacot dropped his weapon and ran. Machau stared after his comrade instead of paying attention to his spear point. It wavered off-line from the Werewolf's chest. The Mage Spawn dashed in, batting the heavy pike aside. Machau held on to the shaft an instant too long.

The Werewolf was on the Utem before Machau's sword was half out of its scabbard. Still worse, even as the Werewolf's claws disemboweled him, the guardsman's body blocked Blaize's shot.

Colass tried to stand by his training, struggling with the string of his crossbow. But when Machau fell, the recruit dropped the weapon and ran for it.

Exercise over, Blaize thought in disgust, waiting for the twang of crossbow fire from the backup archers posted in the first tier of arena seats, usually followed by a volley of pointed insults for the guardsmen in need of rescue.

Neither came. Blaize glanced up to find no bowmen on duty. His squad was on its own, and the wolf-beast was almost upon him.

But it paid no attention to him, charging on in its strange, twisting lope. Blaize tried for a snap-shot, but missed as the Werewolf ran past him, focused completely on the boy. Whether he was after the one who'd caused him pain or just attracted by a running figure, Blaize had no idea. Before he could reload again, the mage-beast was on Colass.

Human screams blended with the Werewolf's triumphant snarl. Blaize unsheathed his sword and went for the furred back. All the guardsmen had been issued leaf-bladed short swords, more effective for close-in fighting on city streets than for subduing savage Mage Spawn in the arena.

A manaclevt blade would be better for this kind of butchery, Blaize thought coldly as he brought his arm down in a quick cross-slash, laying open muscle and sinew beneath the fur.

With a bellow of surprise, the beast twisted round nearly snakelike, snapping at the annoyance. Carrion breath blasted in Blaize's face, a combination of rotten meat and fresh blood. He brought his blade around again, aiming for the Werewolf's snout, already red with Colass' gore. Blaize added some of the beast's own blood to the mix as his steel bit into the Werewolf's flesh.

The monster recoiled, then leaped to the attack. Blaize dove under the threatening fangs and claws, his short sword up to administer a long, shallow graze along the Werewolf's underbelly.

Almost past, the wolf-thing's rear leg connected in a buffeting blow, sending Blaize sprawling on the burning sands. He managed to hold on to his sword and made it to his feet before the beast came at him again.

The next few moments swirled by in a wild, scrambling retreat as the Werewolf feinted and hurtled about. The wide-open space around them left the creature free to circle around the Altem, trying for an attack from the flank or rear. Blaize grimly kept turning to face the rank monstrosity, so each attack became an attempt to get past his short blade. The Werewolf didn't succeed—quite. But Blaize couldn't put the beast down. He inflicted a few more nicks and cuts, receiving some bruises, scrapes, and a bloody but shallow quartet of gashes across his back.

His padded practice jerkin had taken the brunt of that swipe. Half the garment now hung in shreds, its stuffing leaking out—except where it was soaking up the fluids leaking from Blaize.

He shook his head, trying to keep the burning sweat out of his eyes. With a comrade at his side—or at least guarding his back—he might have a better chance.

Machau is lying in a puddle of his own intestines, a cold tactical voice came from the back of Blaize's head. *Colass is down and not getting up.*

He was vaguely aware of a yammering voice and the sound of fists pounding on the door that had let them into the arena. So Jacot was alive—but useless.

It was up to Blaize to kill the Werewolf, and he was running out of time, energy . . . and blood. Already, he felt lightheaded. Was that heat-haze coming off the arena sands, or was his vision blurring? He backed off a little more, trying to put some additional distance between himself and the Mage Spawn.

Blaize's foot came up against something—the shaft of one of the abandoned pikes. Risking a quick glance, he saw that he was halfway down the length of the spear, and that the head pointed toward the Werewolf.

It was time to roll the bones on a desperate chance. Blaize pretended to trip over the pike, dropping to one knee. Howling with triumph, the Werewolf vaulted forward. Blaize grabbed the pikestaff and hauled it up, bracing himself as best he could.

The spearhead caught the wolf-beast in the upper right chest, converting the victory howl into a bloody wheeze. But this was a war-weapon, not a hunting spear, that the Werewolf had impaled itself upon. There was no crossbar to keep it from walking its way up the weapon to reach Blaize.

And that was what, slowly, painfully, the Mage Spawn attempted to do.

Blaize retreated to the end of the pikestaff, which he

braced with one foot. Then he brought his other foot down as heavily as he could on the shaft. With a hoarse bellow of pain, the Werewolf toppled. Even as it thudded to the ground, Blaize flung himself forward, blade extended.

The point of the short sword found the Werewolf's left eye and plunged in. The beast stiffened in a convulsive shudder, then lay still.

Blaize pulled his blade free and took a couple of wobbly steps back. For the past couple of minutes, his whole world had shrunk to the wolf-thing's face, its eyes, its claws, trying to judge where the next attack would come from, how it would be launched. Now Blaize stood staggering in the midst of a rapidly expanding universe. The stepped bowl of marble seats, the triumphantly posed crystal statues—Archer, Swordsman, Elf at Bay, The Wounded Troll—all seemed to act like a gigantic lens, boiling the sweat from his streaming body.

He saw stretcher-bearers kneeling in bloodstained sand, tidying Machau away, gently lifting Colass onto a litter. Farther away, a squad of guardsmen took Jacot into custody. Still farther away, arena groundsmen emerged from the menagerie doors with chains to haul away the dead Mage Spawn.

Another Altem Guard—a grizzled veteran, but in polished armor—approached Blaize across the sands.

"Guardsman Blaize, you will accompany me and report to your commander," he said. "Immediately."

Blaize saluted, then plunged his sword into the sand to clean it as best he could. He wiped off the gritty, clotted weapon on his practice jerkin, sheathed the sword, and followed.

Orders.

But also, it would be good to see Magus Emillon and report about practices that took the lives of young recruits—practices where backup guardsmen were not at their posts.

Following the headquarters guardsman, Blaize marched across the sands to a break in the arena wall, a section removed to allow them to climb up to the first row of seats.

Another twelve tiers of seating slabs rose up in concentric oblongs of marble—not enough to accommodate the full population of Atlantis-in-the-Sky, but more than ample for the elite of the Empire.

Blackness yawned before them, and they stepped into the shadow of a passageway, finally emerging into sunshine at the portico surrounding the front of the arena's curved outer wall, where the paying customers—or, rather, invited guests—usually entered.

The street outside was not made of gold as the legends claimed. But the silica-rich paving stones reflected the mid-day sun's glare almost as harshly as the sands in the arena.

Blaize glanced back as they set off down the greatest street in the Empire. The arched facade of the arena, rising in spotless white marble, would have stood out in almost any other milieu.

But on the Golden Mile, the glittering core of the Empire's heart, the vast structure usually only got a passing glance. When Grand Magus Tezla raised four square miles of his capital five hundred feet into the air, he'd chosen the sections with the most impressive architecture. And in the 140 years since Tezla discarnated, succeeding emperors had lavished the finest building materials in the Land upon Atlantis-in-the-Sky. On this street, more than matchless marble was needed to catch the eye.

The wonders of Technomancy allowed crystals, even gemstones, to be fused or fashioned into structural elements. They passed Orien's Fountain, which seemed to be crafted from a single, tremendous piece of lapis lazuli. Visitors to the Chapel of Heroes entered through a facade of gigantic jade panels depicting warlike deeds. Tezla's soaring temple was fronted by ten enormous columns, rising not in barreled sections but as single alexandrite crystals, shining red or green as the light fell upon them.

Spires and obelisks arose using newer Technomantic skills, cladding Magestone with veneers of other crystals to create edifices that seemed to glow from within.

Unlimited tax monies, labor, and magic allowed the

rulers of Atlantis to pile wonder upon wonder. Even the aristocrats of the Land's other great cities gaped like peasants at the display.

The locals, however, made their way past these titanic works like ants traversing the feet of a grand statue, eyes down, usually oblivious in the grip of their own business. It took the unveiling of some new wonder to capture their attention, unless they were passing some personal favorite.

Following his guide along the Golden Mile, Blaize came upon a construction that had taken his fancy. A teacher from the Academy had taken Blaize's upper-form class out to examine some of the more neglected monuments on the Golden Mile. He'd pointed out the massive stone structure spanning the street, calling it the Altered Arch.

The schoolmaster explained that the arch had risen more than 250 years ago, intended as a triumphal memorial for Tezla's attack on the Knights Immortal. That campaign failed at the Battle of South Pass, but the arch, covered with scenes of victory over the Elves, was already in place. Rather than tear the thing down, artisans had changed the carvings to show Wylden followers of renegade Elemental mages facing Imperial justice.

But, as the teacher pointed out to the Academy students, the sculpted battle scenes still included many High Elves fighting in the ranks of the Empire's enemies.

The suggestion that even Tezla could be fallible had fascinated Blaize. A number of parents had complained about this lesson, however. And shortly afterward, the offending teacher had been dismissed from the Academy.

From the shadow of the arch, they moved away from the Golden Mile, skirting the edge of the Lower Forum. Dotted with heroic statues of Tezla and later emperors and lined with the offices of the Lesser Ministries, this space would have crowned many a lesser city. Compared to the splendors they'd just left, the gold, silver, and marble seemed almost homely. The building facades of the various offices still gleamed in white marble, with colonnades and pediments of polished stone. Even the tiered steps leading up to each building were carved from single blocks of marble, each riser an inch higher than a comfortable step. Not only did it make a more impressive vista, it taxed that much more effort from the suppliants coming to the offices.

Those who worked in the ministries—Blaize's father among them—entered the buildings through rear basements, making their way to their places of business on much more comfortable back stairways.

Certainly there were more than enough suppliants thronging the forum, with drabber-robed government functionaries bustling among them. Then the guardsmen were beyond the open space, following the street into a residential district of island-castles.

Having grown up in a building like these, Blaize knew they were neither islands nor castles, but large blocks of cramped apartments stretching fortresslike from one street to the next. A narrow center court in the middle of each building was lucky to get full sunlight for half an hour each midday. The places were sweltering in summer heat, freezing in winter winds.

They also represented the only home Blaize had ever known before coming to the guardsmen's barracks.

And now they were close to those barracks, entering one of the military zones surrounding the liftgates that allowed access to the city.

Instead of leading the way to the Company Area for Blaize's unit, the veteran led his charge to a different building, a much larger office. Blaize immediately became alert, as veterans do at any change in routine.

Magus Emillon was already in the office, his hair carefully coifed, revealing the single Magestone implanted in his forehead—his true sign of rank, marking him as a magic-wielder for the Empire. Golden armor shone over his dull red uniform, but he carried neither his sword nor his magical staff. Emillon was young for an officer, really an Elite Magical Apprentice. At the moment, his bony face looked even younger as he stood erect as any recruit in front of the desk. Behind it sat a hawk-faced man whom Blaize had only seen at major parades—Lord Scarbro, commander of Capital Defense Legion.

From the looks of Magus Emillon, it was turning into a hard day for guardsmen in Blaize's unit. The young mage usually presented a pale, ascetic facade to the world. Today, his face looked waxy, the dark roots of his freshly scraped beard showing through the flesh.

"Guardsman Blaize," the veteran announced, then left.

"That was a fairly eventful practice bout," Scarbro said. "Two guardsman dead and a third arrested for dereliction—"

"But the test was for Blaize," Emillon said a little too quickly. "The others in the exercise were supposed to be expendable."

Blaize knew better than to open his mouth. It was in the first Imperial Precepts taught in school, supposedly handed down by the Grand Magus Tezla himself: "A superior speaks with the authority of a father. A subordinate's duty is to hear . . . and obey."

This wasn't about negligence in setting guards or failures of safety. The morning had been a test, which Blaize had apparently passed. What if Jacot, Machau, and Colass had used their weapons with more effect? Would they have passed, too? Blaize ached to tell the officer that Colass hadn't been expendable, he'd merely been young. But even phrased with respect, Blaize knew his words would be unwelcome.

Was this a test now? Was he expected to speak, or to keep quiet?

"Guardsman Blaize dispatched two Mage Spawn essentially single-handed." As Emillon spoke, Blaize noted a fine sheen of sweat on the mage's face. That was the first time he'd ever seen such a reaction from one of the magically gifted to someone without magic, which is what Scarbro essentially was. The magus also seemed to keep glancing to his right. Blaize followed Emillon's nervous gaze, to see another entrance to the office—or maybe some sort of closet or storage space. It was an opening in the wall, blocked with an embroidered tapestry.

The hanging billowed slightly as Blaize looked. Could

someone be listening behind there? Had Emillon's powers somehow divined another's presence? But who would make the young mage more nervous than the capital's commanding officer?

Emillon's words tumbled over themselves as he continued. "Besides the bravery expected of an Altem Guardsman, he also showed exceptional skill with several unorthodox weapons—crossbow, pike, short sword—"

"Most commendable, Magus," Scarbro said crisply. "You are dismissed."

Saluting, Blaize went to follow his commander, then halted as Scarbro said, "Not you, Guardsman."

Blaize resumed his stance as Emillon hesitated in the doorway. He was an exception to the usual run of mage-officers, who threw their troops into harm's way as gamesters discard pawns. Although he looked as if he'd be happy to scuttle off, Emillon nevertheless showed a commander's responsibility. "Sir, this guardsman is in my company."

"He is now on detached duty," the legion-captain replied.

The young mage swallowed loudly. "Serving where, sir?"

Scarbro's hawk-face looked like a graven image. "Serving the Empire," he said with an air of finality.

Bowing his head, Emillon left.

The hanging fluttered aside as a new figure entered the room. Scarbro rose from behind his desk and bowed. "You heard, my lord?"

A new note entered the Warlord's voice—the same sort of careful, eager-to-please tone Blaize had heard from Emillon.

"I not only heard, Lord Scarbro, I saw. A scrying-stone was set to overlook the arena. I watched the entire test." The newcomer fell silent, but Blaize had the impression of a long, searching scrutiny. He remained at attention, unable to turn his head to return the look. From the tail of his eye, he got a glimpse of purple and gold—the colors of a senior mage's robes of state.

"Excellent combat reactions, and his improvisation showed a certain quickness of wit." The mage stepped into Blaize's range of vision, his hair and beard a pure white, thin lips set in a considering frown. Deep-set eyes of iron gray continued to regard Blaize as if searching for a flaw. Slowly, the robed figure circled. Blaize took in the high forehead, the bold cheekbones, the jutting beak of a nose. Every line of the mage's face shouted power—and arrogance.

The very air seemed to curdle with strange energies circling the tall, spare figure. Invisible currents tugged at robes whose silk reduced any other fabrics Blaize had seen to the status of sackcloth. Even the man's mane of white hair stirred in the grip of an unseen aura.

This morning's business had brought Blaize to rarefied heights, indeed. His examiner had to be a personage of importance within the Atlantis Guild—and within the Empire itself.

The mage glanced toward Scarbro. "Can we trust him?" he asked as if Blaize weren't there.

Scarbro answered as quickly as Emillon had. "Born and raised here within the Floating City, Lord. Educated through the secondary forms at the Academy. Several tours in the outlands, west and north. A true son of Atlantis."

"As we might expect." The mage stepped forward. His aquiline features, tight as a fist, filled Blaize's view. The Altem felt his body sway, only iron discipline keeping him upright. Had he counted four Magestones set in the magus' brow? Or had his vision gone as weak as his knees?

All he saw now were the mage's flashing iron eyes. They seemed to press into his very soul. Strange, skittering sensations tickled behind Blaize's brow, like spiders dancing on flesh—or very delicate, immaterial fingers rifling through his thoughts and memories. The mage's left hand cupped the back of Blaize's skull, holding him in place, keeping him upright . . .

"Yes. I read all you say, and more. This one is acceptable." The mage stepped back, releasing Blaize, who promptly collapsed to his knees like a puppet with its strings cut.

He strove for balance, to prevent himself from pitching face-forward onto the floor. A hand in a silver glove rose before his eyes. Silver? Only one mage in all the Empire wore those, or had four Magestone implants—

Blaize's whirling thoughts were interrupted as a metal-clad finger came to rest on his forehead. That uncanny insect-skitter penetrated his skull, dancing deep into his brain, and the world grew very far away.

Then a bolt very much like lightning seemed to pass from the mage to the kneeling Altem. Though the only contact was a fingertip, it seemed to deal Blaize a blow far worse than any he had ever received in practice or in combat.

Blaize flopped backward, his whole brow aflame.

"Done," the mage said.

The word echoed between Blaize's ears as he crashed against the office floor.

CHAPTER 2

BLAIZE didn't lose consciousness—quite. But for several long minutes, he was as unsure of his senses as he was of his unstrung muscles. The walls of the office seemed to parade around him in a slow march, led by the woven hanging. They moved in time to a set of low murmurs—he couldn't make out any words. Also, when Lord Scarbro finally helped him to his feet, Blaize realized that he had missed seeing the mage leave and the arrival of a pot of herb tea.

Hauling himself to attention, Blaize watched the steam curling from the teapot and wondered if there was a similar plume rising from his forehead. If a bare touch was enough to knock him down . . .

Scarbro shook his head. "At ease, Guardsman." He pointed. "Sit."

Blaize gladly dropped into the indicated chair—his knees still seemed very tentative about holding him up.

The officer resumed his seat behind the desk. "I imagine you have many questions about the things that happened this morning."

"Yes, sir," Blaize replied. "It seems as if I survived a test—but for what?"

"No doubt you realize it's a matter of some importance, considering the people involved." Scarbro peered at Blaize as he poured a cup of tea and handed it to him.

If anything, Scarbro was underplaying the question. Blaize silently took the cup and nodded.

"But I don't think you realize quite how vital your duty

will be." The veteran commander continued to scrutinize Blaize's face intently. "Do you know who was in the room with us just now?"

"Sir?" The image of the silver glove—of four Magestones stretching across a high brow—swam before Blaize's eyes, and his mouth abruptly went dry.

Scarbro allowed Blaize to take a sip of tea. Then he brought two items up from the top of his desk. One was a silver chain and medallion, set with a tiny bit of crystal about the size of a fingernail paring. His other hand held a mirror. "Take a look at yourself."

Blaize held the mirror between his hands, examining his reflection. A handsome enough face, or so tavern wenches across the Empire had assured him. Regular features, calm brown eyes. He looked paler than usual thanks to exertion and blood loss. His cheeks were a bit more hollow. All in all, though, he seemed fairly hale after being struck with a levinbolt. Blaize half expected to find a burn or scar on his forehead. Instead, he saw merely untouched flesh.

"Keep looking," Scarbro instructed, bringing up the medallion until the tiny crystal touched Blaize's brow.

The mirror shook in the young soldier's grasp as a complicated design appeared on his flesh. He brought up a hesitant finger and ran it across the mysterious image. It didn't run—apparently, it was ingrained in his skin.

"Think of it as a tattoo." The commander's voice was almost gentle. "It's the sigil of Karrudan, Blaize. Do you understand what I'm saying? Who was here?"

Karrudan, the Prophet-Magus, head of the Atlantis Guild, power behind the Imperial throne, the voice of Immortal Tezla's soul. Where all the other mages of the Guild clad their hands in gold, Karrudan wore silver. He was also the only living mage capable of channeling the power of four Magestone implants.

A haze seemed to obscure Blaize's reflection. He blinked, firmly ordering himself not to faint. His eyes refocused, finding his reflection even paler than before. Scarbro put the chain round Blaize's neck, allowing the medallion to fall onto the guardsman's chest. Karrudan's mystic sigil blinked out of existence.

"That's a little piece of Magestone in the medallion," Scarbro said. "You can use it whenever you wish to make Karrudan's sign visible. Any Atlantean leader of command rank—mage-officer and above—will recognize the sigil and know whose work you're doing. It goes without saying that they'll do whatever is needed to get you out of any trouble or to assist you on your way."

So now I know whose work I'm doing, Blaize thought. *But what, exactly, is the job I'm supposed to do?*

Blaize knew better than to ask his superior. But the question must have shown in his eyes.

Scarbro, however, answered with yet another question. "Have you ever heard of the Oracles of Rokos?"

Rokos was the old capital of Kos, a conquering kingdom that created a large empire centuries before Imperial days. Unfortunately, the Academy was more interested in the history of the Empire than in predecessor states. Yet the Oracles of Rokos struck something . . .

"They predicted the coming of Tezla," Blaize suddenly said.

Scarbro nodded. "They foresaw Tezla's birth and career a hundred and seventy-five years before he was born." The Warlord leaned forward, his lips tightening, his cheekbones becoming more prominent. "There is another foretelling from the Oracles—one that suggests the Prophet-Magus might be in danger of assassination."

"Where? How?" The words burst from Blaize's lips.

Scarbro gave him a sardonic smile. "Unfortunately, auguries tend to be deficient in hard facts. The description of the seer's vision speaks of gold and purple robes, a crystal diadem—which could refer to the implanted Magestones—'silver hands,' and a weapon never seen before."

The guard commander shrugged. "Some of the Oracles' prognostications are fairly outlandish. In the same codex, they predict the coming of a race unknown, some sort of gigantic beings of light, which sounds fairly ridiculous to me."

He looked at Blaize. "The Prophet-Magus finds the foretelling of his death equally ridiculous. But others among his advisers put more stock in this vision."

Scarbro frowned at his desktop for a moment before he went on, speaking very carefully. "It is said that Karrudan was not surprised when the Oracles' codex was brought to his attention . . . that Tezla's Avatar had made a similar prediction."

The cup of tea cooled in Blaize's hand as he stared. Tezla's Avatar was supposed to be the greatest achievement of Technomancy, the Magestone-powered Golem where the Grand Magus' soul—his true essence—had transferred after leaving his body. For any Atlantean, the avatar spoke ultimate truth, and the Prophet-Magus decreed it.

Now Scarbro seemed to be saying that the herald of Tezla's Voice was willfully ignoring a holy message.

"It may be pride," Scarbro quietly admitted. "Karrudan is surrounded by all the might of the Empire, military and magical. He also has his own considerable mage-born potency.

"Or it may be policy. This is a difficult time for the Empire. Factions, both political and magical, strive for power. Even the breath of rumor about the Prophet-Magus somehow being vulnerable would cause plots to double and redouble. You've patrolled Down Town enough. How would the common folk there react to such news?"

Blaize slowly nodded. "Riots such as we've never seen before."

Scarbro joined him in grim agreement. "Then think of the outlands, where Rebels already scheme to secede from the Empire, to attack our Magestone mines—"

He broke off, taking a deep breath. "At any rate, the Prophet-Magus has agreed to allow some secret investigations into the possibility of plots against him. Your task, Guardsman Blaize, is to go to Khamsin—there's always some rebellious intrigue on the boil up there. Get among these dissidents, find the rebels or would-be assassins, discover their plans—and expose them."

"Sir . . ." Blaize fumbled for words. "With respect, why would anyone choose me to do something like that? I mean, there must be wiser, more subtle servants of the Empire. Mages—"

"A mage would be the last person we'd send on this mission, Blaize," Scarbro replied. "At the first sniff of magecraft, our quarry would run—or our agent would be dead." The officer gave Blaize another long, measuring stare. "You don't have magic abilities, do you?"

"No, sir." Odd, how he still felt a little pang at giving that simple response. Blaize had lived with the pain for seven years now, since the examiners at the Academy rendered their final verdict. He was no late bloomer. There would be no sudden quickening of magical ability. He lacked even his father's modest talents.

"I'm sure Karrudan searched for that—a final test." Again, Scarbro seemed to read Blaize's face. "There was more to it than that, and there were others tested as well. We needed to find a certain kind of warrior."

He paused, then gestured to the drill field below the office window. "You know that the strength of our army has always been our system. Our troops are trained to move and fight in formation. History has shown it to be a very successful way of making war, but it doesn't allow for much in the way of individual initiative."

Scarbro rose and moved around the desk. "You went to the Academy, so you must have read Tezla's Precepts. With your history, I'm sure you know this one: 'Let the Mills of Circumstance grind common folk to dust. The superior man rises above.' Most writers who comment on the precepts think Tezla's 'superior man' must be a magic-wielder. Is that what you believe?"

Blaize allowed himself a bitter nod. Both during his testing for magic abilities and after the final verdict, that quotation had haunted him.

"Of course," Scarbro said, "most of the commentators were themselves magic-users. Tezla himself never mentioned magecraft. This is your chance to rise from the ranks of the dust-people, Guardsman. What better chance to demonstrate that you are a superior person than to achieve a most difficult undertaking without any intrinsic magic?"

The commander let that thought sink in for a moment, then continued. "Of course, you'll have any Technomantic assistance you'll require."

He tapped Blaize's brow. "That seal will ensure compliance from any Imperial officers. And there's an additional spell on the medallion. None will see it unless you—or Karrudan—wish them to. Call it an extra bit of assurance for you."

Scarbro leaned back in his seat. "I want a bit of assurance as well. Specifically, I wish you to report any information to me immediately—by way of mage-writ."

"Yes, sir." Scarbro's order only underscored the importance of this mission. Mage-writ meant instant written communication—but it was ruinously expensive. Teleporting messages literally burned out the Magestone used in the Technomantic process.

Lord Scarbro nodded. "Report here at dawn. Until then, you're free to finish up any local business. My personal healer awaits next door. After she's finished, I suggest you get as much rest as possible." He gave Blaize another sharp look. "Of course, you will not discuss your new duties with anyone."

Blaize saluted, then hesitated. He wanted to ask—but a conflicting notion cut in. Finally, he cleared his throat. "Sir, I'd like to tell my parents that I'm leaving Atlantis. I can simply say I've been assigned to a new unit."

"I leave that to your discretion, Guardsman."

But Blaize caught the underlying message. *If you're going to survive this mission, you'll have to be very discreet indeed.*

Emerging from the Warlord's office, Blaize underwent the ministrations of Scarbro's healer and left with nothing more than a slight tightness of the newly grown skin replacing the scratches on his back. To work that out, he wandered at random through the military compound, past drill fields and the Technomantic workshops where magical weapons were maintained.

For Blaize, it was a blur, a familiar background—too familiar. Maybe he'd gotten overly used to the city and a soft life. Initial duty in the outlands had turned him from a raw recruit into a real warrior. His second tour, off in the west, had won him promotion. Blaize found himself grinning. This time he'd be matching his wits against the outlanders instead of his sword arm. But any true Atlantean was worth three of the lesser breeds. This was an adventure—

A slight tremor in the ground shook Blaize out of his thoughts. He managed to halt himself just short of the Storm Golem's path. The artificial creature was twice the height of a man, a construct of metal and Magestone. The armor it wore only increased its mighty bulk.

Depending on its orders and the alertness of the mage controlling it, the huge creature might have stopped. *Then again,* Blaize thought, *maybe not.*

As he continued on his way—a bit more carefully—a sardonic thought insinuated itself. *Not the best proof of superiority—stomped to jelly instead of dust by those big, flat feet.*

The near-accident also squashed the circular argument that had been rolling through his head. Blaize couldn't understand this strange, sudden aversion to seeing his parents. No, he wasn't close to them, although they lived in the same city. Contact was usually limited to uncomfortable feast-day dinners.

Even so, Blaize couldn't leave Atlantis without saying good-bye.

He wended his way to his former company's barracks—empty now. The others were posted on guard duty at this hour. After a long splash alone in the company bathhouse, Blaize felt a little more attached to the world. He went to his bunk, opening the chest at its foot. There he sorted his things into two piles. Personal items and the uniform he'd had hand-tailored went into a small satchel, along with the officer's whistle his parents had bought him when he'd been promoted to Altem. The rest of his equipment was wrapped in his blanket for return to the quartermaster.

After taking care of that, Blaize headed to the legionary bank, where he drew out some money and arranged for his pay to be added to his savings. Then, dressed in a set of civilian clothes, the satchel slung over one shoulder, Blaize set off across the city. He crossed the Lower Forum at the other end, noting how the crowd had diminished. Now it consisted of disappointed favor-seekers, slowly leaving the scenes of bureaucratic defeat.

Afternoon sunshine gilded the facades of the clerkly palaces, but Blaize took no notice, heading instead for the shade of the Public Gardens. An island of greenery in a sea of marble grandeur, the gardens had been his playground from earliest youth. As a toddler he'd gone to the "woods," holding his mother's hand, running along the paths, snitching a flower for Mama when he could, marveling at the ten-sided, high-arched temple full of plants, seeming to mix indoors and outdoors beneath its prismatic crystal dome. Mama would always tell him how she and Fada had been married here.

To an adult, the "woods" shrank to a small plaza shaded with trees, the temple to a charming but rather small architectural folly. Blaize smiled at the sight of a groundsman pushing a wheeled barrel, dipping into it to water the plants. Tezla had provided for his Floating City by turning the mighty Roa Vizorr into a reverse waterfall, the river's waters roaring five hundred feet into the air to irrigate the city. Pumps powered by Technomancy piped the water through the four square miles of Atlantis-in-the-Sky. On the other side of town, a thundering fall of waste water cascaded to the sea.

The rich and powerful had direct service and water at the turn of a tap. Humbler folk picked up their water from public fountains. And the plants in the "woods" had their drinks brought to them. Once Blaize's highest ambition had been to be the man pushing that barrel. He straightened, his hand unconsciously going to straighten a scabbard that wasn't there. Times changed.

Still, the garden was pleasantly shady, and Blaize lingered there until the dinner hour neared. Then he headed for a nearby marketplace. Moving through a sea of last-minute shoppers, Blaize invested some of his money in crocks of olives and a mashed-bean salad, a round of soft cheese rolled in cracked pepper, figs, a loaf of fresh-baked bread, several skewers of spiced and roasted meat, and a flask of good wine.

The food smells reminded him he hadn't eaten since breakfast, and each step toward the old, familiar island-castle seemed to be accompanied by a stomach growl.

Blaize's father preferred to style himself Administrator Audrick, no patronymic, but using his managerial title from the Ministry. While many ministerial functionaries of his rank maintained comfortable villas outside the walls of Down Town, Audrick maintained what he called "apartments" in an island-castle a brief walk from his offices.

While the building was genteel, "apartments" was a grossly inflated description of the living quarters. There was a sleeping chamber with just enough room to accommodate a bed for Blaize's mother and father, a minuscule kitchen, a decent-sized dayroom—which served as dining area, study, and family domain—plus a storage area converted into a space for Blaize.

Located on the third floor of a five-story building, the rooms represented the edges of respectability at a ruinous rent. For Audrick, who came from among farmer folk up-river on the Roa Vizorr, the only place to live was in the Floating City, Feshku take the expense.

Blaize still remembered his father setting off for work in carefully mended robes, kept because he claimed he was especially fond of his wife's embroidery on them. It took a few years for Blaize to realize the true reason for such small economies as these. Tuition for the Academy was another heavy expense.

But Administrator Audrick footed the bills for years so

that his son could be educated among the best of the Empire. He paid and kept paying, until the Academy's examiners gave their final judgment on Blaize's magical potential.

On occasion, Blaize spotted his former schoolfellows. Many wore the plain golden robes of apprentice mages, others clerkly drab. Some had the embroidery marking them as administrators, already matching Audrick's position—at the beginning of their careers.

The fact was, Audrick's magical abilities were just enough to raise him above the general run of clerks—not exactly a demonstration of superiority over the dust-people ground out by the Mills of Circumstance.

But then, he had worse results with his hoped-for posterity, Blaize thought as he climbed the stairs. *Me.*

He knocked at a very familiar door, which opened to reveal his mother, Laure.

"Blaize!" she said, surprised.

"I thought I'd join you for supper," Blaize said, stepping in with his purchases and sniffing the air. "Soup and bitter greens? Just as well I brought a few things."

"We could put a little water to the soup," Laure said, the light of mischief in her eyes taking away twenty years.

"Or we could add a few of these things." Blaize smiled in return.

That expression became a little forced as Audrick rose from the chair where he'd been reading. "To what do we owe this unexpected visit?" While Laure had been trying to examine the contents of the bundles Blaize carried, Audrick's attention was on the satchel.

"You wear no uniform and carry a traveling bag." The observations sounded more like accusations.

How like Father, Blaize thought. "I'm being transferred to a new unit," he said.

"Away from Atlantis?" To Audrick that could only be a punishment. His unspoken question hung heavy in the air. *What did you do to deserve this?*

Laure took the packages from her son. "Serving in the outlands leads to quicker promotions," she said. "That's how

Blaize rose to Altem." She looked at her son. "You'll tell us about the new posting while we eat."

Promotion was a foreign concept to Audrick. He asked about the possibilities as they sat at the table. Blaize kept his replies vague, but pointed out that action against the various secession movements offered plenty of opportunity. Hadn't Scarbro mentioned the superior man rising?

Father was soon back to his usual topics. "The Empire must be strong," he proclaimed, gesturing with his spit of roasted meat. "Otherwise those Orcs to the north and west would be reaving along the Roa Vizorr. How would that suit those flea-bitten barbarians up in Khamsin? They complain that Imperial law hurts their precious trade. Don't they understand that it's the Empire's law—and the order it imposes—that allows trade to flourish?"

Blaize nibbled on an olive. It wasn't that he disagreed with his father. But too many parental dictates had been delivered at this table.

"The army certainly plays its part," Audrick went on. "Protecting the borders, maintaining order." For Father, this represented a major concession. When Blaize had first mentioned a military career, Audrick had acted as if his son were taking up work as a ditchdigger.

"You're not going to guard the mines?" Laure asked hesitantly. "I've heard that the Elementalists—"

"Oh, yes, we must beware of what the tree-lovers get up to." Audrick took a long swig of wine.

Laure didn't respond except to look down. But Blaize remembered her happiness among the greenery of the Public Gardens. "The Empire started seizing Dwarves into slavery to work the mines. When the Elemental League sought to stop that—"

"They were driven out—as they should be if they can't support the Empire," Audrick responded. "We don't need them, nor the Necros, whatever they do with their filthy bones."

"My assignment has nothing to do with the mines," Blaize assured his mother. "Mostly it will be scouting." He didn't even hesitate before that last word. Certainly, it was close enough to spying.

Somehow, they got through the meal. Blaize explained that he would be leaving the next morning and asked if he could leave some of his things in his old room. Laure insisted he spend the night.

They had to shift around some of the room's arrangements to open the way to the cubby where Blaize had slept. There was the brazier for the winter and some pieces of furniture that had been retired but not thrown out. Blaize had noticed the small changes in the room outside—a few new pieces, some nicer things, a trace of affluence without the crushing costs of the Academy. He hadn't mentioned it. Mercifully, neither had Audrick.

Laure set out the bedding, as if Blaize hadn't been tending to that himself for years. At last, they stood by the door.

"Will you be leaving very early, dear?" Laure asked.

Blaize nodded.

"If your father and I aren't up—good luck." Her voice choked a little.

"Fare well, son," Audrick said.

"Thank you, Mama. Good-bye, Father." For a long moment, the three of them hugged together. Then Blaize's parents left him, and he turned to crawl into the tiny space where his bedding was laid out.

Blaize blew out his candle and lay down. He must have spent thousands of nights here after saying good night to Mama and Fada—Father. Odd, that strange note of formality had always stood between him and Audrick.

It had only grown worse when the news came from the Academy. Blaize remembered the last night he'd lain here, listening to raised voices from the room outside.

"The Delphanes had the right idea, breeding for magical power." Audrick's voice cut like a knife. "Unfortunately, I made the mistake of being swayed by a passing physical attraction—distracted by the breeding instead of the program."

The next morning, Blaize had gone to the recruiters.

CHAPTER 3

BEFORE dawn, Blaize rose and padded as quietly as possible to the kitchen in search of water to wash the sleep from his eyes. Instead, he found his mother steeping spice herb leaves in a teapot. A jar of honey stood open beside her.

"Honeyed spice tea was always your favorite," Laure said with a smile.

"Thank you, Mother." He poured tea into two cups, and Laure spooned in some honey. Blaize tried to peer across the shadowy main room of the apartment to the sleeping quarters.

"Your father still sleeps." Laure gave him a lopsided smile. "I don't think he was used to last night's wine."

They sat for a few minutes in companionable silence, sipping tea. When Blaize reached the bottom of his cup, he said, "I must get to the compound now."

Laure left him to the water pitcher and the washbowl. After toweling himself off, Blaize returned to his room, dressed, and hefted his much lighter satchel. He left his good uniform and most of his personal effects, taking nothing that would identify who he really was.

When he stepped into the common room again, Laure stood by the door. She opened her arms and enfolded him. Blaize had to bend down as he hugged her. His mother planted a kiss on his brow, where Karrudan had marked him. "Be careful, out there in the wide world," she whispered.

"I will, Mama," Blaize promised. He went out the door and headed for the stairwell.

. . .

Arriving at Scarbro's office, Blaize didn't know what to expect. The Warlord, of course, perhaps some aides to brief him, a mage or two in attendance . . .

Instead, he found Scarbro and a barber.

"I'll take that," the officer said, removing Blaize's satchel and spreading the contents across his desk. Then, to the barber, "Shave his head."

Blaize sat on a stool while his hair was sheared off, then the barber went to work with his razor. He even threw in a facial shave as well. When the barber finished, Scarbro threw him a coin. The man left without a word.

Still seated, Blaize ran a tentative hand across his head. The sensation on his bare scalp was very strange. Even though the day was warm, a brief chill shuddered his body.

"We decided your best bet was to go out as a Caeronn," Scarbro said, sweeping Blaize's things back into the bag. "Caero is friendly with everyone."

Reminded of where he was, Blaize stood at attention.

"That's a habit you'll have to drop quickly," Blaize's commander said. "You'll give people the impression you're still in the army, rather than having left it." He pointed to the wall. "Go over there and slouch. I have a feeling you'll need the practice."

While Blaize stood, Scarbro leisurely looked him over, until Blaize began to feel like the prize pig at a fair. "You did well with your preparations, lad. Nothing to raise suspicion in the sack. Of course, you're still wearing legionary boots."

Blaize looked at his feet. He hadn't even thought of that. "They're all that I have."

But Scarbro waved away Blaize's response. "Just what an ex-army sort would have—especially if he went over the hill before his enlistment was up."

Reaching behind the desk, the officer brought out a bundle. "Travel leathers—suitably broken in. You don't want anything to look too new."

Next came a worn leather baldric and a sheathed short sword, the wire wound around its hilt tarnished. Scarbro handled it with distaste. "That should show it's been a while since your last inspection."

Behind the desk again, Scarbro produced a crossbow and a sack of bolts. "This should complete the image of former Utem Guardsman Blaize."

The officer opened the desk drawer and removed a small washed-leather pouch. It landed with a clinking noise as he tossed it into Blaize's hands. Opening it, Blaize found an odd lot of silver bits—cut portions of coins, chunks of larger bars, shavings, even a raw nugget or two.

"Road-silver," Scarbro said. "It will draw a lot less attention than freshly minted Imperials." He stepped to the door, leaving Blaize in privacy to change into the travel garments.

Moments later, Blaize was ready for the final inspection. The leathers fit well enough; his satchel went over one shoulder, the sword over the other. The crossbow hung from his back. His pouch of quarrels hung from one hip, his hand knife in his belt, and the moneybag was hidden close to his chest—right by Karrudan's medallion.

Scarbro nodded, well enough pleased. "There's a northern pony waiting for you in the messenger's stable north of Down Town," he said. "It's not a cavalry mount."

Blaize saluted, and Scarbro shook his head. "No more of that, now. Good luck, lad." He went to shake hands, then held up one finger, stepping back to the desk. A small pot of ointment came out of the drawer. "One more thing," he said with a grin. "Rub this into the top of your head. It will help that freshly reaped scalp grow brown in the sun—instead of scarlet."

Blaize had to laugh. Some days, it seemed as if the Empire thought of everything.

Rolling thunder from Snow's shot echoed down the valley. Black powder smoke vomited from the muzzle of the handgun into the chill northern air. And a bullet about the width of Snow's thumb hurtled into the target with a solid *thwack!*

Fifty paces away, the roughly man-sized, hay-stuffed target jigged wildly for a second on its wooden frame as the projectile struck.

Snow jerked the pistol apart at its hinged middle, exposing the rear end of the breech block. He dropped a bullet in until it stopped against the rifling in the barrel, brought a twist of paper up to his mouth, and bit the end off. After pouring in the black powder contents of the cartridge, he snapped the halves of the gun back together. A remaining pinch of powder went into the priming pan while he cocked the flintlock striker. Then he brought the gun up, aimed, and fired.

Another low boom billowed on the northern wind, another cloud of smoke, another dance from the target. The gun came down to be broken open. Bullet in the breech, charge of powder, snap together, priming, cocking . . . firing.

Open. Bullet. Powder. Prime. Cock. Aim. Fire.

Repeated.

Repeated yet again.

Snow was cracking the pistol open for yet another repetition when Sigwold's voice interrupted. "Time's up. I'm sure the good folk of Varsfield are tired of listening to you banging away."

Snow glanced back toward the town nestled farther up the valley. "I don't see anyone complaining."

"They should be applauding." The Dwarf tapped the top of the tiny hourglass to dislodge the last few grains of sand. "One minute, and you got in five shots—with five hits—at fifty paces."

Snow shrugged. "On the other hand, the target didn't dodge, charge, fling a spear, or send a fireball at me."

He went through the reloading operation on the handgun again. "A decent weapon for closer ranges. Probably be good for street-fighting."

Extending his arm, he aimed the pistol at the next target in line, a hundred paces off, and fired. The black powder boom echoed, but the target didn't move.

"Not so useful farther away, though," Snow said.

"I think that was a fairly close shot," Sigwold offered.

"Oh, yah. Scared that dummy half to death. Probably have to put new trousers on it," Snow deadpanned.

"We would have been delighted to come that close when we first started testing the smoothbore long guns." Sigwold shook his head. "The short-barreled guns were useless at twenty-five paces."

"I'm sure all this progress has Rayjan the Inventor dancing in his grave." Snow broke open the pistol again, searching among the gunsmithing odds and ends on the wooden bench before him until he found an oiled rag. He cleaned out the breech, then used a stick to run the rag through the handgun's barrel.

Laying the pistol down he picked up his Dwarven fuser rifle. The long gun was a big, brutal-looking weapon, thick in the barrel, with a halberd blade added on below the muzzle. Some of the human fighters called it ungainly, but Snow achieved an enviable accuracy with it.

He popped up the breech block, dropped a ball into place, then slapped the metal container down. A flick of his thumb levered up the plate over the charging bore, while he poured in the contents of a much larger black powder cartridge.

"Most humans complain that thing kicks like a boar sow in labor," Sigwold commented.

Snow grinned. "They don't have shoulders like us." He snapped the plate down, added a pinch of powder to the touch-hole, cocked, and aimed at a still farther target—two hundred paces.

The flintlock striker came down, but there was a perceptible, hissing interval before flame, smoke, and ball gouted from the muzzle. In the distance, the man-sized target jumped, a fresh hole appearing in the weathered canvas of its chest.

Snow looked sour. "I hate when these things hang fire," he grumbled. "Can't be sure if the ball will just dribble out, or if the whole breech is going to explode in my face."

"You got a fair hit," Sigwold said.

"Mmph. Fair." Snow's practiced hands ran through the reloading ritual while he squinted at the next-farthest target. The big fuser rifle came up and boomed.

Sigwold watched carefully. The distance was far enough to make spotting the impact a difficult job. "Belly wound," he reported. "Low and to the left."

Snow grunted. "*Not* where I aimed. I was going for the heart."

"If it's consistency you want for every shot, you'll have to wait till we perfect the new brass cartridges." Sigwold smiled. "Premeasured charges, correctly packed. Explosive wax to start the bang—it will mean the end of touch-holes, priming, flints . . . and fizzle-shots."

"Except sometimes the brass swells and jams the gun, leaving the gunner with a very large, expensive club," Snow pointed out.

"As I said, we still have to perfect it," Sigwold said. "That means there are things to fix."

"What are we perfecting and fixing now?" a voice inquired from behind them. Sarah Ythlim carried a long package wrapped in oilskin balanced over the shoulder of her homespun jacket. But the supple leather of her riding trews and boots quietly hinted at her wealth—not to mention that intangible air of command that graced her aristocratic features.

Snow fumbled with his weapon, still a little shy around the leader of the anti-Imperial Rebellion. Strong, smart, and citified, she was a more powerful woman than he'd ever met before. Though her charisma almost cowed a country boy like him, his anger had acted as a brace against his inexperience at their first meeting. Time and exposure had gentled his late-teenage bravado, and he could only remember how she'd changed him and how he respected her now.

He'd wandered north after finally escaping from the pit mine at Linzfarne, angry at the world—and especially at his father. At the last moment, Pap began dithering about the getting away. In spite of the beatings, watching his neighbors die from the poisonous effects of the Magestone, and losing

Mam to an Imperial spear, Pap had clung to his illusions about the great and glorious Empire.

And a less-than-glorious overseer had killed the old man while Snow and a few others had escaped. Given his frame of mind when he reached Varsfield, Snow might have ended up as a brutal reaver—there were plenty of bandit gangs up in the mountains.

Luckily he'd fallen in with a group of Rebels and met Sarah. She'd shown him an alternative to raging against the world. Snow found what it was like to try to build a future. Oh, the Rebels could still use his skills as a fighter. In fact, they helped him discover his talents with black powder weapons. But the fighting was a means to an end—an end of the Empire that had wrecked his life and the lives of so many others.

"We were talking about the new brass cartridges," Sigwold told Sarah.

She shook her head. "The Tinkers are still working on them. Too bad they won't be ready—" Sarah broke off, turning briskly to strip coverings from the package she carried. "Perhaps you'd like to see something already perfected."

The weapon she drew out of its cocoon was a fuser rifle Snow had never seen before. The gun was finely worked, but compared to his weapon of choice, it looked frail.

Sarah smiled, seeming to read his mind. "Yes," she said. "My lady's hand-cannon."

"I've heard about this," Sigwold said, taking the rifle and glancing over at Snow. "You'd be surprised." He proffered the weapon for his friend's closer inspection.

Snow could see the flintlock striker and priming pan, but there was no breech opening that he could discover. All the metalwork was intricately carved. The striker arm was actually in the shape of an armored arm about to deliver a blow. The priming pan was the wide-stretched mouth of some Mage Spawn or other. The long, ornate trigger guard was a dragon in mid-flight, breathing fire.

He gave the smiling Dwarf a look. "Very pretty."

"It was made by a true craftsman," Sarah pointed out.

"And he could have crafted three more regular rifles in the time he was carving all those curlicues." Snow pointed to the dragon wings. "Those are sure to snag on something—most likely, the poor gunner's shirt. And how are you supposed to load it?" He glanced over at the smirking Sigwold. "Or is this one of your early experiments, where you rammed powder and ball down from the muzzle?"

"No, this is one of our Tinkers' latest efforts," Sarah replied. "And the 'poor gunner' is me."

She smiled at Snow's open mouth. "I'd never ask one of our people to do anything I wouldn't—or couldn't—do myself."

"How—?" Snow managed.

"Thought you'd never ask," Sarah responded with a grin. She grasped the dragon's tail and twisted. One revolution, and the trigger guard was now an inch and a half below the bottom of the gun, attached by a large screw perhaps three-quarters of an inch wide. And a three-quarter-inch opening had appeared in the top of the rifle.

Holding the weapon muzzle-down, Sarah dropped a bullet into the aperture, following it with the contents of a black powder cartridge, saving a little bit for the priming pan.

Another twist, and the trigger guard was back in place. Sarah brushed a few crumbs of black powder off the top of the screw, then aimed her rifle at the three-hundred-pace target. The rifle fired with a sharper *crack!* In the distance, the target jumped.

"If you aimed for the heart, you hit it dead-on," Sigwold said.

"Would you like to try?" Sarah asked, offering the weapon to Snow. He ran through the loading process and fired. His shot, too, was dead-on.

"Impressive." Snow handed the rifle back. "But I'd feel better with a heavier gun like mine in case the fighting gets hand to hand."

"This is the weapon of the future," Sigwold insisted, taking the rifle and cleaning it. "With the next generation of rifle, you'd be able to stand on one side of Throne Complex and hit Karrudan all the way on the other."

"Except that there'd be a quarter mile of palace in between." Sarah's expression was enigmatic as she took the new rifle back. "This is the weapon we need now."

Snow grinned, hefting his heavy Dwarven rifle. "And this is what we'll be fighting with when we get to Atlantis—not to mention those pistols. We don't have time for the future, Sigwold."

The Dwarf shrugged. "If you say so," he said. "If you say so."

Blaize used his sleeve to brush sweat off his face and his heavily tanned, stubbled scalp. After three weeks in the saddle, he was considerably browner and leaner, riding through the town gates of Khamsin as the rear guard of a caravan. The early days of his journey had been straight riding on the Imperial post-roads. Then, as he'd come to look more the part of a wandering sword for hire, he'd sought out traders heading north.

Before his first week as an outrider was over, he'd blooded the short sword he wore, driving off a crew of bandits. The would-be reavers were hardly the hulking Orcs Father had spoken of—they'd looked more like scarecrows. At their first rush, Blaize had feared the caravan was under attack from Necropolis Sect Zombies.

They smelled bad enough to pass, he thought, wrinkling his nose at the memory. But the bandits had proven all too mortal when the guards had ridden against them.

It had seemed too easy to Blaize, who held back from dealing with what turned out to be a diversion. He was in just the position to deal with a pair of bandits who burst from a stand of underbrush, riding through the line of pack mules and trying to make off with one of the load-beasts.

The one who didn't have the mules' reins just pulled up his bony nag and rode off. The other dropped the reins and swung his sword in a wild, looping arc.

Blaize simply kept low and thrust his blade home.

He'd gotten a bonus from the master-merchant in charge as well as favorable references at their destination. Nowhere along the journey had Blaize been forced to use his mystic tattoo for help.

With the payment from his new caravan master, Blaize would just about double the collection of road-silver he'd set off with. Next stop, the baths, and then a shave for his head and face.

His fellow guards would probably be heading for the Street of Brothels. But pleasure wasn't what Blaize was pursuing. Now it was time to begin his business, with a tour of Khamsin's taverns. They'd be good places to listen . . . and even better places to talk.

Four days later, Blaize had lost count of the watering holes he'd walked into. Not that his drinking had gotten ahead of him. It became a temptation, however, after walking through the ovenlike streets. Khamsin was a town of baked brick, an odd, yellowish-gray stuff that seemed to reflect sunlight onto the streets until the pavements became hot enough to cook on.

He had yet to see any trace of greenery in his wanderings. The ranked houses on the streets shared communal gardens, or so he'd been told. But the class of drinking establishment he'd be expected to frequent wouldn't offer such amenities. This pub was much like the rest, dark and stifling, but at least out of the relentless sun.

Blaize sat, looking around. His days on the town had taught him at least two things. The good folk of Khamsin had little love for the Empire. And the drinking life quickly made alarming inroads on Blaize's purse. Also, the citizens of Khamsin drank very thin, bitter beer. The local wine was so acid, it would serve better on Khamsin salads than on drinkers' palates.

He looked at the collection of scruffy patrons around him. Some were old men who had nothing better to do of an afternoon than sit in front of a beer mug. Others were career drinkers, already half-sodden. Several were younger men out of work for one reason or another. Blaize tried to fit himself into that category. Throughout his wanderings, he'd made inquiries about outgoing caravans.

And when people had blamed bad business on the Empire, he'd cursed the Empire, too.

Sitting in the corner of this midden, a half beaker on the table in front of her, was a woman. He'd noticed her red hair in several other places along his drinking odyssey. She was neither a professional drinker nor a professional courtesan.

Pretty enough, Blaize silently opined, *if her face weren't so hard . . .*

He raised his mug to his lips, allowing himself another glance at her. Perhaps the angularity he saw lay more in her stance than her face. Her shoulders were tight, and there was a sort of ingrained fierceness to her expression. Even the drunks who pawed at the waitresses stayed away from her, and she certainly didn't go out of her way to mingle. The woman simply sat, watched . . . and listened.

Either she's what I'm looking for, or she'll be reporting me to the local garrison as a potential rebel. Blaize hid his smile behind another swig of beer and waited for his opportunity to join the barroom conversation. Sooner or later, as it always did, the subject of taxes came up.

"Gold is the lifeblood of the Empire," one of the old men beerily expounded.

"Then the gods-be-damned Empire should be careful with the bloodletting before it kills us all," Blaize spoke up in a loud voice.

The eyes of the other drinkers jumped to him, startled, as he went on. "I'll tell you a little story, true as Necros love bones. My people had a farm down Caero way—"

"As if we couldn't have guessed that from that shining pate," one of oldsters muttered.

Blaize held his breath to send a flush to his shaven head and gave the man a hard look. The whitebeard hastily lost himself in his beer mug.

"I got a letter—Mam and Pap had to pay a scribe to write it—telling of tax troubles. Took a while for it to reach me.

My legion was off to the borders, slamming the door on some Orcs." He took a hard, angry swallow. "Soon as I heard, though, I headed for home. And what do I find? Our farm is now part of an estate, with a fat-faced majordomo telling me to get off the master's land. I wanted to lay the swag-belly's guts out, but I had to find my folk first."

He took another swig, getting into the story he'd composed on his trip northward. "But they and all the neighbors were gone—probably starved to death by the side of some road. My folks gave a son to the army—wasn't that tax enough? Lose the farm we've had from time out of mind. Lose Mam and Pap. I did find out who the new master was, though. Surprise, surprise. He was the local tax-collector!"

"Bleed us all," one of the old men said.

"But the ones who kiss Imperial ass do well enough." Blaize let a slight slur into his voice. "Push up them purple-and-gold robes and pucker their lips. Gods rot all Imperials, that's what I say!"

"You fought for 'em," one of the younger men, a muleteer by his looks, pointed out.

"And now I fight for myself," Blaize snarled, his hand going to the hilt of his sword. "Want to see how?"

The muleteer backed off quickly. "Just saying—"

Blaize drowned out whatever the man had to say. "I shed blood, not gold, for the great, good Empire. And what did I get from it in return? About as much good as I get from this goat-whizz beer." He upended his mug and let the dregs run out onto the sawdust floor.

"Why don't you open a barrel of better brew?" the red-haired woman from the corner said to the tapster. "I'll stand our friend here a drink."

A moment later, she approached Blaize with two mugs and sat at his table. "Tell me more," the redhead said as she sat down. "Just do it in a lower voice. The press-gangs are out, and there's always room in the Magestone mines for those who complain too loudly."

"Who are you?" Blaize asked, trying to sound suspicious.

"My name is Rikka," the woman replied.

"That's a Dwarven name." Blaize looked at her intently. "But you're no Dwarf."

Rikka rolled her hazel eyes. "Well, now we know you're not completely blind from ale. What do they call you, stranger?"

"Blaize," he replied. "How did you get that name?"

"I was adopted—a long story," Rikka said. "Right now, I'm more interested in hearing yours."

So Blaize continued spinning the tale he'd constructed over weeks of caravan night-guard duty. He'd picked up more than enough elements from the times his unit had participated in sweeps through the slums of Down Town in search of deserters. Back then, he'd dismissed what he'd heard as the excuses of prisoners taken for going over the hill.

But stitched together with a good narrative, they'd offer a good set of reasons for a soldier becoming disaffected from the Empire.

Rikka apparently thought so. The angularity was gone from her face, which, Blaize had to admit, was actually quite attractive—high cheekbones and expressive eyes. She asked him about his military service, and Blaize answered with soldiers' yarns he'd heard from various Utem Guardsmen he'd trained with—carefully played down.

Rikka was especially interested when she learned that he'd been posted in Atlantis, asking questions about the city in the sky and about Down Town. Those, of course, were the easiest for Blaize to answer. The less lying he had to do, the easier it would be to keep up this illusion.

"Were you ever assigned to guarding the mines?" The angularity was back, all over Rikka—shoulders tense, face grim, her fingers white around her mug.

"Never!" The outburst was genuine enough. Mine duty would be like Feshku's Pit of Perdition for an Altem Guardsman, the worst imaginable punishment detail. Blaize wanted to spit. The only thing worse than that guard duty was digging in the mines themselves.

"Once someone is sent off on mine detail, they rarely get out again," he said. "And usually they did something to deserve it." He almost quoted the soldiers' description of the mine guards—"Scum guarding worse scum."

Then it hit him—a human girl with a Dwarven name. Where did you find most Dwarves in the Empire? Slaving in the mines. Biting back the remark, he shook his head. "Whatever the guards are, they aren't warriors anymore."

"They fight bravely enough when the mines are attacked by rebels—or Elementalists," Rikka pointed out.

"That only happens at isolated mines in enemy territory," Blaize replied. "The guards have no retreat and little chance of aid. You can get the same sort of 'bravery' out of a trapped rat."

He paused for a second. "Or maybe that's where they send the best of the worst. Inside the borders, where there's less fear of attack, townsfolk leagues away from the mines lock their doors at the sight of an Imperial uniform. Those animals give guardsmen everywhere a bad name."

"Spoken like a true guardsman," Rikka said ironically.

"An *ex*-guardsman." Blaize looked down at his worn leathers with a bitter laugh. "Whatever good I thought I found among them, I still went over the hill."

Rikka's tense attitude softened again. Resting her elbows on the table, she interlaced her fingers and propped her chin on top of them. "So that's your past, Blaize. What lies ahead?"

He shrugged. "A man's got to eat—as well as drink." Bringing up his mug, he took a sip. This beer actually did taste better than the last. "I've been making a living hiring out my sword." He paused. "But it would be better to fight for a cause I believed in."

The line came naturally enough to his lips because he was fighting for a cause—for the Empire that unified humans and protected them from the other races. Thanks to Imperial law, the diverse human tribes each had their place, not to mention the Dwarves. Living under Tezla's Precepts—

"Blaize?" Rikka's voice invaded his thoughts. He refocused on her with a start.

She smiled at him. "If it's a cause you're looking for, I do believe we can find you one."

Chapter 4

Following Rikka out of the tavern, Blaize walked into the last vestiges of sunset. With an inconspicuous movement, he loosed his sword in its sheath. It wasn't that he anticipated treachery from the young woman. He just expected their journey would take them into the poorest slum in town, probably ending in some rat-infested cellar. That was where he and his comrades had usually found the dissidents in Down Town—starving wretches who often flung themselves bare-handed onto Imperial swords.

Instead, Rikka led him through streets of yellow-gray brick buildings to a warehouse in an unprosperous but quiet enough Khamsin neighborhood. Blaize realized they were about two streets away from the caravansary where he was staying.

A pair of workers, one human, one a Dwarf, stood in the entrance, stripped to the waist as they shifted barrels and bales. Blaize had to admit he'd never seen a harder-looking pair of warehousemen. They stopped work when Blaize came into sight, directing cold gazes at him.

Rikka gave an exasperated snort. "He's with me."

The pair wordlessly went back to their tasks.

"A very impressive pair of doorkeepers," Blaize said as they headed inside. "They'd be enough to give even an Imperial Altem pause. Although . . . you don't usually see warehouses being loaded at night." He smiled. "A suspicious mind might wonder if illegal activity is going on here."

Rikka flashed him a grin in return. "As you said so well, a man's got to eat."

Blaize followed her through cavernous, shadowy storage bays, toward a pool of dim illumination in the rear of the warehouse. The light came from a small oil lamp perched on a wood slab laid across a pair of barrels. It barely allowed Blaize to make out the faces of four people sitting round the table.

He immediately went into his adopted personality, rubbing his hands together and asking, "Got a game of some kind going? Is there room for a fifth player?"

A bearded, craggy face turned to take him in with flinty eyes. "What we're doing is talking business, Caeronn. I don't know if that's a game you can play."

"Father—" Rikka began.

The Dwarf cut her off. "My daughter has been watching you for a while. She thinks you're a man who could be about our business. Looks as though you've convinced her. Now you've got to convince me. Are you a likely man, Caeronn?"

Rikka said nothing as her adopted father leaned a little farther into the light. The Dwarf's craggy face was almost hidden in curly hair-bristling eyebrows, a low hairline, a bushy beard—all of it grizzled with gray.

Old for his kind, Blaize thought. He looped his thumbs in his belt, returning the look from the Dwarf's shadowed eyes. "Name's Blaize, and I'm a likely man for all sorts of work." He nodded toward Rikka. "But from what the lady here said, it looked to be something a man could take pride in. Not smuggling and throat-slitting."

The Dwarf's fist hammered down on the tabletop, making it—and everyone around it—jump.

Blaize braced himself. Everyone knew about Dwarven battle-fury. He might well have just sparked a case of it.

"Well, you've shown you're a likely enough man with your mouth." The Dwarf looked round the table. "Let's see how well you do with a sword. All right with you, Tulwar Windfoot?"

One of the others at the table nodded, bringing his face into the light. A Galeshi, judging by the name. The young man's looks underscored his identity as a sand clansman.

Bright white teeth gleamed against deeply tanned skin. So did his dark eyes as he looked over Blaize. There was no way to guess his hair color—Tulwar was beardless, and his head was covered in a green kaffiyeh. "A pleasure, Eginhard."

Blaize let his hand rest on his hilt. "Practice weapons, or do we send for the leech right now?"

Eginhard stroked his beard, a low, deep laugh escaping from him. "You make a point, stranger. Practice weapons it shall be." He held the lamp while the others began disassembling the table, creating a larger open area. Then they pulled out crates, which, when opened, proved full of wooden swords, shields, staffs, even polearms.

Blaize glanced at Rikka, who shrugged. "Sometimes, people gather here to see prizefights."

Another profitable illegality, he thought. *The Empire prefers to keep the returns from the arena for itself.*

Tulwar, tall and lean, did his best to loom over Blaize. The Galeshi glanced from him to Rikka and back again. "If they had called a leech, it would have been for you, farmer."

For the nomadic sand-clansmen, calling someone a farmer was a deadly insult. To call a clansman something like that in front of his woman would leave him foaming.

I wonder if Rikka realizes what he thinks he's doing? Blaize thought.

She did, producing a knife so quickly Blaize didn't even see where it came from. Neither did the Galeshi, who now found the point of her blade dimpling his throat. "Keep on that road, and it will take *you* to the leech, Tulwar," the red-haired woman said.

Tulwar backed hastily away, turning to the armory of sham weapons. He quickly dug out the equivalent of a Galeshi scimitar, a fire-hardened length of wood, and set it whistling in a circle around his head.

Blaize said nothing as he stepped over to the crates. He'd fought Galeshis during his time on the western borders. Their fighting style was much like their tactics—whirlwind attacks followed by lightning retreats.

I need a weapon that will allow me to stay agile in a fight, he thought. *And it wouldn't hurt if friend Tulwar was unfamiliar with my choice.*

He saw a rounded edge poking up from the corner of one of the dustier crates. Kneeling, Blaize dug into the mass of old equipment and came up with a wooden buckler, about a foot across. "This and a short sword will do."

"In truth?" The dubious words came from one of the other men who'd been at the table, a tall, shifty-eyed Khamsin. Or maybe that was just another way of conveying doubt.

Blaize grinned. "Stay with what you know," he said, watching the Galeshi limber up with a series of complicated sweeps and slashes. "And what the other side doesn't."

He found a blunt-tipped practice blade about the right length and shape and slipped off his sword and baldric, removing pouches and knife from his belt as well. Then he worked to loosen his shoulders and stretch his legs. Blaize hefted his chosen weapons, left hand gripping the handle on the buckler, sword in his right, trying a couple of combinations.

They would have to do.

He rejoined the others, finding the group had grown. The pair of bruisers from the door had come to watch the entertainment.

Eginhard looked at Blaize's chosen weapons with interest. Tulwar gave a great, braying laugh. "That cake plate will not save you, farmer."

Blaize simply saved his breath as he went to the spot that Eginhard indicated. Tulwar was already in place. The audience, such as it was, spread in a wide circle.

"All right," Eginhard said. "Begin."

Instantly, Tulwar flew at Blaize, the belled sleeves on his heavy cotton shirt flapping like a bird's wings as he moved.

But Blaize was more concerned with the bird's beak—the curved sword lashing crosswise at him. His buckler was already up and straight out, deflecting the blow. He followed with a lunge, but the Galeshi wasn't there, nimbly backing out of the way.

Blaize wanted to curse—he'd hoped to end this quickly,

in the first passage of arms. Tulwar swore out loud, a complicated-sounding Galeshi cussword. At the same moment, he launched himself again, obviously hoping he'd distracted his opponent. Again, Blaize managed to parry with his buckler but couldn't riposte in time to catch the Galeshi.

Both men began to circle, an admission that this fight would take longer than either had hoped. The Galeshi's dress—the flapping pantaloons and sleeves—distracted Blaize as he tried to gauge his enemy's movement. Tulwar lived up to his epithet-name, moving in incredibly quick bounds to deal slashes and cuts with his make-believe scimitar. Blaize stayed on the defensive, blocking and moving, trying to find an opening.

Another flurry of quick passes, and the Galeshi stood glaring at him in frustration, sweat beginning to dew his face. He had the height on Blaize and the longer sword. Both gave him the advantage of reach.

It seemed inconceivable that Blaize's toy shield, barely larger than a dinner plate, could keep the Galeshi's blows swerving away.

But the secret of the buckler lay in its position, not in its size. By keeping the small shield at arm's length in front of him, Blaize was blocking his opponent's attacks as they originated. This created a cone-shaped zone of safety that protected most of his body. If Tulwar went high or low, a small adjustment of the buckler shifted the deflection zone and thwarted the attack. And when the Galeshi tried to aim attacks that would bypass the buckler, he found himself in unfamiliar, contorted positions—and missed.

On the other hand, while Blaize succeeded in blocking Tulwar's rushing attacks, he still hadn't been able to counterattack against Windfoot's dodging recoveries.

"Will you not stand and fight?" the Galeshi demanded.

Blaize replied by retreating—but only a half step as his adversary charged in again. Tulwar let his slash go broad, and Blaize actively pushed it along with his buckler, at the same time whipping round with his blade.

He rapped Tulwar smartly on the forearm with the flat of

his wooden blade. The Galeshi's usual dodge turned into more of a scramble.

"A touch," Rikka announced.

Eginhard looked as if he'd just been fed a persimmon. "A passing wound," he admitted.

A bloody cut on the sword arm, if this blade had been steel and I'd used the edge, Blaize thought.

"Continue to a death-cut," the Dwarf ordered.

Tulwar looked only too happy to comply, his face red with mortification over being tagged by his opponent.

He crouched now as he circled, taking the bout much more seriously, stamping his feet, flapping his free arm to distract Blaize's attention. This time when he launched himself, his scimitar seemingly went wide of Blaize's protection.

Then the Galeshi brought his curved blade down and back, impacting with the back of Blaize's extended left calf. Blows were supposed to be laid on the flat of the sword, but it was Tulwar's edge that bit with a slicing blow into the nerve plexus behind Blaize's knee. As it was, his lower leg seemed to go numb. A live blade would have left a gash serious enough to bleed a man out, not to mention probably crippling him for life by cutting the hamstring.

"A touch!" the shifty-eyed Khamsin cried out in delight. He probably had a bet down on this.

Blaize could only hobble to the side as Tulwar swept around, bringing his scimitar high for a downward slice at his opponent's head. He seemed to have completely forgotten about using the flat of his blade. And the edge of even a wooden sword could crack Blaize's skull.

I wonder what would happen if he lands on Karrudan's tattoo, Blaize thought as he hauled himself around. He pivoted on his good leg, moving into the Galeshi's line of attack, twisting the buckler so the edge of the shield caught Tulwar right in the upper lip, where his mustache should have been.

The impact brought up the Galeshi even more effectively than a punch in the face. But Blaize wasn't finished. He brought his other arm around in a thrust that showed he knew a thing or two about nerves, too.

In combat, the correct blow would have been to the upper chest—the heart. Instead, Blaize aimed his blunt blade just beneath Tulwar's breastbone—into the solar plexus.

The sand clansman collapsed with impressive realism, trying to draw breath with a suddenly paralyzed diaphragm. He finally began wheezing again as Blaize turned to Eginhard.

"I believe that would be considered a death-cut," he said to the suddenly silent room. Then he rubbed his leg. "Although, I have to admit I'd be limping ever after if this had been the real thing."

A slight thaw appeared in the Dwarf's arctic eyes. "Well, at least you're no blowhard," he said. Then the flint returned to his gaze. "But there's more to being a fighter than winning a practice bout."

Tests, tests, and more tests, Blaize thought with a sigh. "Then give me something real to do," he suggested out loud.

"I'll do that," Eginhard said. "Do you read?"

In quite a few armies, the likeliest answer would have been "no." But literacy was prized among Atlantean troops. Better than half the rank and file could read, with the average much higher among the specialist ranks.

"I can get along," Blaize replied. "As long as it's not poetry."

"Then it's just as well I don't want any romantic odes," Eginhard replied. "I'm looking for rosters and listings—troop and patrol movements for the Atlantean garrison here."

Blaize shook his head. "You don't ask for much, do you? And where do you expect me to get them?"

Eginhard's hard-bitten face took on an almost innocent expression. "Why, from Khamita Castle, of course. The Imperial garrison's headquarters. Bring the information here tomorrow night."

Blaize spent the next morning taking a stroll around the so-called castle. Actually, it was a typical Atlantean fortress, with a few atypical features.

"This was originally the old *shahria*, or royal palace, for Family Khamita," his guide muttered. "It was built on the highest piece of land in the city, and the center was the Great Tower."

The tower was a definite non-Atlantean touch, ten stories of shiny blackness rising above the thirty-foot curtain walls of dressed sandstone. It would make the perfect lookout point to spot an oncoming caravan—or an Orc army boiling across the plains.

Shifty-eyes gestured to the open space around the walls. "All of this was the Grand Market of Khamsin. Merchants came from all over the North to trade during the market month." He spat. "The Atlanteans took four times as much room as the castle and decreed that the surrounding land must always be bare. Now the market takes place outside the city."

The Atlantean siege of Khamsin ended more than three hundred years ago when Tezla's troops marched into the city. To hear this fellow, it might have been last week. *Either he's a fanatic,* Blaize thought, *or his family seriously lost something to Tezla.*

"They created their own town in there," the Khamsin went on. "Barracks, a training ring for cavalry, granaries, even their own bathhouse."

Blaize shrugged. He knew the ways of the army's engineering corps, having put enough sweat into some of their building projects. The sappers kept everything standardized. Anywhere in the Empire, from Napolis in Delphana to this fort in Khamsin, one barracks room looked pretty much like another. Some found that sameness comforting. For Blaize, it verged on boredom.

On the other hand, it meant he'd know exactly what to expect on the other side of the walls—once he got there. The ramparts of the fort followed the contours of the hill, enclosing a shape like a gigantic kidney. Four gateways appeared at the cardinal points of the compass, offering arched entrances in forty-foot-tall fortified gatehouses.

Blaize watched a wagon of supplies coming in and getting a thorough search.

"Not easy, eh?" Shifty-eyes asked.

They continued on a circuit of the battlemented walls, where square towers jutted out at intervals to allow the legionary defenders to catch assault forces in crossfire. Blaize carefully examined each as he passed along. Finally, he stopped. "Here," he said.

His companion glanced along the wall and tower. "What? You'll need a harder head even than yours to batter your way through."

"Not through," Blaize corrected. "Over."

Bidding his guide farewell, he headed for the markets to buy a few necessary items while he awaited the sunset.

Blaize left his inn, walking along the darkened streets. He paused for a moment in front of a well-lit tavern, not considering a drink, but trying for a backward glance. No one behind him seemed interested in his progress, but he caught a hint of movement in the shadows of an alley mouth.

So, he *was* being followed and watched.

Following one of the larger streets to the former Grand Market, Blaize began circling round Khamita Castle, toward the tower he'd scouted earlier. He'd chosen to make his move before moonrise, so the Great Tower rose up like a vast, formless bulk against the stars. Blaize knew he had to be equally indistinct, but he felt naked traversing the barren killing space around the walls.

He crossed it, to end up hugging the base of the hill. Blaize loosened the length of rope worn baldric-fashion across his chest, tying a loop at the end. A quick scramble brought him up to the corner of the tower.

If I have an audience behind me, he thought, *they're in for a show now.* Taking off his shoes, he tucked them in his belt and then reached up, feeling for the crevices between the blocks of dressed sandstone.

From there on, he simply scrabbled upward, fighting for finger and toeholds, keeping a careful eye on the stone ahead of him while trying to ignore the ever-growing potential fall below.

For some legionaries on really boring garrison duty, tower-climbing was a sport. Others found it a more serious matter—an attempt to get back to barracks before the roll was called . . . or the first step in going over the hill.

Blaize had climbed his first tower as an eighteen-year-old under the elevating influence of some winter wine. He'd wished for a drink before this ascent—better to wish for the strength and agility he'd enjoyed seven years ago.

He reached the overhang at the top of the tower and clung in place, holding his breath. At long last he heard footsteps and the faint jingle of armor. Blaize hung on as the sentry passed through the tower and continued along the rampart.

Using one hand, Blaize loosened the length of rope he wore, tossing the looped end upward to snag on the battlement. In the old days, he'd have maneuvered himself over the hump as the climax of his climb, but these weren't the old days. *He* was older.

It took two tries, the slap of the rope sounding obscenely loud. But the line held, and Blaize used it to clamber into the top of the tower. He dropped to one knee, not wanting to be outlined against the stars, and scanned the nearby walls. There was the sentry, marching along his beat. No other guards nearby.

Blaize headed down the interior stairs of the tower to ground level. He dumped his rope, resumed his shoes, and eased open a wooden door onto an empty graveled street.

Well, I'm in, he thought.

He was wearing the purchases he'd made at the market—nondescript clothing that would look enough like an Atlantean uniform at a quick glance. Keeping his pace to a stroll, he made his way along company streets, doing his best to stay away from the open verandas of the barracks.

Here was the main road, opening into a sort of miniature forum fronted by the headquarters building. This wasn't the standard rectangular structure, though—it was a piece of the old palace, with the Great Tower rising from its rear.

Blaize gave the guards at the front entrance a wide berth, heading off to see if there was a side door. He found one, closed, but apparently not locked. A little work with the tip of his knife slipped into the seam between door and jamb was enough to lift the latch. Then a gentle tug on the ring outside, and Blaize was in the building.

The problem was, he had no idea where he was. And as he followed the corridor, which made a sudden dogleg turn, he encountered another problem—an armed guard.

The soldier goggled for a moment, then brought up his spear. If he'd been a true enemy, Blaize might have risked drawing his knife and rushing him.

But they both served Atlantis, so he raised empty hands while the spearhead wobbled into line with his chest.

Blaize gave the nervous guard his friendliest smile. "Take me to your leader," he said.

CHAPTER 5

THE magus divided his frown between Blaize, sitting in front of the desk, and the collection of Technomantic gear spread across the desk's surface.

"You can see I have as much magic as a Khamsin brick," Blaize said. "Why won't you let me see Lord Portarr? Do you think I'm some sort of new Mage Spawn?"

The magic-wielding officer's frown deepened. "I find no magecraft within you," he admitted. "Yet there is something—some small trace—of magic about you."

Blaize sighed. He had hoped to reveal Karrudan's tattoo only to the garrison commander. Unfortunately, that didn't seem likely.

"Lord Mage, I need to show you something—alone." Blaize looked at the pair of guards flanking him with drawn swords.

The magus looked even more dubious. Blaize spread his empty hands. "It can't be that you fear me."

No officer, much less a member of the Atlantis Guild, would let that go by. The magus' face contorted, his pride struck to the quick. "You will burn for that impertinence, Caeronn."

He dismissed the guards with a curt jerk of his head. "Speak," the mage grated. "Save your life—if you can."

Slowly, Blaize fished the silver medallion from under his shirt. The magus snatched up his staff, ready to respond to any sorcerous attack with a magic blast. Instead, his face went pale as he recognized the sigil that swam into existence on Blaize's brow.

"You recognize this?" Blaize asked, tapping the sign.

The mage licked his lips and nodded. "What do you require?"

Although Blaize maintained his confident front, a tiny shudder ran down the length of his spine. This wasn't some Galeshi sword-swinger he'd just faced down, but an Atlantean mage-officer! It took a second for Blaize to get his lips to work. "Lord Portarr."

"This had better be good, Gamelon." Glaring at the mage-officer, the commander of Khamsin's garrison stalked into the office, smelling of sweet wine and musky perfume. His gray hair was tousled, his robe was half undone. He was not happy at this interruption to his private pleasures.

That attitude changed when Portarr saw Karrudan's mystic tattoo. "How—" The Warlord shook his head, trying to clear it. "How may I be of aid to the Prophet-Magus?"

Blaize carefully weighed what to tell and what to leave out. "I was sent here to seek out certain dissidents."

If the mark hadn't sobered Portarr up, that comment certainly did. The commander's bloodshot eyes took on a look of alarm. "The Prophet-Magus is dissatisfied with our efforts against Rebellion?"

Scarbro's words about the swirl of Imperial intrigue whispered in Blaize's brain. It was time for him to be politic. "My concern is activity in Atlantis," he said, considering each word. "But I need to get the trust of some Rebels up here to further my business in the capital."

"You think there could be any connection between some flea-bitten dissidents up here and the dust-folk of Down Town?" It seemed that Gamelon had a skeptical nature in general.

"I think there is communication," Blaize replied, still keeping things vague. "Messages from would-be Rebels in Khamsin might find interested ears in Down Town."

He shifted his attention to Portarr. "A leader of the malcontents, believing me to be a disaffected soldier, sent me to penetrate your headquarters and get information about troop movements."

Lord Portarr responded with a grunt. "It seems you made your way well enough without my help."

Blaize shrugged. "There may have been eyes on me, Lord. I didn't have the option of approaching you openly."

The garrison commander's brow furrowed in thought. "What you seek is trifling, given your commission—and who sends you. The information you've requested would be more useful to smugglers than Rebels." He gave Blaize the hard eye.

"It's possible to be one, Lord, or the other—or both," Blaize replied.

Portarr nodded, then turned to the mage-officer of the guard. "Gamelon, get the duty rosters and let him see the patrol schedules."

Still frowning, the mage went to the pigeonhole files behind the desk. He drew out several sheets of paper and wordlessly passed them to Blaize.

The schedules detailed unit sizes, routes, and timing for patrols in and around Khamsin for the next week. Blaize memorized the list, jotting down a few notes with a charcoal stick on a paper scrap just to make sure.

"And now you'll vanish back over the wall," Portarr said as Blaize returned the documents.

"Again, I suspect others may be looking for me." Blaize glanced at the door and the guards beyond. "It would be best if no word of this visit left this room."

"The guards will be silent," Gamelon grimly promised.

"I'd also request that a mage-writ be sent to Lord Scarbro of the Atlantis garrison," Blaize went on, "reporting that the Prophet-Magus' suspicions of brewing Rebellion were correct."

The mage-officer's frown grew deeper. "I can handle that task," he said.

Blaize simply nodded.

Invoking Karrudan would probably ensure that the message was sent. Beyond that, Blaize could only hope that Scarbro would correctly read between the lines.

Politics just makes everything more confusing, he thought, tucking his notes away in his belt pouch.

Gamelon raised a hand to stay his departure. "I trust that when the Prophet-Magus no longer has use for these Rebels, we will be informed where and how best to deal with them?"

As Blaize nodded, he was struck with a sudden, stunning vision of Rikka dying on an Altem Guardsman's sword. Somehow he kept his voice steady as he replied. "That will, of course, depend on the decision of the Prophet-Magus."

Portarr leaned close enough that Blaize could smell the wine turning sour on the Warlord's breath. "Gamelon isn't just the duty officer of the night guard. He's my ferret among all these Khamsin rats."

"So it might be to both our interests to work together," Gamelon said. "I have an easier way to arrange a meeting than having you climb the fortress walls in the dark of night. In the Street of Metalworkers there is an old bronze statue of one of the Khamita kings—or rather, the remains of a statue. Folk hereabouts have a tradition of touching the statue's toes for good luck."

The mage-officer gave him a narrow smile. "I made a small addition. Touch the toes, then give two taps to the left heel of this statue. That will activate a Technomantic device. I'll then meet you within the hour at the Emperor's statue in the Great Square."

Portarr laughed. "So, I'm sure we'll see you again if you have further reports for Atlantis," he said. "Just as I'm sure you can find your way back over the wall without an escort."

Blaize nodded and rose as the mage-officer called the guards from outside the door. The soldiers came in, carefully blank-faced.

As I would have, if the circumstances had been reversed, Blaize thought.

He saluted the officers and left, retracing his steps through the fortress to the tower door. The coiled rope lay where he'd left it.

Blaize cat-footed up to the top of the tower, where he checked for sentries. When none were near, he looped the rope around one of the crenelations and walked his way down the wall.

When he reached the ground, Rikka and another man stood waiting for him. Both wore cloaks that reached to the ground.

She twitched the end of the rope. "This will tell them there was an intruder," she whispered.

"How else was I to get out with the gates locked?" Blaize replied, his voice equally low. "My job was to collect the information."

Rikka nodded. "And ours to keep the Imperials unsuspecting." She knelt, producing a small bull's-eye lantern. Shrouding the iron box with her cloak, she flicked it open for an instant, sending a beam of light out into the darkness.

Immediately, singing suddenly rang out from the distance—several voices drunkenly harmonizing in a bawdy ballad about a mage who constructed a she-Golem, what he did to it, and what it did to him.

Diversion, Blaize realized.

A challenge was shouted down from the wall and a smart answer returned, the exchange quickly degenerating into back-and-forth insults.

As the argument grew louder, the man with Rikka unslung a crossbow from his back, strung it, loaded a bolt, and fired.

The sound of the shot seemed deafening to Blaize's taut senses, but it coincided with the supposed drunk throwing a rock at the fortress wall.

Blaize caught the sound of metal impacting rock. Rikka pushed him against the stony slope, and the crossbowman joined them. Even as they moved, the rope slithered down to coil at their feet.

Rikka gathered it up as the bowman darted out to retrieve his bolt. Blaize hadn't even heard it fall. "How—" he began.

Capable fingers shut his mouth. "Cross the open space first," Rikka hissed in his ear.

They made their way across the kill zone as quickly and quietly as possible. The guards might not waste their time sending a patrol after a bunch of ostensible drunks. On the other hand, no Atlantean soldier liked being insulted by lowly townsfolk.

A furious shout came from the now torch-lit section of the ramparts, followed by a scream from below. Blaize and his companions reached the shelter of a dark street mouth as the drunks hustled off carrying one of their number, shouting imprecations at the soldiers on the wall.

Tomorrow morning, one of the guardsmen will have to account for his spear, Blaize thought.

"Do you think he was actually hit?" he asked Rikka.

"In that uncertain light, who could tell? Either way, it was time to leave before more spears came flying."

Blaize nodded. "All right. Now why don't you explain that trick with the rope?"

Rikka took the bolt from the crossbowman and held it up. Instead of a conventional arrowhead, the tip of the bolt flared out into a concave cutting edge.

"I'm told pirates use it to cut rigging on ships," she said.

But it takes quite an aim to shear away the slipknot on a loop, Blaize thought, taking the short arrow. On closer inspection, he could see that one tip was crooked. *From where it hit the stonework,* he realized.

"Sorry to damage your tool," Blaize began. He glanced around, discovering that the bowman had already disappeared without a word.

"Come," Rikka said.

She took them on a complicated, devious course through narrow alleyways where the risen moon's light barely penetrated. Blaize was totally lost, except for the knowledge that he was far from the warehouse where he'd met Eginhard. Finally they emerged on a street lined with what looked like derelict buildings. Some appeared to be leaning against one another for support. One tilted precariously forward, threatening to spill itself into the tiny, squalid square. Rikka continued past this hazard to a tumbledown dwelling whose doorway stunk of spoiled food and urine.

This is more like the Rebels I know, Blaize thought, wrinkling his nose as Rikka gestured for him to precede her inside.

A blind beggar who must have lost his sense of smell as well as sight sat outside the hovel, his legs crossed, his body hunched. As he stepped into malodorous darkness, Blaize realized that someone had turned the beggar's bowl over, so any potential alms would bounce off the upturned bottom.

"Straight ahead—you'll find a flight of stairs leading down," Rikka said from behind his shoulder.

Rat-infested cellar, here we come, Blaize thought.

He groped toward the stairway, trying not to think of what he might be stepping on, and fumbled his way down a set of groaning, treacherous boards that barely deserved to be called stairs. Moving in pitch-blackness, Blaize's foot finally encountered a solid floor. He took a step forward and crashed into a remarkably sturdy door, considering the shoddy construction he'd been moving through up to that point.

The door noiselessly swung open on oiled hinges, and Blaize froze, squinting as blazing torchlight assailed his eyes.

Eginhard was the torchbearer and door-opener. He stood in a corridor that looked more like a mine adit. Wooden pillars rose every ten feet, supporting cross-beams that arched under the low ceilings.

Low for humans, that is.

It was an excellent height for Dwarves.

The Rebel leader turned, pointing the way with the torch. "Come along. Mind you don't brain yourself."

Blaize didn't move. "Nice place you have down here," he said. "But why didn't we meet at your warehouse?"

Eginhard looked up at him. "I'm afraid it's closed for a while." Blaize could barely make out the smile on the Dwarf's lips. "We had a little concern that we might have unfriendly visitors—just as we were concerned that the Imperials might have someone following you."

An icy finger traced its way along Blaize's back at the

thought that Portarr or his mage subordinate might try exactly that.

"Luckily," Eginhard went on, "there was no one trailing."

"And if there had been?" The minutest sense of motion behind him caused Blaize to look round at Rikka's pale face and fierce expression. He also noticed the naked blade she still carried.

Eginhard shrugged. "You'd have been taken care of out there, Rikka would have come in here, and the building above would have fallen in. Happens all the time. That cheap Khamsin construction, you know."

Eginhard turned again. "Solid Dwarven work down here in the Warrens," he said. "So come along. And mind your head."

Blaize was still trying to figure what signal had told Rikka to let him live. "The beggar," he suddenly said. "The overturned bowl."

The Dwarf glanced back in appreciation. "Very good, Caeronn. If the bowl had been upright and open, Rikka would have opened your throat, but our archer let us know you were on the up-and-up." He smiled. "Not many would have noticed the bowl was turned down. You might have a future in this business."

They traversed several blocks of Dwarf-made caverns, to end in a rather cozy human-scale basement. Blaize had no idea where he was. If the upstairs alleys were a maze, the underground Warrens' webwork was even more confusing.

Eginhard plunged his torch into a huge jar full of sand. It wasn't needed here. Oil lamps hung on reflectors along the walls.

Blaize stretched to relieve his back after his hunched-over journey. Eginhard stepped over to a somewhat battered oak table and sat behind it. The bottoms of the legs had been sawed off to accommodate his size, Blaize noticed.

"So, what was it you found out?" the Dwarf asked, all business.

Blaize recited the patrol schedule, consulting his notes to supplement his memory. Eginhard sat with his eyes closed, his face relaxed, soaking up every fact—another strange Dwarven ability.

His eyes opened when Blaize finished. "Most interesting. Now we'll have to maintain a discreet watch on the Imperials to make sure their patrols do as you've reported."

He coughed, leaning over to pull an all-too-familiar satchel into sight. "Discretion also demands that we maintain an equally close watch over you."

Blaize swore. "What more must I do to prove myself?" he burst out. "Creep into Throne and slit Karrudan's throat?"

His intemperate words caused a stabbing pain to lance through his head—from the point where Karrudan had imprinted his sigil.

Some of Blaize's distress must have shown on his face, because Eginhard asked, "Have you eaten?"

Blaize shook his head as the throbbing receded. "What I was doing was best done on an empty stomach."

"And you, daughter?" Eginhard turned to Rikka.

"No, Father—for the same reason."

"Then go with the girl. Eat, both of you. I'll send someone along with your things, Blaize." The Dwarf gave the human another long, measuring gaze, then broke into a grin that revealed large, square, yellow teeth. "Rikka was ready to kill you. It's only fair that she feed you instead."

Rikka silently opened another door and led the way through a new section of the Warrens. Her back was stiff with embarrassment—not an easy stance to keep when marching hunched through Dwarf-height tunnels.

"I don't blame you, you know," Blaize said.

The redheaded woman stopped, looking back. "What?"

"You did everything you could to get me out of Khamita Castle safely. Of course you had to take the necessary precautions when you took me to meet your father. And if I were going to betray him . . . well, I could only wish for someone to go that far in protecting me."

The odd thing was, Blaize realized he was telling the truth to this enemy of the Empire. For whatever reason, he wanted things to be easy between himself and Rikka.

At least her gait wasn't so angular as she guided him onward. The tunnels now filled with the scent of baking bread. Blaize's empty belly rumbled at the smell. A second later, as if in response, Rikka's stomach growled, too.

She turned with a thin smile. "If you can hold on just a little longer, we'll be there in a moment."

They turned down a side corridor, the baking smells growing ever stronger. The tunnel dead-ended at a ladder, which Rikka climbed. She pushed at something at the top, disappearing through the ceiling.

Blaize followed and found himself in a large brick oven—warm, but obviously empty. Rikka squirmed out of the grate. The smell of baked goods was so strong, Blaize feared that drool would be sopping over his chin.

"Mama!" a child's voice cried out. Blaize pushed his way out of the oven to find a five-year-old boy embracing Rikka. "You were gone so long, Mama!" the little one said. He had large eyes and sharp little foxy features, crowned by a mop of disorderly red hair.

"Well, now I'm back," Rikka said matter-of-factly, as if she came crawling out of the oven every evening at this time.

But Blaize could see the soft smile she gave the little boy as she knelt with him. He turned wide-eyed to see a stranger emerge after his mother.

"I also brought a guest," Rikka said to the aproned Dwarven woman who obviously ran the bakery. "And we're hungry enough to take care of all your day-old stock."

"No hope of that," the baker-woman replied with mock sternness even as a smile quivered on her plump face. She removed the kerchief holding back a mass of coarse black hair and snapped the cloth at the boy. "Everything around here is devoured while it's still fresh. Especially the jam tarts."

"Ohhhh," the little boy defended himself. "I asked first—and I said please."

"And thank you after you ate it?" Rikka gently teased.

Blaize was out and on his feet now. "Bruna, this is Blaize," Rikka said, making the introductions. She remained kneeling, her arms around the boy. "And this is my son, Kennet."

"We have some stew by the fire, and a loaf of seed-bread right out of the oven," Bruna said briskly, moving ahead of them. Her head barely came up to Blaize's chest, and she seemed about as wide as she was tall as she headed down the hallway. "There should be enough for two more mouths."

"Maybe if I'm really lucky I'll get a jam tart," Blaize said with a smile. "Although I always need help finishing them."

Kennet's bright fox-face looked up with a hopeful expression.

They sat at a small table in the back of the bakeshop. The stew was good, the bread even better—crusty, but soft and warm inside. Blaize used a chunk to sop up the last of the gravy on his plate, took a sip of cider, and leaned back in his seat with a contented sigh.

Throughout the meal, he'd watched Rikka with her boy, listening to Kennet's report of his day—who had come into the shop, how he'd helped Auntie Bruna, the boys he had played with. Watching the responses play across Rikka's face, he'd been struck by a feeling of . . . sweetness. Blaize remembered quiet afternoons in the gardens with his own mother.

Bruna bustled in, taking away the empty plates. A moment later, she returned with a pair of jam tarts and a steaming pot of tea. Blaize broke his tart in two, aware of an expectant gaze.

Kennet edged over to him shyly, his eyes wide. "Is it true you used to be an Imperial soldier?" the boy asked in a hushed voice.

Blaize gave him a man-to-man nod, keeping his face serious and a chuckle hidden well inside. He remembered his own youthful awe when the legions of Atlantis marched by. *What is it about little boys and soldiers?* he wondered.

The boy leaned eagerly forward. "Then could you show me your tail? Please?"

"Kennet!" Rikka said, her face flaming.

"When I'm good, Mama tells me stories of the Elves and

the Dwarven-folk," the boy plunged on. "When I'm bad, though, she tells me about Trolls, and Lizard-men, and Mage Spawn with claws and tails. And Auntie Bruna always says how the Imperials go on about their laws, but the soldiers never get off their tails—I just wanted to *see*, Mama."

Throughout all of this Rikka sputtered apologies. Bruna broke into whoops of laughter, her dark eyes crinkling with merriment. Blaize was sore-pressed to keep from joining the Dwarven woman. He was jealous when the baker retreated to her ovens.

Instead, he gravely assured Kennet that soldiers did not, in fact, have tails, that Auntie Bruna was just using a figure of speech.

When calm had been restored, Kennet accepted half the jam tart, but he just nibbled it. Obviously, Blaize's humdrum explanation had taken some of the magic out of the boy's young life. He climbed into his mother's lap and soon fell asleep.

High color still burned in Rikka's cheeks as she held Kennet in her arms. Somehow, it brought out the spray of freckles across her cheekbones, something Blaize hadn't noticed before. Just as he'd somehow missed the fact that, in repose, Rikka's face was heart-shaped, and the gentle wave in her auburn hair as it brushed her shoulders when she shrugged.

"I'm so sorry," Rikka said in a stifled voice. "How could he have gotten such a crazy idea?"

"Children get them," Blaize said gently.

In Atlantis, the little ones think soldiers are the heroes of the Empire, he thought. *But Khamsin kids see us as some sort of exotic Mage Spawn.*

He nodded toward the sleeping child. "Was he born in the mines?"

Rikka stared. "How did you—"

"A young woman with a Dwarven name, a Dwarven adopted father . . . it wasn't all that hard to figure out."

She nodded. "Kennet was born in a mine. So was I. It was a big place, lots of Magestone—and lots of Magestone poisoning. If it weren't for the Dwarves, we humans trapped in the pits wouldn't even have a chance of survival. A Dwarf midwife, Rikka, saved my mama—and me—when I was born."

"And your mother named you after her."

Rikka nodded in silence.

"And Eginhard?" Blaize asked.

"I ended up an orphan," Rikka said quietly. "The Magestone—it just burns the life out of humans. When my mother died, Eginhard and his family took me in. They'd been in the mine for generations, but he was determined to get his family out. It just took years . . ."

Long enough at least for her to gain and lose a husband, Blaize thought.

Rikka looked up, her expression suddenly fierce. "My boy was never going down into the mines. We trekked all the way from the Blasted Lands to get here. But it was worth it."

As she looked at him her eyes hardened, and her low voice grew harsh. "Maybe you saw a different face of the Empire before your parents lost their farm. Me, I never even saw a face. The Empire has always been a foot on my neck—on the neck of everyone I know. I have to change that."

"Even if it risks your son?"

Rikka looked down. "Kennet stays with Bruna when I have to do my work. We made a pact. If—" She cleared her throat. "If I never come back, he'll stay with Bruna."

Her voice was quiet and calm, but her features took on the stressed angularity they had when Blaize had first met her.

"I believe you," he said. "You don't have to convince me with your warrior face."

She blinked, then scowled. "My what?"

"Your warrior face," he repeated. "It comes on whenever you talk about your work—and why you do it. I've seen it in the legions, too. The fellows who tell the funniest jokes, who are the softest touches for a loan, who love their mothers and are kind to little children. They can't go into a fight wearing the same face they use for those other things. So . . . they change."

The tension gradually drained from Rikka's face as she stared at him.

"Do you?" she finally asked.

"I don't know." Blaize's words were barely audible. "I've never looked."

They sat in silence until Eghinhard's next guide came to lead him away.

Chapter 6

Snow reined in his horse on the shoulder of the hill, scanning the horizon yet again. His vantage point gave him a long view of open grassland, with the hint of taller peaks in the distance.

This was not a healthy place to stand and watch. The open vista was the steppeland of the Fist, and the space between the hills and the mountains offered the easiest route of march for warriors leaving or entering the home of the Orcs.

Often enough in history, this vista had crawled with thousands of reavers as the Orc warhosts combined into mighty hordes, pillaging and eating their way through the northlands. Almost six hundred years ago, the Orcs had plundered as far as Caero, capturing and wrecking much of the city.

The growing strength of the Empire put an end to the days of Orc raids in strength, but the odd warband still rode out to grab what it could. Not even Imperial military might and Technomancy allowed Atlantis to control the Fist.

That was one reason why Sarah Ythlim decided to send half of her supply of black powder through the steppes. Another reason was her belief that all races must join together to thwart the Empire.

Snow could respect her reasoning—but then, Sarah wasn't the one who'd had to shepherd a pack train through the mountain valleys from Varsfield to Enos Joppa, then across the flatlands and into these hills. He couldn't even imagine how the black powder had made its way from the slopes of Nepharus Mons into the Fist.

One thing was clear, though. Snow, Sigwold, and their

team of packhorse drivers had made their way across more than a hundred miles, much of it rugged country, in slightly more than a week.

The Orcs, traveling across flat grasslands, had yet to turn up.

Snow was about to turn away, when his mount nickered, breathing deeply. The horse was a half-feral cross-breed, part of its heritage hailing from the northern ponies that wandered the plains. Its greater size suggested a plow horse in its background, probably brought to these climes by humans attempting to settle the area. Disaster for those settlers—Mage Spawn or Orc marauders—had left that equine ancestor free to mate with the local ponies.

The result was a rangy hybrid with a fierce disposition and the strength to carry a rider of Snow's size. At the corral where the pack train had chosen horses, nobody else had wanted this big brute. When Snow had approached him with a saddle, he had snapped at Snow's arm and head. Sigwold had joked that horse and rider shared the same temperament.

For Snow, it had simply been a practical decision. His bulk might not have killed a pony, considering the large loads on the pack animals, but he was damned if he'd ride with his feet trailing the ground on either side of an animal any smaller.

Mount and rider had formed a cautious alliance during the journey from Varsfield. Since Enos Joppa, they'd at least had a trail of sorts to follow. From this stand of hills onward, however, they would cut cross-country to Khamsin. The question that worried Snow was whether the full cargo would be heading south, or would it only be his half?

Sarah may have been wise to split up the shipment as it went through the wild lands. But Snow and his people had been waiting two days now.

Snow's mount stirred nervously again, taking in deep breaths, smelling something. The breeze was from the north, so Snow turned in that direction, squinting, trying to find something out of place on the broken, rocky hillsides.

He almost turned away, when he caught a trace of movement

from the tail of his eye. Cued now about where to look, he made out dusty greenish shapes heading into a valley between rises.

Either our Orc friends chose the difficult way around, or that's trouble coming our way.

"Well done," he said, patting his horse's shoulder as he turned him around. "What happened, you had a brush with their cook-pots somewhere along the line?"

He arrived at the camp and warned of oncoming Orcs. The men armed themselves and took defensive positions. Sigwold mounted up and joined Snow to meet the visitors.

"Better to be ready in case of surprises," Snow said, resting his axe-haft across the pommel of his saddle.

"It seems our green-skinned friends have little sense of time." Sigwold also carried an axe, having decided his crossbow would be a clumsy weapon to use while mounted. It was now in the trembling hands of one of the horse-drovers hiding among the rocks.

"Those jumped-up Mage Spawn haven't a sense of anything except greed—and hunger," Snow retorted. "They could have decided to eat the packhorses instead of shifting the powder. Or maybe they were seized with a whim to go raiding instead of meeting us. This could be a completely different bunch, unaware of the agreement between Sarah and the kzar."

"You just don't like dealing with strange races, Snow—a narrow-minded human failing." Sigwold hefted his axe.

"I'd happily deal with them—if I could use my rifle."

Sigwold's head-shake was emphatic. "No outsiders are supposed to know about them. We'd have to do for all the Orcs—and you know how hard they are to kill. Otherwise, the raider-bands would be all over us like flies on Ankhar dung. We'd lose our best weapon, secrecy."

He paused. "We'd also probably lose our lives and our cargo. If you think Orcs are bad enough, what about Orcs with black powder weapons?"

"I'm thinking of that already," Snow replied. "I grew up a farmer, and I know what the Orc Raiders already do to farms—and to farmers."

"Make stew out of them?" Sigwold tried to joke.

Snow spat. "I've never seen Sarah make a mistake before. But having anything to do with these Troll scat . . ."

Sigwold shrugged. "When you're as weak as we are, you have to take allies wherever you find or buy them." He glanced at his friend. "Perhaps you'll let me do the talking. I think a diplomatic hand is needed."

Snow's face tightened. "Here they come."

The band totaled about a score of Orcs and Goblins—light cavalry, ten Cave Butchers and five Cave Archers. The overdeveloped upper bodies on the true Orcs made them look top-heavy on their Cave Lizard mounts. Snow wondered how the spindly beasts carried so much weight.

They spread out, Goblin archers standing with arrows nocked, searching for targets among the rocks surrounding the campsite.

The Cave Butchers rode with bare blades. Now they began clashing them against their rough Ankhar-bone armor, starting a war-chant. "Huuuuuuuu . . . huuuuuuuuu . . . *huuuuuuugh!*"

A lone rider rode forth. His Cave Lizard had an odd, capering gait as he came forward to confront Snow and Sigwold.

The Orc leader had a little more armor on him than his companions, with a bit more decoration, mostly pilfered human work roughly hammered into place. He rode in typical Orc stance, half hunched over his mount's head. A rank stench assailed Snow's nose as the Orc approached. There was no way for Snow to tell whether it came from the half-cured hides the green-skinned warrior wore, or from unwashed flesh.

Best not to ask, Snow thought. *Sigwold would probably find it undiplomatic.*

The Orc had a curved slashing sword in his hand, and a hand-and-a-half straight blade. As a token of peace, he neither clashed his weapon nor chanted.

But his greeting wasn't promising.

"Maggot-human stink fills Grugh's nostrils." The Orc's

voice sounded like a bubble surfacing in tar. "What do you do in our land?"

"Your land?" Sigwold asked. "This isn't the Fist."

"Wherever Orcs ride, that is their land," Grugh replied proudly. "I ask again, what do you do here?"

"We wait," Sigwold replied. "Perhaps for you?"

"So what is there to keep me from taking what you have, killing you, and using your bones to pick my teeth?" the Orc demanded.

Sigwold faced him squarely. "Kzar Kraksha wishes otherwise."

"And if I do not ride with Kraksha's warhost?"

Snow brought up his axe and leaned in so his face was inches from the Orc's. "Then we'll die, but whoever wins will pick their teeth with your bones, too, Orc. Because you'll die before us."

Beyond them, the clashing and chanting came faster and faster.

But Grugh leaned back, laughing. The sound was like stones being ground together. "Good answer! We ride with you to the maggot-human cesspit—the place you call Khamsin."

Snow and Sigwold exchanged glances. Grugh knew their destination. Apparently this was their escort after all.

The Orcs stopped their noise, and their leader straightened himself in the saddle, calling back orders. Five more Goblins appeared, leading heavily laden packhorses. "Grugh follows Kraksha's orders. You pay us?"

"We'll pay the amount Kraksha agreed to," Sigwold replied.

Grugh shook his head. "Want more."

Snow tightened his grip on the axe-haft.

"Broke open barrel of spice," the Orc said. "We want it. Sprinkle on roast horse, tastes good."

Snow and Sigwold exchanged glances. "All right," the Dwarf said. "You can have the broken barrel."

Let's just hope they don't toss any "spice" into their campfire, Snow thought.

Grugh gave them a toothy grin. "Good." Then he looked worried. "Humans infest the land for many leagues around their cesspit. The armored maggots—the Imperials—send out warbands to kill whatever they find."

"We know about the patrols," Sigwold said. "Our people in Khamsin are working on it even now."

Rikka entered Eginhard's Warrens office, to find him deep in conversation with a worn-looking man in stained riding leathers. Several runners stood nearby, almost quivering with eagerness as the Rebel leader consulted with the newcomer. As they spoke, Eginhard scribbled cryptic notes on scraps of paper.

Finally he said, "Get Tommo Wayrider here to some food and a bed."

None of the runners moved, all of them waiting for the big message. Eginhard pulled a face, picked out one of the scraps, and handed it to one of the sturdier lads. "This is the response. Set off directly after you've settled Tommo and gotten the directions from him."

Puffed up with pride, the young messenger stepped off with his exhausted-looking predecessor. The other runners crowded round Eginhard's desk as Eginhard started distributing the other messages. "This is for Benni Stabler, to gather our horses. Make sure this gets into Joab Cutpurse's hands *only.* Why are you asking me where he'll be? I'm sending you to find him."

After a series of these rapid-fire orders, the group seemed to explode from around the desk. Now only Rikka was with Eginhard. He leaned back in his seat, massaging his face with his hands.

"Events are moving," he said, his voice half-muffled.

Eginhard dropped his hands, his craggy face pink with barely suppressed excitement. "That was an outrider from Sigwold. The package has been on the road from Varsfield, and it's almost here. I've just sent him a return message with a safe meeting place."

He gave Rikka a crooked grin. "Your friend Blaize came

along at just the right time. Thanks to his little burglary, we know where all their patrols are heading. I've kept watch on the castle, and the tin soldiers have all marched or ridden off exactly on schedule. It will make things much easier meeting Sigwold."

"He's not my friend," Rikka said.

"Sigwold?" Eginhard said, feigning shock. "He's my brother—your foster-uncle."

"Will you stop playing the clown, Father? Blaize is not my friend."

"You spend considerable time with him."

Rikka couldn't keep the tart tone out of her voice. "And why would that be, with you continually throwing us together? What a terrible, suspicious mind I must have. I thought you had me keeping an eye on the new recruit. Or was this so that Kennet could have a man in his life?"

Eginhard shrugged. "You could choose worse."

"Oh, I can't believe you, Father. What am I to do with you?"

Eginhard gave a substantial rap to the tabletop. "You're to prepare for a considerable trip with me, leaving tomorrow. We're leading the escort to meet Sigwold and his pack train, then we're heading for Caero. There we'll meet Sarah Ythlim, Valerian, and the other leaders of the Rebellion. From there . . . Atlantis."

"You're not joking?" Rikka said. "The time has finally come?"

"It has, daughter. We'll need a good dozen escorts—more, counting you and me." Her father frowned for a moment. "Who else? Tulwar, of course. He's good on the road."

They went back and forth, listing other possible fighters. Some were rejected. They weren't good riders, or they were needed in Khamsin, playing too key a role in the organization's structure.

"You're the head conspirator in Khamsin, yet you're going," Rikka said.

Eginhard shrugged and grinned. "It's good to be the chief." He sobered slightly. "Rikka, any of our most trusted people would give their right arm to go on this foray. But Khamsin has a place to play in the Rebellion, too. The uprising here is going to need leaders."

Rikka nodded, going through a mental list of names.

"What about Blaize?" she said suddenly.

"He's new to the Rebellion," Eginhard said in a considering tone.

"But you've already said he did good work for us," Rikka answered. "He knows how to handle a sword, he's ridden as a caravan guard, he's a Caeronn, he knows Atlantis . . ."

She finally caught the look on her father's face. "And he's not my friend!" she finished in a louder voice.

Eginhard broke into laughter, trying to wave her anger away. "All right, fine, I believe you. Tell him to be ready. Treat him to a last meal, if you want."

Rikka turned way, feeling a certain warmth on her face.

As she headed for the door, the laughter abruptly died away behind her.

"Rikka," her father called.

She turned back to find the serious face of Khamsin's chief conspirator looking at her. "Don't tell Blaize what we're carrying—or what they'll be for."

"You still don't trust him?" Rikka asked.

"I prefer to call it being careful." Eginhard now watched her with a father's eyes. "It's a good attitude in this business we find ourselves in, and in other parts of life. You don't want to give your trust too soon."

He shrugged. "Go now. Talk to him."

Blaize had spent the last couple of days bunking with an extremely closemouthed Khamsin named Jorj. He never found out the fellow's epithet-name. Perhaps it was "the Silent." Blaize didn't even find out about the "Jorj" part until the morning of the second day, when somebody happened to mention it at breakfast.

The obvious suspicion was that Jorj was on the run from the Imperial authorities. Whether it was a criminal or a patriotic matter, Blaize had no idea. The only other solid information he had was that Jorj was a remarkably quiet sleeper—except one time during the night when he began to shift around and moan.

It was nothing lascivious. Whatever Jorj was dreaming about, it had him pretty upset. Blaize had debated waking the man but decided against it. He was glad when the fit ended. Jorj woke up swinging.

True to form, the Khamsin didn't discuss it.

But Blaize found himself glad that their bunks were on opposite sides of the small room.

Another question nagged at Blaize, but he never got a chance to discuss it with his bunkmate. Was Jorj there as a watchful eye for the Rebels, or did he believe that Blaize was a Rebel doing that job on him?

After two days, Blaize was sure of one thing—he would kill for a chance at some sunshine. All that kept him from going crazy were visits from Rikka. They had talked a little and eaten a couple of meals together.

Blaize found it pleasant—if Rikka was a watchful eye, she was a much more attractive one than Jorj.

So, when she entered the bunkroom a little before suppertime, Blaize greeted her with a smile.

"Come and eat, then get a good night's sleep," she said. "We'll be out of here come morning."

They followed the underground ways to Bruna's bakeshop, where a veritable feast awaited. Blaize took in the roast fowl, grain salad, greens, fruit, and the steaming round loaf spread out on the table. There was even a jug of wine.

"Now, in the army," he joked, "if they fed us this well, we knew we'd be sweating it off for the next week."

"I wouldn't know about that," Bruna retorted primly. "But I've seen some samples of what they loosely call waybread." She sniffed, rolling her little anthracite eyes. "Could be better used to patch shoes."

That comment—and the farewell feast—suggested that Blaize and Rikka were actually going out of town. But Rikka remained aggravatingly vague about their destination. They were going out to meet some people and give them whatever help they needed with a mysterious shipment.

It was while they were eating that he got the hint that this might be a longer—and much more dangerous—journey.

Kennet should have been in five-year-old heaven, a roast fowl leg in one hand and his face full of grease. Instead, his shiny features were clouded. "I don't like when you go away, Mama," he said with a child's directness. "Why do you have to go on this ship? Will you be gone for long and long?"

Rikka's expression showed the same unhappiness. "I don't know how long this trip will take, Kennet. You'll be a good boy with Auntie Bruna, won't you?"

"Oh, yah. I like Auntie Bruna." Putting down his food, the little boy snuggled closer, looking down. "But it's not the same as being with you."

Rikka hugged him tightly, ruffling a finger through his wild red curls, unmindful of Kennet's greasy condition. Only after that did she start wiping his face.

Kennet bore the cleaning stoically. Then he glanced up at Blaize. "Are you going on the ship, too?"

Blaize noticed that Rikka didn't correct the boy's misapprehension. "Yes," he replied, "I'll be going, too."

"Then you have to take care of Mama," Kennet said decisively, "like Auntie Bruna takes care of me."

"Auntie Bruna will always take care of you." Rikka's voice shook a little as she said that. Blaize noticed her big hazel eyes were clouded, full of tears.

So were Bruna's.

Just what is this journey supposed to entail? Blaize wondered.

Kennet's sharp little features were fierce, almost glaring at Blaize. "And you'll take care of Mama, no matter how far away you go, all right? Even as far as—as—"

The little boy struggled to come up with the name of some place impossibly far away. "Even as far as Atlantis!" he said triumphantly.

"I promise," Blaize solemnly assured Kennet. He glanced at Rikka, expecting perhaps a mother's exasperated eye-roll, or maybe a laughing response.

Instead, Rikka's arms went tightly around her boy, and there was a flash of her warrior's face.

Atlantis struck a nerve, Blaize thought, trying to keep his easy smile. "But your mother is a big, grown-up person, Kennet. I don't think she'll need that much taking care of. She'll probably be telling *me* to wash behind my ears—and not to burp too loudly if I eat too much roast fowl."

"You're not supposed to burp—ever!" Kennet cried, scandalized. That took his mind off the impending trip, even as Blaize began putting the fragments he'd heard together.

It took a little while. The table was cleared, dishes washed, and although Kennet insisted he wasn't at all tired, his mother and honorary aunt took him off to bed. By that time, Blaize had assembled a fairly comprehensive mental picture.

An important package is coming from somewhere outside of Khamsin—maybe outside the Empire. But it seems to be going to Atlantis. That argues much more organization on the part of the Rebels than Gamelon—or Karrudan—suspects. Whatever the package is, it might very well have something to do with the predictions of the Prophet-Magus' death.

The question was, what should Blaize do about it? Should he travel on with Rikka tomorrow to find this package—and look for a suitable place along the way where the authorities could intercept it?

Or should he contact Gamelon and have the Khamsin garrison sweep up the Rebels before they set off? He imagined guardsmen breaking into the Warrens, capturing Eginhard, marching off with Bruna and Kennet—Rikka dying on an Altem's sword . . .

And right after you promised to take care of her.

The mental battle between putting off an unpleasant action and instantly carrying it through began to make his head hurt. It was a really blinding twinge of pain, right where that damned tattoo—

The pain became blinding, casting a white haze across his

vision. It took Blaize a moment to realize he'd risen and headed out of the shop.

Blaize was so dumbfounded, his body reached the outer door before he tried to command himself to stop. Except for a momentary hesitation, he found himself continuing out into the street.

Stop! Turn! Go back! Sit! With increasing desperation, Blaize tried to exercise some control over his limbs. It was as though his body belonged to someone else.

Abruptly his mind spiraled down into darkness, yammering in terror. This wasn't like getting stinking drunk or having a limb fall asleep from lack of circulation. His body had apparently been stolen from his mind.

Fury overrode his fears, driving his soul back up from the darkness. He became dimly aware of sensation, and his vision returned. His headache was gone, replaced with a tingling feeling, strangely familiar.

Now he remembered—the sensations were dim echoes of those ghostly spider-legs that had danced along his nerves when Karrudan touched his forehead.

The mage hadn't just imprinted him with his sigil. Karrudan had planted some sort of spell, to take effect if and when Blaize encountered any direct threat to the Prophet-Magus!

Blaize tried to see where he was, but even his eyes defied his will. They stayed straight ahead, looking down a darkened street. He had no idea where he was, only entering the rear of the shop, and that from underground.

His body carried him to a passerby. "How would I get to the Street of Metalworkers?" Blaize heard his voice demand.

Actually, it wasn't exactly his voice. It was his voice doing a flawless impersonation of Karrudan.

After receiving directions, his body set off at a stiff-legged march. Blaize strove desperately to regain some kind of control. Feshku's Pit, he'd be happy just to make himself fall down! Every once in a while, he lurched, more from irregularities in the paving than because of his own efforts. Passersby would probably think him drunk.

The Street of Metalworkers turned out to be close enough, and Blaize easily found the statue Gamelon had mentioned. Indeed, it was just the remains of a statue, a pair of legs cut off at the knees, two bronze stubs arising from a battered stone plinth that had been knocked down and then restored at a slightly drunken angle.

Blaize's body approached it at a wobbly stalk, one hand fumbling up to touch a surprisingly shiny toe where the contact of thousands of hands had worn away the verdigris.

And, although he tried with all his will to stop it, the other hand reached up to press against the statue's left heel, tapping twice.

Blaize's senses couldn't tell if the Technomantic call had gone out.

Instead, he lurched toward a Khamsin peddler returning home with his stock, and Karrudan's voice required directions to the Great Square.

"That's not a good idea, Caeronn," the peddler said. "I've heard the press-gangs are out in that area."

"Tell me," Karrudan's voice insisted.

The little man with his sack full of geegaws began to look a bit afraid. He gave the directions and moved away as quickly as he could.

Blaize's body lurched off on a new course.

He encountered the press-gang just a few streets away from the Great Square. They were dressed in something resembling Atlantean uniform. Or perhaps an Orc's conception of that gear. What armor they had was half-corroded or badly mended. The tunics and breeches didn't fit correctly.

And, of course, they didn't carry swords, only clubs.

The leader carried a torch, which caused the golden hoop on his ear to glisten. His tunic was soiled with old food and probably worse.

"Hold there, Caeronn." The leader raised the burning brand to get a better look at this apparent drunk. He stepped into Blaize's path. "Legionary boots—probably a deserter. Fair game, boys."

"Get out of my way," Karrudan's voice rumbled from

Blaize's throat. An unheard, despairing cry echoed in Blaize's mind at his futile efforts to get himself to turn, to run.

His limbs didn't respond, of course. So there was no way for Blaize—or his body—to see the wooden cudgel swinging for the back of his head.

CHAPTER 7

SNOW was not in the best of moods. The travelers were enduring yet another night of camping without a fire, which meant uncooked food and a freezing night out on the plains. On the other hand, it made it harder for any passing patrols to spot them.

The messenger from Khamsin had blundered onto the pack train just as the long shadows were turning into true evening. Snow found himself feeling sorry for the kid after his brush with the Orc guards.

Standing in camp, the young rider was a sturdy enough Khamsin youth. Judging from the looks he kept shooting at the Orcs, he was now wondering if this adventure he'd been so eager to join was a good idea after all.

Snow decided to take pity on the boy. "Why don't we give him a fresh horse and send him back to the city?" he asked Sigwold. "That way your brother will know we received his message."

The lad flinched as Grugh poked him with a huge, sausagelike finger. "Shame," the Orc leader said in his gurgling voice. "There's good eating on these."

Looking at the boy's pale face, Snow reminded himself that their time together on the trail had proven Grugh to be something of a humorist, although of the cruder sort. For instance, he'd pinned the name "Lukush Buttwound" on one of his warriors. The epithet had come from the unfortunate Orc's all-too-close brush with an arrow during a retreat. It was inconceivable for Grugh and his comrades that Lukush's rear end, skinny even by Orc standards, should have been hit.

So, hooting laughter had given Snow proof that Orcs could tell a joke. His problem now was telling when the escorts were joking and when they were serious.

Luckily, Grugh began laughing.

Sigwold, meanwhile, knelt with a bull's-eye lantern, deciphering the message Eginhard had sent. The brothers had their own private code, and Sigwold spent some time going from the scrap of paper that the rider had delivered to the map he'd been using to chart their course.

Finally he shuttered the lantern and arose. "I think Eginhard has chosen a good spot," he announced. "It's a crossroads near an extensive stand of brush, so we'll have concealment but be able to keep a watch. And he assures me the area should be free of Imperial troops."

"No armor-maggots? Good." The Orc drew himself up on his Cave Lizard. "Not that we are afraid of them. Not even Lukush Buttwound. But it is good if they are not there. Easier."

Snow knew what the Orc wasn't saying. If there was a clash with the Imperials, the humans and even the Dwarves could, if necessary, disappear into the populace, aided by local supporters. The Orcs, however, would be trapped deep in enemy territory with nowhere to hide and every inhabitant's hand raised against them.

That enmity might be deserved, but it showed a certain lunatic bravery for the Orcs to keep on their course and do what they'd said they would do.

"Best news of all," Sigwold finished, "the rendezvous is an easy ride from here. We can take things slowly and carefully."

"I'll ride out at dawn with a couple of the lads to check things out." Snow turned to Grugh. "That's not to say anything against your people. They just might seem a bit . . . conspicuous."

The meeting broke up, and Snow took the Khamsin lad by the shoulders, turning toward the line where all the horses were picketed. "Now let's get some food in this young man's mouth, get him a fresh mount, and send him home!"

As they moved off, Sigwold joined them. His voice was low as he said, "I just hope Eginhard's information about the patrol schedules is as solid as his assurances."

Snow could only shake his head. "Confidence is a wonderful thing."

"Oh, yes," Sigwold agreed sourly. "Until it blows up in your face."

Inarticulate with fury, Eginhard tore loose two handfuls of his own beard. "I don't believe this!" he bellowed at his foster-daughter. "How could you have let the Caeronn get away?"

"We went in to put Kennet to bed," Rikka said miserably. "I wanted to say good-bye."

"And while you did that, Blaize, it seems, did the same." The Dwarf took a long, deep breath. "I'm sorry, Rikka. It's my fault, too. I told you to take him, when I should have kept Blaize down here in the Warrens."

He laid both hands on the tabletop, as if pushing his anger into it. "What did you do when you realized he was gone?"

"We went outside the shop and asked around. One of the neighbors heard him asking directions to the Street of the Metalworkers." Rikka hesitated. "At least a Caeronn asked for those directions. But the woman who told me about it said he was drunk."

Eginhard's brows lifted until they almost disappeared into his hairline. "And was Blaize drunk?"

Waving her arms, Rikka said, "I wasn't paying all that much attention. Kennet was my concern—I was trying to soften the news that I was going away." She frowned, replaying her memories of the evening. "Blaize got very quiet after dinner."

"Well, you obviously aren't drunk," Eginhard said. "What was he doing? Guzzling?"

She shook her head. "No. But we were drinking wine. All I've ever seen him drink was beer."

"Sometimes different tipples hit people differently,"

Eginhard admitted. "But Blaize didn't just wander outside to take a leak. He went to the Street of Metalworkers. Why?"

"I don't—" Rikka stopped.

"What?" Eginhard leaned over the table.

"I took Kennet once to the Street of Metalworkers to see the statue of the Lost King and rub his foot for luck. For luck!" Rikka repeated. "You know what gamblers Caeronns are. Suppose Blaize had heard about it—"

"And went off to get a little luck before his big journey." Eginhard nodded.

"Maybe he got lost finding his way back."

"I'll put out the word to look out for a drunk Caeronn." Eginhard sighed. "At least he should be pretty noticeable with that shaven head. If we find him—when," he amended, after a glance at Rikka's face, "I will take personal delight in sobering him up myself. With lots of very, very cold water."

Rikka managed a shaky smile.

Eginhard just growled. "Young fool."

He called for runners, sending them across the city.

It took less than two hours for word to come back about the drunken Caeronn who'd confronted a party of slave-takers . . . and been taken.

Blaize regained consciousness to find himself facedown in some sort of wagon. Every rattle and lurch of the unsprung vehicle sent another sickening jolt through the back of his head, which seemed about ready to burst.

Sickening . . . He wished he hadn't thought of that word, as he clamped his lips, trying to impose his will on a stomach determined to spew everything he'd eaten that evening.

The filthy taste of bile filled his mouth, but Blaize managed to ride out the wave of nausea.

Eyes closed, he tried to remember what had happened to land him here . . . the feast with Rikka, the strange spell that had controlled him . . . and the confrontation that had left him knocked out.

He tried to move his arms—and succeeded, in a limited

way. Shackles encircled his wrists, and he was buried under at least one and maybe more layers of inert bodies.

The wagon hit some obstruction with a major jolt, sending a lance of pain that Blaize could even see behind his tightly shut eyes.

A groan escaped his lips.

A muscle-corded arm casually dug among the unmoving forms until it touched Blaize, got a response, and hauled him up.

Blaize found himself flung into a corner of the wagon, almost paralyzed by the new bolt of pain shooting through his head. He saw three figures sitting on the plank seat opposite him. They coalesced into one, the leader of the press-gang who had blocked his way. The heavyset man still wore his army surplus armor, and rode with a club across his lap.

The gang leader gestured with his cudgel. "Sit."

He reminded Blaize of an Altem he'd served under as a raw recruit. The veteran soldier had had dead eyes like this man—right before he'd gone mad and killed three comrades. Blaize painfully pulled himself up on a seat. Planks ran around the inside of the wagon, offering ample if splintery sitting room.

A man on a horse rode up, another member of the press gang. "First one up, Armon?" he said to the leader. "Aw, Troll scat. Nobody bet on this one. Thought he'd cracked his head."

"Shut it," Armon replied tonelessly.

Blaize raised a careful hand to the back of his head, winced at his own touch, and took it away. His fingers were sticky. When he looked at them in the half-dawn light, the tips had a blackish color.

Clotted blood, he realized. Without hair, his shaven scalp had taken the brunt of the blow. But if he had no padding, he also had no hair to stick to the blood clot.

"Touch it again and you'll start it bleeding again," Armon said. "Let the leech at the mine tend it."

Blaize felt another twinge. His hand went up in an unthinking gesture.

The tip of Armon's club caught him in the chest—a hard poke. "I said don't touch it." Armon's voice didn't change tone, but the threat was somehow clear.

Blaize dropped his hand. He looked around at the wagon. Besides Armon, two gang members flanked the driver, and four more rode horses surrounding the conveyance. Armon didn't look worried at being alone in the back of the wagon with all the recent captives. In fact, the dead-eyed man seemed to enjoy his position.

About a mile farther along, another of the victims began stirring. He lurched up to his knees in a rattle of chains, looking around wildly. "Noooooo!" he cried in a cracked voice. "I've got a wife—children. You have all these others. Let me go!"

"Sit," Armon said flatly.

But the captive surged to his feet, trying to leap off the wagon. The guards with the driver began to turn, but Armon was already on his feet. A quick backhand blow of his club caught the obstreperous prisoner on the side of the head.

The man dropped back into the bed of the wagon and lay unmoving.

Blaize immediately went to help him, only to encounter the tip of the cudgel again. "I told you to sit."

"But he could—"

"He could cost us five Imperials if the mine procurement officer won't take him." Armon's voice was cold. "This one might be more trouble than he's worth." The press-gang leader looked at the other unconscious bodies, some of them now stirring. "But if what happened to him keeps the rest of you in line . . ."

Blaize sank back on the raw wood of the plank. His life was worth five silver Imperials.

How much road-silver did he have? Unbidden, his hand went to his belt pouch—or rather, where his pouch had been. The press-gang already had it, of course.

He sagged forward, dropping his head into his hands. Inside his shirt, Karrudan's medallion shifted against his chest.

Blaize felt a moment of surprise that the slave-takers, obviously practiced at stripping their victims, had missed it.

Blaize briefly debated showing Armon his tattoo. But the gang boss was so far down the Imperial hierarchy, he wouldn't be able to tell Karrudan's seal from Tezla's knob.

And he'd probably steal the medallion in the bargain, Blaize thought.

He closed his eyes, head hanging, trying not to feel the bone-shaking jolts as the vehicle rattled along.

By the time the sun was above the horizon, all the prisoners had revived and were lining the sides of the wagon. Most sat hunched over, hands or arms across their eyes. A couple glared at their captors.

Blaize spent his time studying the landscape with a soldier's eye. There was a slight rise to the ground, and stony outcrops appeared more and more frequently. Not good land for farming. It had been left to grass, scrub, and occasional stands of trees.

Until the last quarter of a mile. Where there had been trees, Blaize now just saw an expanse of rotting stumps. Apparently, it had been a chop-and-drag operation, the cutters not even bothering to trim off the limbs. As a result, the earth was scarred and furrowed, the top growth scoured away. In rain, it would be an endless mud-hole. When the sun got higher and the breeze picked up, the air would fill with dust.

"Is this from the Magestone?" Blaize asked.

One of the outriders laughed. "They ain't cleared enough of the wild stone to cause a big kill-off yet. Nah, they logged everything to build Minetown."

"So it's a new mine," Blaize said.

"So new, we're still calling the base camp Minetown. Don't got a name yet, till the 'perial mapmakers write one down. Diviners found the stone not too long ago, so it's still a job of digging down. That's why we went after you lot instead of the little guys."

Armon frowned, spitting over the side of the wagon and onto his subordinate. "Not as much money in getting Dwarves. Got to get the garrison to seal off their quarter and then cover our action. That costs money. Not to mention what we lose when the soldier-boys go hunting on their own."

They reached Minetown before the dust got too bad. "Town" was a grander description than Blaize would have given it. This place was more like a fortified gateway, its turfed palisade wall using up the bulk of the felled trees in the region. The walls on the official buildings inside still gleamed with the whiteness of raw wood. Around them a shantytown clustered like rubbish deposited by a strong wind, housing the women and children of the original population concentrated on this site. Beyond yawned the vast strip mine for which this whole complex served as sole entrance . . . and exit.

The wagon rolled through a gate barely wide enough to accommodate it. Blaize wondered if they'd have to enlarge the opening when the mine went to full production. The vehicle rattled on to what would have been the commander's office in a regular Imperial fort. Here the other sides of the main square were lined with guards' barracks.

Armon and his assistants removed the manacles, and the prisoners were chivied into a rough line under the watchful eye of a squad of armed guards. It reminded Blaize of his first day in the army—although with a much lower class of recruits.

The headquarters door opened and a mage-officer came out. From his dreamy eyes and the acrid, spicy smell that clung to his robes, he'd been busily inhaling some narcotic essence to beguile the tedium of his duty.

It took him a moment to come down to earth and begin the inspection. Even then, it was actually the clerk who followed him who classified the day's intake as five-, four-, or three-Imperial specimens.

As the slaves headed to the infirmary for the medical exam, the mage-officer was sufficiently aware of things to complain to Armon. "We don't need more of this type. We need steel drivers to break the rock. Broad shoulders, for hammer-men."

Armon's look was as eloquent as if he'd spoken aloud.

You don't pay enough for us to tackle big men with broad shoulders. Let the boys with swords pick them up for you.

"These wiry ones will be useless except for toting baskets."

The man behind Blaize went into a racking, consumptive cough.

The mage glared at Armon. "If that." His eyes focused on Blaize. "That one might at least be trained to hold the steel."

He's an officer, Blaize thought. *He has to recognize Karrudan's sigil.* "Lord Mage—" he began.

That was as far as he got before the guard commander backhanded him across the face. A ring on the mage's finger tore Blaize's lip.

"I do not speak to slaves," the officer announced to the empty air. "Slaves do not speak to me."

Blaize didn't see the mage-officer again. It was the clerk who officiated in the infirmary while the leech, an older woman, certified the new inmates' health. She turned out to be an excellent judge of slave-flesh. She had the carefully blank eyes of someone who has seen too much ugliness in life. But her hands were deft and surprisingly gentle as she repaired the damage to Blaize's head, fore and aft.

As she finished with each slave, the clerk assigned them to their work gangs. Then they marched off to their lives of servitude.

Blaize wound up toting a basket—a waist-high wicker construction used to transport dirt and crushed rock from the floor of the pit up to the surface. Getting there—and back again—meant a torturous trip along a trail that spiraled down the sides of the pit. One trail, two lanes.

"Going up, you carry your full basket on the inside, next to the wall," explained Trav, the more experienced basketman Blaize had been teamed with. "Empty baskets go down on the edge."

"Would have been easier if you had ledges with ladders between them." Blaize considered the dizzying fall beside him as he marched downward. "Safer, too."

"Our Imperial masters want only one road, that leads

right into their arms," Trav said in a low voice. "Ladders could be moved somewhere else, so that people could bypass Minetown and reach the surface. The Empire doesn't want escapes."

"Why do they even need us?" Blaize burst out in frustration. "Why not use magic blasts to smash down to the Magestone and Golems to gather the stuff up?"

"Raw Magestone doesn't just kill human folk—it kills Technomancy, too." The older man's voice was tired, as if he'd explained this many times before. "Spells and such don't work down in the pit. So the only way the Empire can use Magestone to get Magestone is to fight for it. Otherwise, the Empire pays in blood—convicts, slaves, rebels. There's always a plentiful supply." His thin lips twisted. "Khamsin, for instance, has lots of rebels."

By the time Blaize had made one circuit—down and then back up again with a filled basket—his muscles ached, but it wasn't all that bad. He said as much to Trav on the way back down.

Trav gave him a flat look from under grizzled eyebrows. "Fine," he said. "Just keep it up from now until sunset."

Like most of the other carriers, Blaize had stripped off his shirt as the sun beat down. He'd taken the precaution of hiding his medallion in spite of the invisibility speil. The old man ran knowledgeable eyes over his partner's muscled chest. "Basket work is where a slave starts off and ends up. You're too healthy to waste here. After a couple of days to work you in, you'll probably end up holding steel for the hammer-men, or doing pick-and-shovel work."

The oldster gave Blaize another crooked smile. "They don't like to put a potential weapon in a slave's hand right from the start. This way they sort of break you into harness first."

Blaize took in Trav's gray hair and wiry frame. "You say this is where the slaves start off or end up—which are you doing?"

"Oh, I'm ending," the slave replied in a flat voice. "Just a question of how many loads I have left in me." They reached the bottom of the pit, where men shoveled dirt and cracked rock into their baskets. "Less than you." He nodded at a hunched figure straining to move his full basket. "More than him."

They moved off with their full baskets. "Sounds like you don't care," Blaize said, heaving his load up onto his shoulder.

"That," Trav wheezed as he got his load into place, "is the first thing you have to learn around here."

They were halfway to the top when the older slave Trav had pointed out fell to his knees. Blaize went to help him, when an overseer came charging down. They were posted all along the roadway like some sort of traffic directors. Each carried a long staff.

The end of this overseer's staff now poked ungently into Blaize's chest. "You want to carry double, make up for his share?"

There was no way Blaize could do that for the rest of the day. He shook his head.

"Then get back to your basket." The overseer leaned over, screaming into the collapsed slave's face. "Up to the top or over the side. Your choice. Do it—now!"

The white-haired man rose on wobbly legs, pulling at this load, and the line moved on.

Blaize looked hard at Trav, who merely shrugged. "Have to learn for yourself, kid. Here in the pit, you can't care."

They were halfway back down into the mine, on the outer edge of the road, when the white-haired man stumbled again. One moment, he was on the road. The next moment, he wasn't there.

Outcries came from below, where the old man was probably bouncing across lower coils of the road.

Blaize turned to Trav. "Is there some sort of head overseer?" he asked. "How do I find him?"

The head overseer had short-cropped, grizzled gray hair like a veteran Altem Guardsman. Unlike a guardsman, he had a gut that strained the fabric of his tunic. His lips seemed curved in a continual smile, but his eyes were as expressionless as polished gray pebbles.

He's too low on the chain of command to recognize the tattoo, Blaize thought. *I can only hope he's smart enough to bring it to the attention of the mage-officer.*

"So, you had to see me—and privately." They stood alone by a freshly exposed Magestone outcrop. "Make it quick. It's not healthy to stay here too long. What do you want to report, a criminal conspiracy or a Rebel plot? It doesn't matter. You'll be staying here."

Blaize drew the silver medallion from behind his belt, raising it to his head. "You see this?"

A slight spark appeared in the overseer's eyes. "Very nice. It still won't buy your way out."

"Not that." Blaize tapped his forehead. *"This."*

Now the other man's genial air vanished. "A crazy act isn't going to help you, either."

The medallion had a polished back, offering Blaize a blurred reflection. It was good enough to show that Karrudan's sigil had not appeared.

Blaize stood dumbfounded, trying to control his skittering thoughts. Then he remembered Trav's comment on the way into the pit—about wild Magestone interfering with Technomancy.

It certainly had in this case.

"Wait," Blaize said desperately. "I have to show you up on the surface."

"Maybe in Khamsin, or Caero?" The overseer snatched the medallion from Blaize's hand. "This will pay for my time and attention . . . for today. If you come to my attention again, you won't like what happens."

He turned away, utterly confident that Blaize wouldn't try anything. Of course, he was armed, and Blaize wasn't.

And even if Blaize tried, what more could he do? He was at the bottom of a great pit, with countless guards blocking the one way out.

No wonder Trav had told him not to care.

He was here for the rest of what probably would be a short, hard life.

CHAPTER 8

RIKKA watched as Eginhard leaned against the bale of hay he was using for a desk. It gave under him, adding another degree of annoyance to his already harassed expression. Since Blaize's capture, he had cleared out the Warrens and every other Rebel hangout that the Caeronn had seen. Bruna and Kennet had been uprooted from her bakery and moved to one across town. Dwarves were already at work filling in the tunnel from there.

And the ramshackle building masking the other Warrens entrance Blaize knew about had collapsed that morning.

Eginhard had moved his operation to the upper loft of Benni Stabler's place. It smelled of horses, hay . . . and used hay. Joining him up here were the fighters chosen to meet the pack train and the lieutenants who'd run things in Khamsin while Eginhard was gone.

"We won't be going directly north," Eginhard said. "Benni is already moving horses out the West Gate. We'll take a wide detour north and east to confuse any potential searchers, which means a gathering place. It will be on the unfinished Imperial Road."

"The one that ends up as an unpaved path and splits off to Enos Joppa," Tulwar said.

Eginhard nodded. "You won't have to walk that far," he said, "only to the blasted tree."

"There's a little gorge nearby—it's hidden from the road," Benni Stabler said. "My boys will be holding the horses there."

Those more involved with smuggling nodded. The tree was a familiar rendezvous.

"And we now meet at moonrise instead of this afternoon." Eginhard's annoyance showed again at pushing the time back. "I've already sent a message to Sigwold, telling him of the delay and warning him to watch for unexpected Imperials. They shouldn't be out that way—Blaize didn't know the details."

He shot a glance at Rikka, then shook his head. "If the Caeronn does betray us, I'll cut out his heart and offer it as a sacrifice to Marway."

"What about trying to rescue him?" Rikka asked.

Her foster-father made a brusque gesture. "You know we have more important business at hand."

"I can remember when the most important business of your life was getting out of a mine," she replied. "With your family—with me and Kennet."

Rikka looked round at the faces of the other men in the loft. None would meet her eyes. "We know where the press-gang was heading, to the new pit being dug north and west of town."

"It's out of the way," Eginhard muttered.

"Out of the way for a direct ride northward," Rikka argued. "Not so far, considering the route you're taking now."

The Dwarven leader looked to his lieutenants, who responded with shrugs or noncommittal expressions. "You're determined to press this, daughter?" Eginhard asked.

"I'm going to make the attempt," Rikka said.

Eginhard looked down at his straw "tabletop," then met her eyes grimly. "If there are to be more to this rescue party, they'll have to volunteer."

None of the men in the room spoke, although Tulwar grinned at her. But then, he always grinned at her, hoping to soften her heart.

Rikka looked away, rounding on the Rebels who'd dealt with Blaize.

"Mikarl?"

The Khamsin who'd guided Blaize for his burglary looked even more shifty-eyed than usual. "He cost me money in that sword-bout."

"Jon Bowman?"

The crossbow artist who'd helped during the escape from Khamita Castle silently shook his head.

Rikka began to feel a little desperate. She turned to Blaize's bunkmate from the Warrens. "Jorj? How about you?"

"He seemed like a good fellow." Jorj sat hunched on another hay bale, his elbows on his knees, his fingers laced together. Rikka noticed his hands were trembling. "But . . . I just got out of that mine. I'm not going back there."

"Are you sure you want to risk such a fate, daughter?" Eginhard asked.

Rikka didn't even reply. *I'll just have to be a rescue party of one,* she coldly thought, turning away.

"Didn't ask me," a lazy voice said.

She nearly spun round to look at Tulwar Windfoot. "I didn't think you would be interested," she told the sand clansman.

He shrugged, balancing his sheathed scimitar across his knees. "More hands make less work."

The thought of putting herself under obligation to Tulwar made Rikka curt. "Then you'll have to stop lounging on that hay." She turned to Benni Stabler. "We'll need three horses—to leave immediately."

Although the mounts were obtained immediately, it was late afternoon before Rikka entered Minetown. She'd had to arrange a rendezvous and time with Eginhard. Then certain supplies had to be purchased, as well as the appropriate costume. Rikka also wound up walking several miles, collecting the necessary props in the despoiled countryside.

Last, and most importantly, she had to linger in a stand of brush, waiting for the proper companions to cover her entrance.

When the straggling group of women passed her, Rikka joined the end of the parade. Like them, she wore a shapeless peasant dress of drab-dyed homespun, giving her a thick-bodied, perhaps pregnant, aspect. A brown knitted shawl covered her red hair. Her arms were full of twigs, withes and osiers, the raw materials for basket making. Women and children might not work directly in the pit, but everyone in Minetown contributed to the effort, even if it was merely weaving baskets.

Rikka walked through the gateway in the palisade without incident. Although the guards were supposed to keep a strict tally, they were much easier with incoming traffic than outgoing. How many people would be eager to break into Feshku's Pit?

After dropping off her load, Rikka made her way to the makeshift central square and the infirmary. There she joined another line. This was the time of day for the women, and there were many ahead of her. Most were pale and strained, some ill, some pregnant, some with sick children. Rikka hadn't eaten since last night, nor had she slept.

She probably fit right in.

At last, it was her turn to see Graciela, Minetown's leech. Rikka kept her shawl wrapped around her hair and face until they were alone together in the examining room. The healer's eyes went wide for a moment when she recognized Rikka. But she put a hand on the younger woman's shoulder as if she were checking some complaint, saying in a low voice, "You're taking a risk."

Graciela, the stolid leech-woman, was the Rebellion's contact in Minetown.

"The press-gang brought in a new intake today," Rikka said.

Graciela nodded. "Poor devils. Most will be lucky to last six months."

"Was there a Caeronn among them?" Rikka gave a quick description of Blaize.

Again, the healer nodded. "Hard to miss, with that shaven pate. Ugly bruise on the back of the head, broken skin . . . and a torn lip from Magus Therion's ring. Your friend must have interrupted the afterglow of Therion's *erl*-essence sniffing."

Graciela's lips tightened. "If the mage doesn't learn a little restraint, he won't last six months, either."

"He's not—," Rikka began, then stopped. "I guess he is a friend." The idea seemed somehow unsettling, so she hurriedly went on, trying to sound more businesslike. "He's one of us, swept up last night. We need him for an operation."

"So you're going to break him out?"

Rikka nodded. "Do you remember which gang he was assigned to?"

"They always keep them under canvas up here for the first night. A last taste of fresh air," Graciela said. "Tomorrow, they'll be down in the pit, working around the Magestone, to see which of them will turn out most susceptible to the stuff."

The healer's expression wasn't pleasant. The next day would be very busy in the infirmary.

"Perhaps we'll change their schedule," Rikka said with a grim smile. "Much could happen between now and the morning."

She rearranged her shawl and left the infirmary.

Now she'd have to wait for dark.

Coming up with his last load of the day, Blaize moved like an older man than Trav. Again, it was like a horrible parody of his first days in the army. This time he was reliving his first hike with full gear. Muscles he never knew of screamed with pain at every step.

But worse than the physical aches was the feeling of despair. He'd walked miles today, and gone nowhere. His armor and military pack had purpose; they might have been heavy, but they were arranged with movement in mind. Toting a basket loaded with earth and stone on one shoulder left his back and body feeling contorted and his soul feeling empty.

Then, too, no matter how much heat the sun had pounded into the pit, Blaize spent the day wading through the cold suspicion of his fellow slaves. Trav had barely spoken to him after Blaize asked to see the head overseer.

The older man had just shaken his head at Blaize's first

request, and he'd shaken his head again on seeing Blaize's face when he emerged from the meeting.

Trav didn't ask what had gone on. It wasn't his business, and he didn't care. But he had become . . . careful with Blaize.

And Blaize could understand that, too. Trav had to protect himself. He'd be down here for the rest of his life.

So might Blaize—but his lifetime might turn out to be short indeed. In this brutal little world, some other slave would probably convince himself that Blaize had informed on some sin or infraction. Blaize's time in the army had shown how a guilty conscience could turn to anger and then deadly action.

And if it comes down to that, Blaize asked himself, *would a life like this be worth a fight? Better maybe to allow myself the easy way out.*

He shook his head. One day down here, and he was already hoping for the release of death.

People have escaped from the mines, Blaize reminded himself. *Rikka did.*

He dumped his basket, stacked it where the others stacked theirs, and looked dully around. He'd be hatching no plans tonight. His brain was almost too tired to come up with coherent thoughts. Blaize could just about manage following the crowd to the cook-tents.

The food was simple, produced in mass—some sort of grain and vegetable gruel with occasional chunks of mystery meat. A ladle of the stuff was dumped on a slab of bread, and turned to the next.

Blaize wolfed it down with an animal enjoyment even as he moved off the line.

A shoulder rammed into him. It belonged to one of the larger men from his work gang. The fellow glowered at Blaize.

Blaize simply sidestepped and went on eating.

The other man would have liked to carry things further, but the guards and overseers were coming in.

Most of the other prisoners had eaten with the same

speed Blaize had. The guards now organized the gangs into single-file lines and marched them out.

The lines were to make things easier when Blaize and the others reached the open-sided tents that were their sleeping quarters. Each file became a coffle as the guards snapped a leg cuff onto slaves' ankles. The cuffs were attached with a short length of chain to a longer, heavier chain, which ran the length of the tent, firmly attached by ring bolts to a pair of huge bollards at either end.

The only amenities were straw-filled pallets for each man, with waste pots placed in reasonable proximity. Privacy was nonexistent.

Blaize couldn't care less. He dropped onto his pallet, ignoring its rough, greasy feel and the stink of sweat and unwashed flesh.

A slight twinge from the back of his head reminded him of his bruise. Cautious exploration revealed only some tenderness. Compared with the distress from his strained muscles, that counted as cured.

Good leech for such a Tezla-forsaken place, Blaize thought muzzily. In another moment, he'd dropped into a deep, dreamless sleep.

With nightfall Rikka got rid of the baggy, shapeless dress. Beneath it she wore a riding costume, trousers and shirt, both in dark colors. She kept the shawl. It covered her hair and face and presented a familiar silhouette to any guards that might see her.

Rikka also shifted the coil of rope she'd worn wrapped around her waist to her shoulder.

She hadn't wasted her time in the waning daylight. After finding a good spot among the tumbledown houses of the shantytown, she'd timed the sentries on their rounds.

Not much variation there. The new shift had marched the same beats, keeping the same times as their predecessors.

After sunset, Rikka let the guards go a few more rounds to get used to the darkness—and to get bored. Then she moved for the ramparts.

The spot they'd agreed upon was a good hundred paces from the fortified gate. Rikka brought up another item that had added bulk to her middle—the bull's-eye lantern. She'd already lit it in the cover of the shanties. Now she leaned over the sharpened tops of the palisade logs and opened the latch on the covered lantern, once, twice, three times.

At the third flash, a night-bird sang in the darkness beyond, Tulwar's return signal. Rikka unslung the rope. A loop was already fixed in one end. That went over one of the sturdier logs. She crouched to wait.

A moment later, Tulwar joined her.

Still crouched, they regathered the rope and were off the wall well before the next guard came by. They made their way among the improvised dwellings, built with whatever the Imperials didn't want.

Rikka knew them well. Such constructions had been home to her for more than half her life.

She waited until they were well away from the wall before opening the lamp again and blowing out the stub of candle inside.

"You know where they're keeping him?" Tulwar asked in a whisper.

"Yes, but he'll be chained. You'll need these." Rikka passed over two more items she'd picked up before leaving Khamsin—a hammer and chisel.

"You think of everything—even if it's not needed." The Galeshi sounded amused.

"And what were you going to use?" Rikka inquired sharply. "Your teeth?"

Slipping from shadow to shadow, they moved on through the silent camp.

Some soldier's instinct stirred Blaize awake. He opened his eyes to find Tulwar Windfoot standing over him, scimitar upraised.

Blaize gawked for a second, not sure if this was some sort of dream—or a nightmare. He tried to move sleep-fogged, stiffened muscles, open gummy lips . . .

With a grimace that was almost comical, the Galeshi dropped to one knee, putting a light hand on Blaize's mouth while he mimed for silence. Then he turned to face Blaize's cuffed ankle.

Pushing himself up on one elbow, Blaize saw what must have awoken him. Tulwar had stretched his leg chain across the head of a hammer. Now he raised his sword again, bringing it down in a swift chop.

Blaize's estimate of Galeshi swordsmithing rose sharply as the scimitar's cutting edge sliced through an iron link as if it were butter.

Although Tulwar had done his best to keep the operation as quiet as possible, there was a little noise as the blade clashed against the hammerhead.

It was enough to rouse someone two sleepers down from where Blaize lay. He immediately recognized the character who'd purposely bumped into him at dinner.

Then, the big, slope-shouldered slave had given him a look of challenge.

Now, as Tulwar whirled to point his scimitar at the stirring figure, the man stared at Blaize with mute appeal. Then he glanced beyond Blaize, his eyes going wide with alarm.

At the same moment, a voice slurred, "Wha're ya doin' here?"

Tulwar ducked down as Blaize turned on his side, still pretending to be asleep, to see what was going on. Light flooded the area as a man with a lamp came close. Blaize recognized the head overseer. The man advanced unsteadily, and his eyes certainly weren't on Blaize. No, the paunchy man's attention was all on a female figure wrapped in a shawl.

"Come here lookin' f'yer man?" The overseer put a proprietary hand on the female figure's shoulder, pushing away the shawl to display thick, red hair.

Rikka!

"Maybe I'll do inshtead." The drunken overseer went to wrap his arm around Rikka's waist.

An instant later, he stepped back, a puzzled expression on

his face. The lamplight showed a spreading stain on the overseer's uniform. It was below the left breast and to the side, where a knife might slip between the ribs and reach a man's heart.

Rikka squared off against him, a reddened blade in her hand.

The overseer was already dead, but Blaize knew strange things could happen with wounds like these. Once he'd watched a man run a hundred paces after taking a blade in the heart.

This one tried to shout an alarm.

But Blaize was already vaulting up, reaching for the overseer. One hand clamped on the dying man's chin, covering his mouth, fingers crushing against his nose. Blaize's other hand grabbed the lamp before it could fall.

Seconds were all that was left for the overseer, and he must have known it. He tried to twist away, his hands plucking at Blaize's wrist. But his struggles were weak, ineffectual. The hands fell as the slavemaster's last breath hummed gustily against Blaize's palm.

Then the fight—and the life—left him, and the man collapsed bonelessly.

Blaize caught the dead weight with his body, fighting to maintain his clumsy hold while making sure the lamp didn't crash.

Rikka joined him, and together they lay the dead man down.

"Keys," she said, wiping her blade on the overseer's uniform and going for his belt pouch.

Blaize found the master key on a chain around the dead man's neck, and the medallion the man had taken earlier that afternoon. The chain was broken—Blaize cursed under his breath.

One he gave to Rikka. The other he slipped under his shirt as she ran over to the chained slaves.

Rikka and Tulwar made quite a team. Working down the line, he'd awaken each slave with a hand on the mouth, ensuring silence while she undid the leg cuffs.

Tactically speaking, freeing as many slaves as possible was a clever gambit. Their unpremeditated, improvised attempts to break out would certainly keep the guards and overseers busy while Rikka followed her escape plan.

On the other hand, introducing so many random elements might serve to wreck that plan. And precious time was flying away . . .

Still, Blaize did not intervene. Rikka might have had some solidly practical—or perhaps some personal—motives to come in here and help him. But, remembering the way she talked about the mines, he realized her root cause was a burning belief that *no one* should be in these places.

By the time the whole coffle had been released, the freed slaves were starting to make noise. Some were already running off. Even Rikka realized it was time to go.

As she came toward him, Blaize noticed Trav standing slack-jawed, looking oddly older than he had today on the line. Apparently this late shot of hope had paralyzed the man who'd chosen to give it all up. Then Blaize spotted his aggressive chainmate kneeling over the dead overseer, coming up with the man's knife and sword.

"Rikka, the key," Blaize said quietly.

She gave it to him, and he tossed it to the now-armed former slave. "Do what you can," he said.

Then a cry of pain came out of the darkness, and a yell of "Escape! Guards! To me!"

The knot of unchained slaves exploded, some heading for the shantytown, some going for the walls, some just running.

Rikka surprised Blaize by heading along the rim of the pit toward one of the farther sections of the palisade. As they reached the ladder leading to the ramparts, a guard appeared, torch in one hand, spear in the other.

"Halt!" the Imperial ordered, hefting his spear and preparing to yell for reinforcements.

Rikka's arm moved in an incredibly quick gesture, and the guard toppled backward over the wall. Blaize had just a moment to spot the knife-hilt that had sprouted in the man's right eye-socket.

Without missing a beat, Rikka swarmed up the ladder. Blaize noticed she'd lost the shawl she'd been wearing. He now saw that it had hidden a coil of rope hanging from her shoulder. She secured it to one of the palisade logs, and then they were going over.

Blaize hit the ground with a thud that reminded him of all his aching muscles. Now Tulwar was hurrying them along toward a distant scrub thicket. "Nearest cover I could find," he said as they crashed through the underbrush. A nervous equine snort came from nearby. Tulwar was already making soothing noises.

Moments later, they were mounted and pounding down the road. Behind them the walls of Minetown were coming alive with torchlight.

As they rode, Rikka drew up beside Blaize. The rising moon illuminated an odd expression on her face. "So now you know," she said.

Blaize shook his head. "Not after one day. But I can understand—and thank you."

He then turned to Tulwar, who, in spite of his horse's pace, seemed to be lounging in the saddle. "My thanks to you as well, Galeshi, though I can't understand why you came. At our last meeting, you'd have been happy to kill me."

"That is why I *had* to come," Tulwar replied with a wry smile. "In my anger, I struck to kill. You saved me from the consequences of a foolish action. When you got drunk and let yourself be captured, how could I not balance the debt by rescuing you from your foolishness?"

Blaize had no answer for that. He just tried to get himself comfortable in the saddle and rode on.

Chapter 9

After they cleared the zone of devastation around Minetown, Rikka left the Imperial Road, turning onto a barely scratched trail through scrubland. From his glimpses of the stars when there weren't trees in the way, Blaize judged they were heading southwest.

Rikka continued to take the lead, and Blaize and Tulwar followed her along an intricate series of trackways and back paths. Some of them didn't seem to be paths at all, just wider spaces between bushes. Blaize had to keep on guard to make sure he wasn't struck in the face by errant branches.

Smuggler's ways, he realized.

They continued on, sometimes in darkness, sometimes in moonlight, until Rikka reined in her horse. Blaize leaned forward to look over her shoulder. The trail they were on intersected a larger road. All around them was second-growth forest, with thick underbrush cutting the view to a few yards.

Rikka gestured to Tulwar, who gave her a flash of very white teeth, then pursed his lips and let out a low, warbling whistle—the call of a night-bird.

With a whispered laugh, Rikka turned to Blaize. "He does it better than I can," she said in an undertone.

A moment later, the recognition signal was returned from the bushes on the opposite side of the road. Rikka gently kicked her mount into a slow walk. Blaize and Tulwar trailed along behind her.

A rider emerged from the shadows across the way, and they rode together along the road for a short distance, until what seemed like an impenetrable wall of brush suddenly shifted aside to reveal an opening.

This was a larger, better-maintained secret road. There was enough room for people to ride side by side. But they continued on in single file along the shadowy path until they found an open space, a rocky gorge cut in the side of a hill. During the spring rains, it was probably a swift-moving stream. Now it was dry, providing a hiding place for Eginhard's troop.

Blaize recognized a few faces among the waiting riders. Jorj, his former roommate, grinned. "Don't think I'd ever get drunk enough to volunteer for a career in the mines," he said.

The shifty-eyed Khamsin who'd guided Blaize to Khamita Castle leaned forward in his saddle. "Is your head all right?" he asked with totally counterfeit commiseration. "The hangover part, I mean. We can't do much about the thinking abilities."

"Shut up, Mikarl," Rikka said.

But those were just the opening volleys in a barrage of rude wit about Blaize's drinking capacity, his gambler's luck, the strength of his skull, and whether he should be allowed out alone.

Eginhard finally brought it to an end, his voice rumbling as he rode over to Blaize, looking him up and down. "No more wine for you until we finish this business. Right, lad?"

If they want to believe the wine went to my head and led to this, all the better for me, Blaize thought.

"Right," Blaize said, putting out his hand.

Eginhard gripped it. Then he released it, grabbed his reins, and started his horse moving. With that silent signal, the cavalcade moved out.

Blaize joined them and rode.

The rhythmic, loping gait began to have a predictable effect—not surprising after unconsciousness, a day of forced labor, and a bare few hours of sleep. Blaize began to nod, then dozed in the saddle, leaving most of the navigation to the tough little northern pony he straddled.

Luckily it was a smart little beast as well, keeping to the middle of the pack as the troop moved through the night-shadowed countryside. When his mount finally came to a stop, Blaize almost fell from the saddle.

A hand grabbed his arm, keeping him in place.

"At least you don't snore," Rikka said, a serious expression overtaking the twinkle in her hazel eyes. "Come on. Father wants you."

They rode out ahead of the others, following the track as it curved up to a vantage point on a hillside.

Eginhard sat on his horse, frowning at the vista below. A pair of larger roads met and crossed, creating an irregular clearing in the midst of another section of scrubland.

"Our destination is just beyond that," the Dwarf said, nodding toward the crossroad. "And look what's getting in our way."

Blaize could see. Strung out along the road paralleling their route was an Imperial mounted patrol, a good dozen men on horseback plus a couple of crossbowmen on the six-legged mechanical Scorpems.

Blaize remembered hearing that Portarr had established a riding ring in Khamita Castle. The Warlord was no fool—he'd worked to improve the garrison's tactical weakness.

Atlantis' Empire had been built by the campaigns of an infantry army, aimed at crushing organized resistance in any of its conquests. Levitating fortresses provided rock-solid supply lines, although they could only move along ley lines. Even with operations limited to the invisible radians of concentrated magical force, the mobile strongholds were impervious to raiding cavalry. On the battlefield, infantry formations had held enemy armies in place to be blasted with long-range Technomantic weapons. Golems then moved forward in shock attacks, with the infantry advancing to mop up any resistance.

Horse cavalry simply hadn't been needed.

But there was a difference between crushing enemy

armies and holding land against hit-and-run raiders. In the west, hard-riding Galeshis and even mounted Prieskans could swoop down on Imperial outposts, attack trade and supply convoys, or intercept tax shipments and outdistance the Empire's troops when they responded.

Powerful and tireless as steel and Magestone Golems were, they only matched the speed of a running man. Once the raiders rode out of sight, it was almost impossible to track them down.

The Atlantis Guild's answer was a Technomantic fix—the Scorpem. Modeled on an insect-form, these fighting machines scuttled along on six triple-jointed limbs, the longest section coming as tall as a man's shoulder. They carried a single rider and offered a variety of weapons—pincers, and a shearing blade the size of a horse's head in front, not to mention a sharp-toothed whirling buzz blade set in the segmented tail. As designed by the mages, they were fearsome things. Actually handling the complex mechanisms in harsh terrain revealed numerous shortcomings, however. For the present, Scorpems were in short supply in the outlands, and the ones in service weren't all that dependable.

Atlantis' cleverer commanders hadn't waited for the Technomancers to overcome their mistakes. They'd imported tall horses from around Atlantis and put their infantrymen on them, extending the reach and striking range of their patrols.

Blaize had first ridden a horse patrolling the plains out west . . .

His thoughts were shattered by Eginhard's next words—especially when their meaning penetrated.

"Marway curse their Imperial guts," the Dwarf swore. "This is all your fault, Caeronn."

Blaize turned, staring. What Eginhard said was all too true. After receiving the signal for a meeting and not having Karrudan's agent turn up for it, Gamelon and Portarr would doubtless think Blaize had been removed—or killed—by the Rebels.

The commander and his lieutenant would change the patrol schedules. No sense in letting the Rebels enjoy any advantage at their expense.

But if Eginhard knew or even suspected that, why was Blaize riding beside him? More to the point, why was Blaize still alive?

Luckily, the Dwarf read Blaize's look of consternation as one of incomprehension.

"Your brilliant performance with the wine flask led to you getting picked up by the slavers, which led to Rikka arranging that mass escape . . . which led to unscheduled patrols out searching for fugitives." The look Eginhard gave Blaize indicated a wry skepticism.

"Better sharpen up, boy," the Dwarf told him. "We've got to take out that patrol—and you're going to lead the charge!"

"The charge?" Blaize repeated. "Shouldn't we have more of a plan?"

"We made one while you slept in the saddle," the Dwarf replied. "Part of it is that you're leading the charge."

Eginhard was obviously in no mood for discussion. Years in the army helped Blaize translate the look he was getting: *Soldier, shut up and soldier!*

Wordlessly, he followed Eginhard as the rest of their party reached them. The pace picked up as they headed downhill, bursting onto the roadway behind the rear guard of the patrol.

Blaize drew his sword.

"Go!" Eginhard yelled.

Blaize spurred his mount from a trot into a canter, then into a full gallop. Well, this was where an Altem Guardsman should be, at the forefront of any attack.

But he felt a strange emptiness—not hunger, though Tezla knew he hadn't eaten much in the last day. No, it was the thought of riding *against fellow guardsmen*. They'd all be fighting for the Empire. But if Blaize's mission was to succeed, the patrol ahead would have to die.

Guardsmen's heads began to turn. Behind him, Blaize heard the pounding of hoofbeats as more of Eginhard's fighters got onto the road.

Tulwar yelled a Galeshi war cry.

The tail end of the Imperial column had now reached the clearing ahead. Already, they were shaking out into a line formation while still on the move.

Something whizzed past Blaize's left ear—a bolt from one of the Scorpem crossbowmen.

Blaize tried to get more speed out of his tough little pony. He knew the guardsmen weren't retreating. They were trying to put a little more distance between themselves and the onrushing Rebels before they turned and unleashed their countercharge.

If they succeeded, that could be very bad indeed.

The numbers were about equal, but the Imperials were mounted on tall horses from the southern plains, while Eginhard's people rode smaller northern ponies. The difference in mass would be felt in a shock attack.

And then there were the two clattering Scorpems, made of heavy metal with a buzz blade in their flexible tails and a blade and pincers where a head should be. The Imperials' horses had obviously trained with the noisy contraptions long enough to get used to them. Confronted with these clacking metal monstrosities, though, the ponies were likely to bolt even before the Scorpems got close enough to use their armament.

Blaize turned in his saddle to shout an order—or at least a strong suggestion—for anyone with a ranged weapon to aim for the Scorpem riders.

He saw the silent crossbowman, Jon, let off a bolt.

These are experienced fighters, Blaize told himself. *They don't need me to tell them their business.*

The crossbow quarrel would have landed right between the shoulders of the right-hand Scorpem's rider. Unfortunately, his mechanical mount's tail flicked up. The missile hit segmented steel with a flat *whack!* and caromed off.

As for the Scorpem crossbowman, he twisted in the saddle and fired back. Despite its many-legged scuttle, the Scorpems offered a remarkably stable seat—and firing platform.

A second after the flat *twang* of the crossbow, a cry rang

out from the crowd of horsemen trying to line up beside Blaize. Jorj flung up his arms and then flopped from his saddle like a rag doll. His hands didn't even go to the crossbow bolt jutting from his chest.

First blood to the Imperials, Blaize thought. His hand was so tight on his sword, the wound wire of the hilt bit into his palm.

Eginhard's troop was spread out in a ragged rank to his left. But the Imperials were turning.

They'll go through us like a fresh-forged sword through snow, Blaize thought, stretching his own blade straight out to the length of his arm.

That was when the volley of arrows sleeted from the brush behind the Imperials.

Whoever the unknown archers were, they obviously knew their business as well. The heavy fire concentrated on the Scorpem riders. In an instant, despite their armored cover, the two crossbowmen looked like pincushions, sagging lifelessly over their now-still mounts.

Riders came tearing through the underbrush—Orcs, for the most part, with a scattering of humans and Dwarves. A helmeted human with a near-Orc-sized chest and a battleaxe rode in the lead.

The surviving Imperial riders milled around, unsure which threat to meet. That marked them as novice cavalrymen. Veterans would have been forming up or at least riding hard to escape being encircled.

Surrounded, bereft of the Scorpems, and outnumbered, the Imperials were now just dead men on horseback.

The onrushing lines of attackers crashed into them. Blaize's view of the swirling fight that followed fractured into a series of separate images.

With one swipe of his weapon, the burly axe-wielder who led the ambushers from the underbrush emptied an Imperial saddle.

The battle lust in an Orc Cave Butcher's red eyes dimmed as he took an Imperial lance in the chest after cleaving another enemy's arm off.

Blaize charged in to administer a final stab to the lancer, catching him in the side while he was still trying to pull his weapon free.

The Imperial bugler raised his horn to his lips, either to rally his troops or to call for help. Whatever his plan, it was forestalled when a feathered shaft suddenly sprouted from his throat. Instead of a bugle call, all he gave was a bubbling gurgle as he toppled off his mount.

A grim-faced Imperial—an Altem Guardsman, from his uniform—kicked his mount into motion. The larger southern horse collided with one of the northern ponies, shouldering the smaller, stubbier animal aside.

At the same time, the Altem's long sword flashed out, all but decapitating the pony's rider, one of Eginhard's men whom Blaize had never met.

Rebounding from the crash, the pony fell, squealing in pain. It flailed out with its hooves, catching another pony in the hock. A gap opened in the cordon of riders hemming in the Imperials.

Urging his horse on, the Altem sent his mount in a leap over the downed pony, making a desperate break for it.

Blaize hauled on his own pony's reins, bringing the animal around so he could cut off the Imperial's retreat.

Hunched in his saddle, the guardsman ruthlessly lashed his horse with the reins, trying for every bit of speed. When he saw he wasn't going to beat Blaize, he reverted to his earlier tactic, aiming to ram.

But Blaize's pony had more room. It nimbly sidestepped the thundering horse, forcing the Imperial to overextend as he wildly lashed out at Blaize.

The slash went over Blaize's head as he crouched over the neck of his pony, whipping backhanded, his arm moving like an uncoiling spring. The tip of his blade connected as the guardsman hurtled by.

His horse's hooves pounding, the fleeing Imperial let his long sword drop as he clapped a hand against the side of his neck. A gush of bright red escaped from beneath his palm and between his fingers.

The man's arm dropped as he reeled in the saddle, staring back openmouthed at Blaize. The motion turned to a graceless flop as the Altem thudded to the earth.

Rikka cantered over on her mount to catch the runaway horse, giving Blaize an irritated look.

"You almost got hit by Jon, blundering into his line of fire like that."

Blaize looked in the direction she'd come from to see Jon the crossbowman standing on the ground, aiming his weapon. Beside him, Eginhard sat in his saddle, holding the reins for Jon's pony in one hand and an axe in the other.

"I was serving as horse-holder," Rikka said, patting her sheathed knife. "My blade is a little short for this kind of work."

Blaize felt a stab of relief to realize she hadn't been in the fight.

"Though it looks as if it's all over now," Rikka went on.

The shrill sound of Tulwar's Galeshi victory-yell had Blaize hauling his pony around almost in embarrassment, realizing he'd turned his back on the skirmish. He raised his sword arm up, then let it fall down again.

Rikka was right. No more Imperials remained astride their horses or Scorpems. The Orcs were already off their lizard-mounts, blades rising and falling to make sure none of the guardsmen were shamming.

The barrel-chested axe-man who'd led the attack from the rear rode through the Rebel lines, joined by a Dwarf with an equally red axe.

"Ha, brother!" Eginhard cried, tossing the reins he held to Jon as he kicked his pony forward. "Well met!"

Snow pulled a cloth from his saddle pack and set to work running it across the head and haft of his axe. Once the stains were gone, he let it dangle by its strap from his saddle pommel. Clean tools had always been a fetish for his father. But Snow had found that clean weapons sometimes meant the difference between life and death.

It wouldn't be a bad idea to rub down his horse after

its gallop. Snow took off his helmet and rested that on the front of his saddle, too. He wouldn't mind washing himself as well.

That would have to wait until they'd cleaned up this miniature battlefield, which in turn must wait on finishing the necessary diplomacy.

The Dwarven brothers had both dismounted, embracing each other. Snow rode over and swung from the saddle as Sigwold presented Eginhard.

"This is Snow," Sigwold said. "As you see, he's a good man with an axe."

"Well, I could see he wasn't Sarah," Eginhard growled. The Dwarf looked with some expectancy toward the copse where the attack had come from. "Speaking of which . . ."

Sigwold shook his head. "Not here," he said. "She has other parts of the plan to set in motion—people who have to be ready. If all goes as planned, we'll meet in Caero."

Eginhard shrugged philosophically. "I suppose Sarah has many threads to pull together." He turned to Snow and gripped wrists in the Dwarven fashion. "Nice ambush, young man—very neatly timed."

Snow shrugged. "You got the warning to us early enough that we had everyone prepared and positioned."

The Dwarf pointed along his back trail. "We saw them coming from the top of that hill—heard them, too, with those stilt-leggity things. Technomancy may be powerful, but it's not quiet."

Eginhard grinned, looking off to his right. "My daughter, Rikka." He introduced a slim redheaded woman who rode up leading an Imperial cavalry mount.

"And this is Blaize, who was happily asleep in the saddle when we first saw the Marway-be-damned Imperials coming this way."

The lean young Caeronn ducked his shaved head, his regular features twisting with embarrassment.

"Well, he certainly woke up when he was needed," Snow replied, shaking hands. "You led that charge without knowing we were there as a backup? And I saw you take that Altem, short sword against long."

"Doesn't have as much authority as that axe you were swinging," the Caeronn responded. He ran a gently probing finger along a filthy bandage, wincing.

"Better have that changed." Snow glanced at Eginhard. "Do you have a leech?"

The Dwarf shook his head. "I just brought fighters. Here comes Tulwar with the butcher's bill."

The robed Galeshi had lost some of his battle zest. "Three men have cuts that don't look too bad," he reported. "But Orrin is dead. Sword slash that nearly went right through his neck." Tulwar shook his head. "And Jorj—that bolt hit him in the heart."

Sigwold was getting the information for the pack-train party. "One man wounded, but he can ride. We lost an Orc, though. Lukush Butt—"

Grugh, the Orc warband leader rode up in time to hear. "Lukush Diedwell," he corrected Sigwold emphatically.

"We leave you now—no battle feast," the Orc said. "You have your people here. Better we be on our way to the Fist before the armor-maggots come to see what happened to this brood."

"We'll do our best to see them hidden," Snow promised. "Lukush, too."

He sent the Grugh and his people off with a couple of Imperial mounts, though he shook his head. The horses would probably become dinner at the Orcs' first campsite.

The rest of the loose horses would be divided among the northern drovers and the Khamsins. The tall animals were prized in the North—cross-bred with ponies, their hybrid offspring would fetch much silver. With their Imperial army brands, however, they couldn't be brought to the city itself.

Eginhard's wounded men and the hurt Varsfielder would take the mounts for sale to the free outposts beyond Enos Joppa, sharing the silver from the booty.

That still left seventeen dead bodies, two Scorpems, and

all traces of any combat in the area to be cleared away—preferably before any more Imperial patrols came riding along.

Snow clapped his hands together. "All right," he said, "we have work to do."

Chapter 10

Blaize joined the others as the leader of the ambush called everyone around. Snow ran a hand through thick black hair worn long enough to pad the interior of his helmet.

"All right, we won this little set-to," he said. "Now we have to bury the evidence. There's an open space back in the brush—let's start digging." Drovers from the pack train were already coming out of the copse with picks and shovels.

A remarkably well-prepared little caravan, Blaize thought.

Then came the grisly task of moving bodies or swearing under the weight of the Scorpems. None of the living knew how to operate the machines. And when Sigwold's experiment with the controls set razor-sharp pincers slashing at Snow's head, they both agreed to the brute-force approach.

Others had already begun the job of digging a pit, but with so much earth to move, they had to improvise, using horse blankets from the captured mounts. Even working in shifts, the men started complaining when they got about eight feet down.

"Are we burying them or digging for Magestone?" one of the drovers demanded.

"Let me know if you find any," Snow responded. He was as filthy as the rest, having served a turn at the bottom with a shovel. Now he'd regained his axe, which ended the argument for a little while.

At ten feet down, though, Sigwold said, "That will do—load them in."

First, they dumped the Scorpems into the pit. They ended

with two layers of stiffening bodies covering the mechanical beasts. Snow vanished over to the pack train and returned with a metal container, which Blaize quickly recognized. Somewhere in the Land, an Incendiary Golem was missing a fuel tank.

The Rebel used his axe to slash the tank open, then slopped the contents over the top row of bodies—the Rebel dead and the Orc. Sigwold was well downwind, using flint and steel to ignite a torch. When Snow finished, he threw in the empty fuel container as well.

Sigwold sent the now-burning torch after it.

With a mighty *fwooomph!* the incendiary fluid caught. Brief, intensely burning flames licked out of the pit, causing some of the watchers to make a quick retreat.

Blaize had slipped to the rear of the crowd right after seeing the fuel tank. He glanced at the distant pack train, wondering what other surprises the Rebels had tucked away on their beasts.

The blaze subsided quickly, throwing up little smoke. *Another commendation for Imperial Technomancy,* Blaize thought. The top layer of dead had been incinerated to the bone.

So much for trying to identify them, he thought.

Sigwold waved a shovel. "Now we fill it in."

The men set to, shoveling, dumping blanketfuls of earth, even kicking the stuff into the pit.

The Dwarf called a halt when they'd created a small mound. Snow and a few of the northern drovers appeared, leading the pack animals and the men's mounts.

The lead horses were skittish, nostrils wide at the lingering scents of burning and blood. But with a drover on either side gentling them, the beasts came willingly enough, trampling the dirt level with the rest of the clearing.

"Enough." Sigwold glanced up at the sun's position. Blaize followed his eyes, astonished to discover that the day was still in the forenoon.

"By sunset I want to be well south of Khamsin," the

Dwarf said. "And well away from any more of these Imperial outriders."

As soon as all the horses were reloaded, they set off along the other leg of the crossroad—the way at right angles to the path taken by the ill-fated patrol. And although Sigwold strove for speed, it was the progress of the laden packhorses that set the pace.

The rhythmic travel began to tell again on Blaize, especially after the last of the battle's adrenaline ebbed away.

Rikka must have sensed his struggle to stay awake. She dropped back in the line of march from her father's side. Joining Blaize, she got him into conversation as they rode along. Just light talk, but it was enough to keep Blaize conscious as his horse jogged away the miles.

"I think that poor pony you're riding is more tired than you are," Rikka teased. "After all, he had to do all the running and jumping in that fight. Your part was restricted to waving your sword."

"That's what you're supposed to do when you're in front of a charge," Blaize replied with a rueful laugh. "My trusty mount spent most of yesterday surrounded by hay. I was excavating. Getting filthy."

He ran the back of his hand across his mouth, smearing a combination of road dust and dirt. Blaize almost reached for the bandage wrapped around his head, but stopped himself. No sense getting it any dirtier.

"If you want, I'll change that for you when we stop," Rikka offered.

"Ah, so you're a leech?"

"No," she said, raising her head haughtily. "I'm a Mending Priestess in disguise."

That got a laugh from Blaize, especially when Rikka brushed at her own dust-caked leathers. "You have to admit this is more practical than those low-bodice gowns they usually wear."

"I might prefer the other," Blaize teased back, ducking a sweep from Rikka's arm.

"You'll be glad Sigwold taught me how to fix battle injuries after I'm done with you," she said, mock-threateningly.

"After what you've already done *for* me—," Blaize broke off, looking at the red-haired woman. "You saved me from living death, Rikka. My thanks for that. Last night must have been long and wearying for you, too. How do you feel?"

Rikka gave him a lopsided grin. "I'll be glad enough when they finally call a halt."

She squinted up at the sun, which was well into its decline toward the horizon. "Can't be too much longer."

Blaize thrust out his right hand at arm's length, the thumb and little finger stretched as far apart as they could go. The spread was about the distance the sun traveled in an hour's time. He pivoted on the little finger, doing a rough calculation. "More than two hours of eating dust," he said with a sigh. "I hope wherever Sigwold takes us, there's some water." Blaize worked his lips as if trying to get rid of a bad taste. "The inside of my mouth feels as if it's been packed with dust."

Rikka reached to the back of her saddle and came up with a water bottle. "You'd better have some of this, then." She sounded exasperated. "Don't you know that if you don't keep water in yourself, you tire even more easily?"

Blaize did know that—one of many hard lessons he'd learned out on the western plains. It was why he'd drained his own water bottle before the fight, to bring up his energy level.

Since then . . . well, it was obvious fatigue had clouded his good sense.

"Thanks," he said, taking the leather bottle. He took a small sip to cut the gummy taste in his mouth, and then a longer draught. "Ah. Delicious."

Rikka snorted in disbelief. "Sitting between the sun and my mare's flesh, it has to be lukewarm and taste like leather." She took a sip and wrinkled her nose. "*Uncured* leather."

"Compared to the condition of my mouth, my lady, it

tasted like the finest Delphane vintage," Blaize assured her, his flowery language getting a laugh in return.

Then it was Rikka's turn to grow a bit more sober. "You remember when you talked about my warrior's face?" she asked abruptly.

Surprised, Blaize nodded.

"I think you've got one, too," she said.

"I thought I might," Blaize admitted quietly. He looked over at the slim, redheaded woman beside him, almost afraid to meet her eyes. "Was it . . . ugly?"

Rikka shook her head. "You looked as though you were trying to total up a very complicated sum in your head," she said. "Very . . . remote. But also very concentrated."

They rode on for a few moments in silence, sharing an almost conspiratorial smile.

"All right, then," Blaize said. "As long as I didn't have my tongue sticking out."

She handed him the water bottle again. "Better have some more," Rikka said. "You're beginning to sound delirious."

They traveled on in good spirits and joshing camaraderie. Sigwold directed the caravan off the road and onto a cross-country run—probably to avoid the next town and any possible inquiries. Their route hugged the edge of the hills, until Snow rode back, declaring a halt.

The bare plains stretched off to the south and east, everything painted a reddish hue as the sun kissed the top of the hills to the west.

More importantly, the sunlight glinted off water ahead of them. It was little more than a stream, winding its way from the hills toward a larger watercourse that fed finally into the Roa Vizorr.

Blaize's tired pony raised his head at the scent of water and began picking up his pace.

The men cheered, turning their final advance into an im-[illegible]mptu charge. They rode their horses right into the water, [illegible]ooves stirring up the bottom silt. The thirsty horses didn't care, leaning their heads down to drink. When the riders started to join them, Sigwold's voice cut across the scene.

"Enough of that," the Rebel leader said. "Get out of there before you get yourselves and the horses sick. You'll have a chance for more—after we have the packs unloaded, a camp set up, and all the mounts checked out."

He beat some dust off his chest. "Then maybe we can think about getting cleaned up and cooking some food."

Blaize was one of the few who hadn't joined the general rush. He'd reined in beside Snow, Sigwold, Tulwar, Eginhard, and Rikka. Now he angled to take his pony a little upstream of the others, where the horse could drink clear water. After allowing a quick drink, he tethered his mount to a tree trunk and joined in the work.

A stand of trees formed the center of the camp, offering some shelter from the elements. The packhorses were unloaded there, and the cargo then covered over with canvas. A couple of tents went up, too, for the leaders and for Rikka.

All the horses were watered. Some of the men went off to gather deadfall to fuel a fire.

Free at last, Blaize headed away from the developing camp, following the stream above all the activity until he found a section that was blocked by scored rock, forming a shallow pool. There he removed his shirt, laving away some of the grime that had accumulated on him.

After taking a deep breath, he plunged his head into the water. The bandage wrapped around his brow loosened, but the pad at the back didn't come free.

Excellent, Blaize thought in exasperation. *It's stuck in place.*

He pulled his head from beneath the water, runoff dripping onto the surface of the pool.

When it stopped and his reflection began to reappear, Blaize twisted back to his shirt to retrieve the silver medallion still hidden within.

Kneeling at the margin of the pool, he slipped the sodden bandage off his brow and brought up the Magestone medallion.

The mark of Karrudan appeared on his skin.

Away from the baneful influence of wild Magestone, the Prophet-Magus' spell seemed to work again.

But as he examined his reflection in the moving water and fading light, it seemed to Blaize that the magical sigil had become slightly blurred.

It could be your imagination, or wishful thinking, Blaize cautioned himself.

But if the raw Magestone had partially effaced the symbol Karrudan had imprinted on his forehead, it might also have disrupted the spell set within his skull. The magical tattoo had been blasted into his flesh with sufficient power to knock Blaize off his feet. But the geas implanted on his brain had been a more delicate business. Blaize shuddered, recalling sensations like insects skittering along his nerves.

Through all his years in the army, Blaize had trained his body to react quickly and decisively when needed. Having that control wrested away at the whim of some wizard . . . that made him deeply angry.

It was a fact of life for the Imperial guardsmen that their mage-officers often wagered away lives like gamblers casting lots. But those warriors ordered to stake their lives in battle at least had the chance to struggle for their own survival, no matter what situation they found themselves in.

Karrudan's game, however, had reduced Blaize to a mere pawn, without even the freedom to fight for himself. The realization burned.

It's one thing to risk all for a great cause, Blaize thought, *but what does it say about the cause when its leader won't trust his followers in the struggle?*

Tezla's Precept, drummed into him so many years ago in the Academy, rose up in memory. A subordinate should obey superiors as a child obeys a father.

Except my father was always a petty tyrant, Blaize thought. *In the Academy, I found that ironic. Now it becomes—a mockery.*

Along with anger came a worse emotion—fear. Blaize had dealt with that on the battlefield. Not for him the brainless bravery of some Utem Guards, who couldn't see dangers for their battle lust, nor the fanatical savagery of some of his Altem comrades. Blaize had always balanced the dangers against what needed to be done and then steeled himself to do it.

Now, though, he couldn't be sure how his body would react in a given situation—or if he'd be in command. That bred a wholly unique fear for Blaize to wrestle with.

When I drew sword to lead the charge this morning, I didn't know if I would head forward or turn on the warriors behind me. Hard enough to battle fellow guardsmen, without not being able to depend on my own sword arm.

Still worse, the rot of doubt, once established, seemed to spread to all the beliefs Blaize had once held dear. The great work of the Empire seemed to shrink. He suddenly recalled the words Lord Scarbro had passed on to him, words that must have sustained the officer during his rise to power. The Mills of Circumstance might grind others to dust, but not the superior person.

Yet to the most powerful magus in the Empire, it seemed all men were dust, to be used with equal contempt.

Another voice invaded Blaize's mind—the training guardsman from his earliest days as a raw recruit. *"On the battlefield, doubt is death. Remember that, Troll scat! You can't stand around and wonder if what you're doing is right. That's how you get a sword in your guts. Do your best—and if you wind up dead anyway, well, at least you can hope for a hero's burial."*

And yet, what could he do but doubt when he might suddenly find himself the prisoner of his body again? Attacking people . . . attacking *Rikka*!

Blaize squeezed his eyes shut, trying to blot out that suddenly disturbing thought. He didn't know Rikka had joined him until he heard her voice in his ear. "I came to take a look at that head of yours."

Blaize almost leaped up, until he realized she referred to his wound, not Karrudan's mark. He tossed the medallion into his shirt again and bowed to show the bandage. "It's stuck in place."

"Happens often enough. Even a little blood will form a crust." Rikka set out her equipment—a pannikin of warmed water, soap, salve, and a razor.

"Do you usually serve as the local leech?" Blaize asked.

"Some believe a woman has a finer touch." She dribbled warm water under the sodden bandage, trying to loosen the clot from the dressing.

"Ouch!" Blaize cried as Rikka pulled the bandage away. "So much for that myth."

"Shut up." Rikka pressed a clean pad to the wound, then sniffed it. "Seems to be healing cleanly. No pus."

She applied soap around the injured area, her fingers gentle. Then she scraped with the razor. "You're better off with this bare pate—no hair to get in the way of the healing."

Another damp pad washed away the lather, and then Rikka dried the spot and applied salve. A dry pad went over that, with a bandage to hold it in place wrapped around his brow.

"It should stop hurting and start itching by tomorrow morning," she informed him.

"Many thanks, Lady Healer." But when Blaize raised his head to look at Rikka, he could see she was no longer in a joking mood. Her expression wasn't harsh. She just seemed to sag with exhaustion and sudden sadness.

"So much nursing," Rikka murmured, her eyes closed. "Mama wore herself out tending my father while carrying me. Magestone poisoning took him anyway."

Blaize felt a little guilty. Had Rikka's foray to the mine last night stirred unhappy memories? "I'm sorry," he said uncomfortably. "You were named for a healer-woman, weren't you?"

Rikka nodded wearily, her shoulder resting against his. "Saved Mama when she had me. Later, though, even with me helping, Rikka Midwife couldn't do much when Mama grew ill. It was the Magestone again—used her up like coal in a forge."

"How old were you then?" Blaize asked gently.

"Seven," Rikka replied. "That's when I went to Eginhard

and his family. We almost got away when I was twelve. But we got caught and had to bide for years."

She leaned more heavily against him, her voice barely audible as more memories of those years came forth. "I didn't want to be a miner's wife, they die too young. But then I met Gared and we had Kennet. Two years later, Gared got the poisoning." Her eyes squeezed tightly together. "More nursing."

Blaize could see this mood was nothing he could turn aside with a light jest. So he spoke seriously. "Do you have other patients to see to?"

Rikka sat straight for a moment, opening her eyes. "I helped Sigwold with the worst cases. And now . . ." She sighed. "I'm too tired. It just caught up with me in a rush."

Blaize hurriedly pulled his shirt back on as Rikka reached out to him, shaking her head in the fading light. "Could we just stay here a few more minutes?" she said sleepily. "The others have Sigwold."

Does that mean, Blaize wondered as she leaned against him again, *that I have you?*

Chapter 11

Returning to the camp with a sleepy-eyed Rikka, Blaize resolved not to mention their discomfiting interlude. In fact, he decided to put all confusing thoughts aside and concentrate on the simpler aspects of life. He curried his pony's shaggy coat, ate several pieces of stringy boiled salt meat wrapped in spiced waybread, and managed to get a pair of blankets. Then, stretching out on the hard ground, he slept like a dead man.

Eginhard and Sigwold had a little mercy, leaving Blaize out of the watch rotation. When he awoke the next morning, Blaize felt as if he'd finally reentered the world of the living—especially after getting himself a mug of herb tea and some unspiced waybread with honey.

He was trusted enough now to hold some of the barrels as the packhorses were loaded, under the supervision of the remaining northern drovers. Snow was out with some scouts, off across the stream. So there would be more cross-country riding today.

Blaize closed his eyes, calling up the images of the maps of the area he'd studied. They had circled the city, keeping to the open country between Khamsin and Wolfsgate. How would they approach Caero? The quickest way would be to come from the north and east, although that would make it all too plain that they came from Khamsin. At this point, though, he figured that they'd have to head north to catch that road.

Or they could circle on to the south and west and come upon the road that came up from Luxor. That might be a better plan for escaping the eyes of Gamelon's Caero counterpart. But that would mean at least an extra day's travel.

Not for the first time, Blaize found himself wishing he had a better idea of the Rebels' timetable—and, perhaps, a glimpse of whatever strange cargo the Northerners were bringing into the Empire.

Seems unlikely that I'll get answers to any of those questions very soon, he thought.

Shrugging, Blaize mounted his pony and eased into the line of the march. Soon Rikka came to join him, and they killed many a mile talking. Blaize gave her army stories, especially some of the wilder things that happened along the western frontiers. They had the advantage of being true—more and more, he came to hate lying to Rikka. Better to tell her about the patrol where the Scorpem accompanying them had gotten stuck in reverse gear, rather than inventing any tales about his Caeronn boyhood.

Rikka didn't talk about her childhood in the mines. Most of her stories were about discovering Khamsin with her foster-father and -uncle.

"Sigwold got work as a jeweler when we arrived," Rikka said. "He was always amazingly good with his hands. Wasn't long before he had his own workshop. I was apprenticed to him."

She directed a look at Blaize's open shirt. "If I had the tools, I bet I'd be able to fix the chain on that medallion you're carrying. I could check with Sigwold to see if he has what's necessary on hand. Or if you're afraid I would botch the job, I'm sure my uncle could—"

Blaize quickly shook his head. The last thing he wanted was that too clever Dwarf getting a good look at Karrudan's magically charged medallion. "No need," he assured her. "I'll get it fixed when we get to Caero."

"Does it have a special meaning for you?" She faltered, choosing her words carefully. "Maybe it came from a special person?"

The Tezla-damned thing has only meant misery for me, Blaize thought. *And as for the person who gave the gift being special, I thought Karrudan was almost a god. Now I begin to suspect he's just a man—and not a very good man, at that.*

"No," he replied aloud. "It's my savings. Never believed in that army bank. I suppose you've seen enough mercenaries to know how they wear their wealth—silver and gold buttons, other trinkets. You know, things you can pull off to make payments after you lose all your road-silver."

Like I did to the slavers, Blaize thought ruefully. "I guess I'll have to give up a few links off that chain until I can get myself a stake."

They rode on in silence for a little while, until Blaize turned to Rikka and smiled.

"So, jewelry-making, leechcraft . . . did Sigwold teach you the way of the knife as well?"

Rikka shook her head. "I learned that from some more disreputable human and Dwarven friends. Father . . . Eginhard settled us on the edge of the Dwarven Quarter. He thought that way I wouldn't stand out so much." Her expression got a bit more serious. "It was not an area where Imperial troopers were very welcome. Folk connected them more with slave-takers than law and order."

"If the soldiers ever got off their tails?" Blaize asked comically.

That got a laugh out of her. "Exactly. The neighborhood had as much law as the inhabitants could back up. So I had to learn a way to protect myself. I might not have been as deft as Sigwold when it came to shaping metal . . ." Rikka shrugged. "But my hands were quick in handling it."

"You proved it to me—and to Tulwar, now that I remember it."

She snorted. "Tulwar fancies me—along with every comely woman he happens to meet." Then, more seriously, "After Father got established in shipping and warehousing—among other activities—we had little trouble from anyone who lived in Khamsin. But there are a lot of people just moving through the city. Drovers, muleteers, camel-drivers . . .

petty merchants coming for fairs." She looked a little disgusted. "Some of them needed discouraging."

"And then there's your other work," Blaize said quietly.

She turned in her saddle, eyes blazing. "I've seen you work with your sword, you've seen me with my knives. Do you have some sort of problem now?"

Blaize shook his head. "It's a pretty foolish problem," he admitted. "I find myself wishing you were only finishing out your apprenticeship as a jeweler, and I was . . . well, anything but a sword for hire."

Rikka stared at him for a long moment. "But we are what we are," she said.

She doesn't even know *what you are,* a soundless voice accused from the back of Blaize's skull.

"We are what we are," he agreed, his shoulders slumping as they continued across the plains. "And the good gods know there are bigger problems to be found in the Land."

Rikka cast sidelong glances at Blaize as they rode along in silence. The last words he'd said were not the sort she expected to hear in a cavalcade like this.

Most of the hired swords she knew were loudly proud of their abilities at killing people. A few of the men who worked on Eginhard's more criminal enterprises were true cutthroats. Anything they did for the cause of the Rebellion was strictly for their own profit. It either dropped silver into their own pouches or weakened the ability of the Empire to enforce the law.

Other swords for hire—even some riding in this group—followed war as a trade, practicing their skills, unwilling or unable to find a more peaceable way of life. Some, like Tulwar, seemed to have heard too many hero sagas as children. They rode the Land with a ready sword and a thirst for adventure.

And some, like poor Jorj, became Rebels out of sheer desperation, determined to change the world or die trying.

Like Jorj, many of that sort of Rebel died.

Rikka had seen them all in her job as a Rebel recruiter.

She'd learned how to steer them, make them useful for the cause.

What sort of fighting man, having just killed two enemies, wishes for a more peaceful world? The question led to an even harder one for her. *What sort of Rebel am I?*

There was a bit of Jorj in her, she had to admit. No one who had escaped from the Magestone mines didn't burn to eradicate those earthly versions of Feshku's Pits.

But Rikka also grimly practiced with targets and in hand-to-hand encounters to hone her talents for survival. Kennet had already lost a father. Despite the pact she had made with Bruna to care for the boy in case of failure on any mission, Rikka was prepared to do whatever was necessary to ensure her return.

That included killing.

She saw nothing to celebrate in that, though. How many times had Kennet climbed into her lap, clamoring for some tale of glorious battle and desperate deeds? The more desperate the situation, the less glory Rikka found. Instead, she concentrated instead on telling Kennet the odd tales, the ridiculous adventures.

As Blaize did in telling of his experiences in the west, she suddenly realized.

Rikka was so engrossed in these thoughts, she didn't notice Eginhard making his way back through the caravan until he came abreast of her and Blaize.

"Sigwold wants to see if your scouting is as good as your sword work," the Dwarf said to Blaize. "Ride on ahead to yonder hills and find us the easiest way through."

Blaize nodded and picked up his pony's pace, moving to the head of the column and beyond.

Eginhard continued to ride with Rikka as they watched the young man vanish off toward the horizon.

"Not so long ago, you nearly tore out my tongue when I called that Caeronn your friend," Eginhard finally said. "Now you seek him out to ride and talk with."

Rikka could feel the warmth rising in her face at her foster-father's words.

"Others besides myself have commented on this . . . partiality," Eginhard went on.

"And what have those others had to say?" Rikka was angry, but she kept her voice low. "Are the fine Khamsin boys complaining that I've given my heart to an outlander? Or is Tulwar complaining that the goods will be damaged before he finally comes up with my bride-price?"

Now Eginhard's face went red. "I'm no Galeshi to sell a daughter to the highest bidder. But I worry for you, Rikka. Blaize seems a likely lad, but he's a stranger—"

"Gods above and below!" Rikka burst out. "You've put him through enough tests. He entered an impregnable castle for you, and killed two Imperials yesterday morning."

"He also vanished on us, and got seized by slave-takers. You had to risk yourself to rescue him," Eginhard pointed out. "For me, that went beyond a test. It was a trial."

Rikka glared at her father. "You never liked Gared, either."

"Oh, aye." Eginhard's voice rumbled like thunder. "*There* was an attachment that worked out well. You ended up alone, with a babe to worry about."

For a second, Rikka could only suck in air. She felt as if she'd been slapped.

"Nay, nay." Eginhard stretched out a hand to her. "That was temper talking. I know you loved Gared and I know he loved you. As for Kennet . . . I can't imagine the world without him now."

His craggy face was creased with worry as he looked at her. "But this Blaize is a wanderer, an ex-soldier—"

"A rented blade," Rikka finished for him.

"All we know of him is what he chooses to tell us," the Dwarf went on. "There could be a wife left behind in his wanderings—no doubt a string of camp-women, too."

The image of the silver medallion Blaize kept hidden by his heart suddenly danced in her mind's eye. Why had she only noticed it now after such a long time? Was it wishful thinking that had kept her blind?

Some of her feelings must have shown in her face. Eginhard stopped, biting his lips. "You never showed an interest in that sort of man before. And even if he returns your feelings, is it for you alone, or . . ."

Could he accept me with another man's child? The question had already presented itself to Rikka. Some men had caught her interest, but they'd ignored Kennet. Others had played up to the boy, trying to use him as a route to her favors.

Blaize had gotten along well with her boy—with a pang, she remembered Kennet demanding that Blaize take care of her.

And then I had to go out and rescue him, Rikka thought with a spurt of humor.

She came back to herself, to find Eginhard nervously eyeing her smile.

"Blaize does seem . . . different from the ordinary run of men I've met," she said.

"That's as may be," Eginhard replied gruffly. "But even if he were a High Elf paladin, I'd worry about you losing your heart to him. Especially right now, given the business we're about."

"Then, Father, you'll be happy to know that Blaize feels the same way—even though he doesn't know what we ride to do."

"In that case, I'd say the lad shows more sense than I imagined."

But the idea of a sensible Blaize stirred a whole new—and unwelcome—line of thought for Eginhard. "And has he asked you much about our cargo and where it's bound?"

"He hasn't," Rikka replied, happy to be able to give a definite fact instead of her own wishful thinking. "He hasn't asked at all."

The only practical route through the hills was a track heading south and farther east.

So it looks as through we are heading for the old Luxor-Caero road, Blaize thought as he made his way back to the caravan. Finding a way that could accommodate the train of heavily laden horses had taken more time than he liked.

Sigwold, Snow, and the others might already be impatiently waiting at the foothills for his return.

His pony carefully climbed up the rugged hillside, which Blaize hoped would give him a view of the plain below. He sighed with relief when he spotted the pack train. There it was, close enough to be in good view, but still sufficiently far off that he could rejoin them before they reached the hills.

In fact, it seemed the caravan had stopped at a small creek for water and a rest in the shade of the trees whose roots were fed by the stream.

As Blaize watched, three small figures separated themselves from the main group. Two were Dwarves, and the third was a barrel-chested human. Obviously, Eginhard, Sigwold, and Snow.

But why were the caravan's three leaders going off alone? They seemed to be heading farther downstream, where the stream made a tight curve, creating a thicker copse of trees that would hide them from sight.

It might also hide me from their sight if I ride in that direction, Blaize thought.

His showing in the fight with the Imperial patrol had finally ended the spate of drunk jokes, and in spite of some good-natured grousing about him monopolizing the only available female company, Blaize had settled in well enough with the other fighters.

He hadn't wanted to make himself conspicuous again with too much curiosity about what the caravan carried and where it was going. So, aside from rhetorical questions like "What in Feshku's Pit do you have in here—anvils?" while he struggled to load or unload the pack animals, Blaize hadn't paid much overt attention to their mysterious cargo.

Now it appeared that Snow and Sigwold were about to reveal some of its secrets.

Blaize wanted a look, too.

He started down the face of the hill, choosing a route that would bring him to level ground, with the trees between him and the caravan. Whenever his usually surefooted pony hesitated to pick his way, Blaize cursed the delay.

They'll be gone before we even get off this Tezla-damned hillside, he silently grumbled.

Not that Blaize could indulge himself with a wild gallop once he reached the flatlands. A plume of dust might still be spotted. He held the pony's pace to a reasonable speed, doing his best to aim for thick, healthy grass.

Halfway to his target, a new and disquieting thought hit him. *What if it's a trap? Maybe they want me to commit myself to spying on them—then they'll have reason to do me in.*

But no crossbow bolts flew from the shadows under the trees, no horsemen came thundering from behind cover to take him. If anyone should happen to spot him, he could simply say he chose the shelter of the trees for his ride back to report.

The stream—and that thicker copse where Snow and the others had gone—was much closer now. Blaize got out of the saddle and began leading his pony, one hand over the animal's nose. This was no time for friendly nickers of greeting to fill the air.

Moving as silently as he could, Blaize slipped into the underbrush around the trees. He was lucky, finding a thin section of greenery that gave him a glimpse right to the banks of the stream while still screening him from sight.

Snow, Sigwold, and Eginhard stood in the shade, but Blaize could see them well enough. He was still too far away to hear clearly. In any event, they seemed to be speaking in undertones.

Sigwold was placing a cork in a small keg while Eginhard regarded a pile of black powder held in his cupped hands. He seemed to be addressing a question to Snow, who nodded vigorously while brandishing a strange-looking implement in his right hand.

Not an implement—a weapon, Blaize realized as he got a better look. It appeared to be either a short polearm or a long-hafted axe. One end seemed to be a club, but the halberd head was unmistakable. The shaft was extravagantly made of metal faced with wood. It seemed a clumsy combination of weapons.

Could this be what has Lord Scarbro so worried? Pikes and swords would rout any rabble armed with those things, Blaize thought, frowning in puzzlement. *Crossbows could bleed them white. Magical weapons would crush them before they could stab, chop, or swing.*

The powder might be something more dangerous—poison, perhaps. Yet Eginhard seemed to have no trepidation holding it in his hands. He dumped the stuff into the river and then brushed his palms together, even licking a finger and making a face at the taste.

He took the club or whatever it was from Snow and seemed to be complaining about the balance. Snow took hold of the end—and pulled off the halberd blade!

Rikka's father raised the staff and seemed to sight along it as men sometimes did to test the trueness of a blade. He pointed the thing almost directly at the stand of brush where Blaize crouched, hidden.

He ducked lower. Could this be some sort of Technomantic weapon?

Then Blaize remembered how the blade had come off. *Perhaps these contraptions were made to be disassembled for easy smuggling.* Materials alone must have cost a fortune, and the weapons showed a craft that cried out "Dwarven work!"

Yet any Dwarf craftsman who turned out such ungainly imitation weapons would have been turned out of his smithy.

Could they be clumsy human copies of Dwarven work? Blaize wondered. *Or copies, perhaps, of weapons made for Dwarves?*

Blaize had no more time for conjecture. Eginhard was handing the weapon back to Snow. They would be rejoining the pack train—and so should Blaize.

He backed carefully through the underbrush. This was not the time to snap a twig.

Clear again, Blaize remounted his pony and rode back

onto the plain. Then he swerved so that the trees no longer hid his approach.

He'd gotten his wish and seen what the caravan carried—a cargo of powder and expensive, fanciful implements of war that couldn't stand up to anything already in the Imperial armory.

Still, the workmanship . . . Blaize was reminded again of the Empire's Technomantic weapons.

He shook his head to rid it of that crazy notion as he rode onward. No matter how well organized they might seem to be, where could these Rebels get the Magestone—and the magic—to create weapons that could rival those of the Atlantis Guild's mages?

CHAPTER 12

SNOW managed to keep his face blank, but one hand kept idly returning to the haft of the axe hanging from his saddle, running meditatively up and down the wood.

If the estate steward noticed, he nonetheless kept his place blocking access to the well. And he still didn't stop the tirade he directed toward the pack train. "Be away with you!" he shouted. "This is Master Ramosi's land. We do not give free water and shelter to vagabonds."

The site of the conflict was little more than a wide spot in the Luxor-Caero road, a handful of mud-brick houses that had once been a peasant village. Now they were abandoned, the lines of neglected roofs and walls softening under the effects of spring rains.

After turning onto the road, the pack train had encountered several such deserted townlets. Snow and the others had stopped at some of them, using the wells to water their beasts, sleeping in some of the less tumbledown adobes.

Debt and failure had emptied the villages of peasants as their farms had been swallowed up by the growth of estates. This set of half-ruinous buildings, however, turned out to be near a gleaming new manor house.

The steward had come out to berate them, waving his staff of office. With his potbelly stretching the top of his linen kilt, the bald-pated head servant hadn't impressed any of the riders, even though he also wore a baldric with an old Imperial sword.

The blade has probably rusted into one piece with the sheath, Snow thought sourly. He knew that the sword wasn't presented to the steward as a weapon, but rather as a symbol—the master granting the power of life and death on the estate.

Besides his dubiously useful sword, the steward had a gaggle of agricultural workers standing well behind him, armed with the usual farm-implement miscellany: sickles, pitchforks, and flails. They didn't look very confident in their chances of success against the riders.

A justified worry, Snow thought. He and the rest of the warriors could go through these farmers like wind scattering wheat chaff. However, their job was to shepherd a perilous cargo to Caero and beyond, not to pick fights with local landowners while heading in the direction of the Imperial garrison those landowners would call upon.

"We're not vagabonds," Snow said, trying to keep his voice mild, "but wayfarers. The law states that landowners must maintain all wells along the Imperial roads—"

"Not Master Ramosi." The servant gave them a smug smile. "He has several estates, besides his mansion in the city, in addition to which, he's a particular intimate of Chief Magistrate Khiza. I'm sure the laws don't apply."

He directed a withering look at Rikka. "We especially aren't going to share the master's bounty with wandering strangers—and their whores."

Eginhard's axe suddenly appeared in his hand, and he nudged his horse forward. "That happens to be my daughter you've laid your filthy tongue upon, you bald-headed Troll scat," he said in a stony voice.

The steward looked between them, his mouth working. "But you're a Dwarf, and she's a—"

"Daughter!" Eginhard barked, bringing his horse—and his axe—another step closer.

Trying to raise his staff, the steward instinctively retreated, nearly tumbling himself down the well.

"To me!" the potbellied man squealed to the other servants.

They clustered on the other side of the well.

"The master will hear of this!" The steward puffed up like a bullfrog as he threatened everyone.

Now Sigwold brought his mount forward, leaning from the saddle with his most diplomatic smile. "So, tell me, my man. Is the next well along the road also adjoining Master Ramosi's land?"

Furious at being addressed that way, the servant barked, "It is all Master Ramosi's land!"

Sigwold maintained that cheerful smile. "Then, I guess you'll have to race us there and see if we drink that water. Maybe we will, maybe we won't. Certainly you won't know." He turned to Snow. "Shall we be off, before Master Troll Scat here gets a running start?"

Sighing, "So much for diplomacy," Snow made a hand gesture.

The pack train lurched into movement. Was it Snow's imagination, or did all the riders do their best to coat the gobbling steward with as much road dust as possible?

The road linking Caero, the old Kosian Sun Capital, and Luxor, the Moon Capital, was more than seven hundred years old, predating Tezla's Empire by a good three hundred years. Atlantis' Imperial government maintained the roadway now, but the trees lining each side of the ancient roadway were the gift of centuries.

At least we have shade if not water for this stage of our journey, Snow thought.

He glanced over at Sigwold, who rode beside him, looking pleased with himself. "I hope you did the right thing," Snow said.

"I kept my brother from popping that human pimple with his axe—not to mention keeping that fool of a servant from drowning himself in the well."

"Perhaps I acted hastily," Eginhard rumbled. "But I didn't like that prancing fool in the skirt saying what he did about Rikka."

Snow then glanced at the Caeronn who rode beside Rikka. Favoring her foster-father with a defiant look, she'd brought her friend up to journey at her side since he'd returned from a scouting trip.

"I suppose I should at least be glad you didn't feel the need to defend the lady's honor," Snow said to Blaize.

The rider colored under his tan. "I didn't think it would help the situation," he admitted.

"Exactly my feelings." Snow rounded on Sigwold again. "You're sure we'll face no consequences from our run-in with that little turd?"

"He's a big man on the estate because he speaks with the master's voice to everyone who works there," Sigwold said lazily. "In the city, though, he becomes an even smaller turd than we saw. Magistrate Khiza won't want to hear some jumped-up servant's complaints—nor will Lord Tackett, the garrison commander. And if he goes to Ramosi, to whom the powerful might listen, the fellow admits he wasn't able to do his job."

"Which would lose him the position," Eginhard said with satisfaction. "You're right. His type will scream at those poor folk working Ramosi's fields, but he'll say nothing to anyone else."

"He reminded me of some of the mine guards." Rikka's voice dripped hatred. "How did such huge estates come to be? Where are the people who lived in all those empty houses?"

She looked at Blaize as she asked those questions. Snow remembered Eginhard's description of the Caeronn's background. Apparently the family farm had vanished into an estate like Master Ramosi's.

So in Blaize's memory there was probably an empty village like the one they'd just left. His restraint impressed Snow all the more. It was also obvious that the Caeronn had taken his manners as well as his swordsmanship from the Imperial army. He stayed silent around what he considered to be superior officers.

"Where was your people's place, Blaize?" Snow asked.

Faced with a direct question, the young man answered. "To the east, on the far side of the river."

He didn't need to say which. The Roa Vizorr was the main geographical feature in the region.

"That's where the estate thing started," Blaize went on. "My folks had to pay boatmen to get their grain to the local markets, and the farms were too small to think of shipping downriver. A few bad years, and they lost the farm."

"You mentioned something about it winding up in the local tax collector's estate," Rikka added.

"I wonder if friend Ramosi has much to do with taxes," Eginhard wondered aloud.

"What I want to know is how it *happens*," the girl said.

"It's just another way the Imperial machinery is running down," Sigwold said.

Snow had heard it before, but the others hadn't.

"What do you mean?" The question came from Blaize, but he'd only just beaten Eginhard.

"It's a theory that Sarah has," Sigwold replied. "You know the Ythlims were always merchants, so they tend to see gold-and-silver reasons for everything. But I think it makes sense."

"Maybe that's because you're a machine-type person," Snow jibed.

"So what is this theory?" Eginhard demanded.

Sigwold took a deep breath. "The Empire is like a giant machine," he said. "Taxes go in one end, and various things come out the other. Armies, for instance. Forts. Upkeep on roads, like this one we're riding on. Technomancy. Silk drawers for the Prophet-Magus."

Snow made a rude noise. Sigwold ignored him.

"When Tezla started things, the machinery was new and ran efficiently," the Dwarf went on. "Taxes weren't too high, the armies were expanding the Empire, uniting all the human tribes, and people could see all sorts of marvels coming out. Even when Tezla did something expensive, like creating Atlantis-in-the-Sky, the common folk could believe that things worked."

"And then?" Rikka asked.

"As the years go on, the machine gets creakier and

creakier. The Empire doesn't unite everyone anymore. The Necromancers ran off to set up their own kingdom and plot. Then the Elementals were thrown out—"

"While the Dwarves were dragged in," Eginhard growled.

"The two main things to come out of the machine nowadays are the army and the Magestone mines," Sigwold went on. "One protects the borders and the other keeps Technomancy going. But they're both very expensive. More taxes have to be fed into the machine."

"Because they're sticking to the gears," Snow said.

"Add more taxes to the costs of running a small farm, especially if there are extra expenses, and a couple of bad years can mean disaster." Sigwold spread his hands. "If someone else comes along with ready money, a large plot of land can be put together. The owner can squeeze out other economies—using fewer people, paying lower wages. And a larger crop means other possibilities of taking it to market. You end up with estates."

"And what about the tax collectors owning them?" Rikka wanted to know.

"Snow said part of it," Sigwold replied. "Some taxes stick on the gears, which makes the machinery even more inefficient. Still worse, people try to twist the machine to do things for them. Tax collectors take money and create estates. Do you think those estates are going to pay their fair taxes?"

"So you need more taxes from different places," Snow said.

Sigwold nodded. "They land on the city-folk, the shopkeepers and craftsmen, the workmen. Taxes appear on things everyone needs, like salt." He looked at Blaize. "And there are less and less farm lads available to go into the army, because the small farmers are starved to death, working on estates, or gone to cities, where they starve, get diseases, or end up not liking the Empire very much. You served for a while in Atlantis, lad. How many recruits does the army get from Down Town?"

Blaize blinked. "Not that many," he admitted.

"You make it sound like the Empire is going to fall apart any day now." Rikka shook her head. "I don't think so."

"The machinery is still grinding along," Sigwold said. "And it will keep going until it runs out of taxes, soldiers, or Technomancy."

"Unless we kick it over." Eginhard patted the haft of his battle-axe.

But Sigwold shook his head. "If the machinery falls, it will make a Tezla-be-damned crash. And a lot of unpleasant folk would end up rooting through the pieces. Orcs, for one. Necros for another."

Eginhard hawked and spat. "Pit-worthy bonesuckers."

"Marway knows who else might turn up, thinking this is their great opportunity," Sigwold said.

"So that's our choice?" Rikka demanded in disbelief. "The Empire or the Necropolis Sect, or maybe something worse?"

"What Sarah hopes for is winning the time and space to set up some new machines," Sigwold said. "She's started one in the North—Prieska, too. They're smaller, run more efficiently . . . and most importantly, they give more people a chance."

"That last I'll fight for," Snow said. "The rest just gives me a headache."

"Maybe you should loosen that helmet of yours," Sigwold shot back. "You want to tear down the people who ruined your life. Me, I've got to hope we can build something out of this."

"I want the mines closed and the people in them freed," Rikka said fiercely. "If that means breaking some gears, so be it."

Eginhard nodded, snarling his agreement.

Snow noticed that Blaize said nothing, his face set in a soldier's blank mask—except for a pair of very tight lines that had appeared between his brows.

That one's no stupid soldier, Snow told himself. *He may not say much, but he's chewing over everything he heard.*

He continued watching the Caeronn as they rode on in sudden silence. *Be interesting to see what this fellow spits out when the time comes . . .*

Why couldn't they send me off scouting now? Blaize kept his gaze on his tightly clenched hands as they held his pony's reins.

He was afraid to meet anyone's eyes, not with the thoughts presently wrestling one another in his head. For all he knew, the pony's hooves could be drumming against the sunny sky—Blaize's world felt that much out of joint.

What he really needed was solitude while he tried to reconcile Sigwold's matter-of-fact dissection of the Empire with everything he'd ever been taught.

At least everyone had stopped talking. Apparently they were also lost in their thoughts. Blaize thought of offering to ride on ahead, but decided that would only call attention to himself. Better to follow the old army adage—never volunteer.

A casual farewell and a ride to somewhere else in the column would be equally conspicuous.

Why did Rikka drag me up here in the first place? Blaize grumbled silently. *She seemed to have something she wanted to prove to Eginhard.*

Whatever that was, it had resulted in an excruciating afternoon. Gone was the easy give-and-take of other days. Conversation had languished as he'd ridden along, silent and miserable, certain he was being scrutinized even though no one seemed to be looking at him.

It was like being with the mage-officers in the army, he thought. *If you had nothing to report to them, what else did you have to talk about?*

Blaize pushed the irritation away. He knew himself well enough, unfortunately, to recognize his spurt of anger against Rikka and the others for what it was . . . an attempt to escape thinking about the things he'd just heard.

Exerting a little pressure on his reins, Blaize got his pony to slow his pace almost imperceptibly. Soon he began to fall behind the leaders of the column.

He was glad that Rikka apparently didn't notice him lagging back. Her conversation would be an all-too-agreeable escape from the thoughts he had to deal with.

From childhood, even before he'd entered the Academy, Blaize had been taught to glory in the essential *rightness* of the Empire. The divine Tezla had mastered Elemental Magic and Necromancy, and then used his knowledge to create Technomancy—magic augmented and strengthened by the use of Magestone. With such power at his beck and call, he'd lead the Atlantis Guild—the most gifted human mages in the Land—into a new age of magic and supremacy. Then Tezla had turned to the ancient dream of uniting all the human tribes. Not only had the emperor-magus succeeded, he'd won new respect for humanity from the more magically powerful races. The result was a realm of peace and plenty for all.

Of course, some factions had been unable to stand that. The bonesuckers—death-magicians—had abandoned the Empire, founding the Necropolis far to the north and incessantly scheming to bring others into their sect. The Elementalists, Elven magicians of life-energy, had tried to set their will over the Empire and been banished.

But the glorious, glittering fact of the Empire made all their efforts look paltry.

Subsequent experience had taken some of the shine off that burnished image of school days. Divinely inspired it might be, but the Empire depended on humans, who often proved all too fallible. Officers, especially mage-officers, could have little grasp of reality. Unfairness and misfortune were a part of life, although there was always a suspicion that those experiencing bad fortune had brought it upon themselves.

Soldiers might grouse about the evident shortcomings of Imperial life, but they'd die for the Empire nonetheless.

So, hearing Sigwold discuss the Imperial system as if it were a machine—and a badly operating machine, at that!—disturbed Blaize.

Especially since so many of the points Sigwold made matched Blaize's own observations. The rich and powerful did twist the machinery to gain their own ends, just as Karrudan had twisted Blaize's own brain. Where did the slaves in the Magestone mines fit into the Empire's goal of peace and plenty for all? What about the farmers being forced off their land? Atlantis-in-the-Sky was a glorious achievement, but what about the starving Down Towners who lived on the ground in the Floating City's shadow?

Blaize had nonetheless stayed loyal to the ideals of the Empire, even when he could see actual practice not measuring up. Some things, quite frankly, he'd ignored. The unpleasant subjects of Magestone miners and starving farmers were far away from the outposts he'd defended in the outlands, or in the great city. Other problems he could look upon as diseases, where the Empire could heal itself.

But Sigwold's vision of overloaded machinery beyond repair . . .

That frightened Blaize. It suggested Tezla's Mills of Circumstance had gone horribly mad, grinding everyone and everything to powder.

You're born into a way of life that may have its faults, he thought. *But you live with them, because that's the only way of living.*

But suppose, as Sigwold suggested, other machines could be started—other ways of living?

The Necros had created one, dark and nasty as it was. As a guardsman, Blaize had helped to squash a few of the Sect's plots. What he'd seen had turned his stomach.

And he had no desire to join the Elementalists. Their view of the world seemed to have very little room for farms, cities, and humanity in general.

All he'd heard of Sarah Ythlim had concerned sedition and rebellion in the northern country. If she was truly building a better machine, perhaps he should hear more about it.

But for her experiment to prosper, the machinery of the Empire, good and bad, must fall. That thought grieved Blaize. He had battled Necropolis pit-fighters, Orcs, wild

Galeshis, and Mage Spawn. If the Empire ended, there would be no army. Who would defend the tribes of humanity?

"So here is where you got to." Rikka's voice broke in on his introspection.

She gave Blaize a quizzical look as he blinked, glancing around. He'd been so deeply preoccupied, he hadn't paid any attention to his surroundings—a dangerous lapse for a warrior. Apparently, he'd still been reining in his horse, since he now rode just ahead of the caravan's rear guard.

"I didn't expect the conversation to get so deep," Rikka said, with a nod toward the head of the column. "Did it make your head hurt as much as Snow complained?"

"It made me think of what I knew about the Empire," Blaize replied.

"I just wish it would be as easy to stop as wrecking some machine." Rikka's voice filled with iron.

"Stopping the Empire will take a long fight," he agreed. "And setting something up to replace it may mean an even longer struggle—generations, even."

He looked at her. "I'm afraid of the world we'll be leaving for Kennet."

Rikka stared at him, eyes wide, as they rode for a moment in silence. All Blaize heard was the jingle of harness, the snorting of a horse . . . and then, in the distance, the laughter of schoolchildren.

He frowned. That couldn't be right. It had the same sort of tone as the cries he remembered echoing down the streets around the Academy—the sound of malevolent schoolboys.

It came a bit nearer, resolving into a sort of chittering backchat among several voices.

And Blaize knew what it was. He remembered a patrol out west, looking for a fallen comrade, finding the body and a green, child-sized form so busy feeding that they'd surprised it . . . and the noises it had made when it tried to escape.

"Imps," he said.

Rikka was thrown by the sudden shift. "What?"

"We've got Imps on our trail. Up in the trees." Blaize squinted, trying to get a count. The small, green winged bodies were hard to spot against the foliage. He saw them better with the tail of his eye, catching movement, then turning to focus on it.

"I see one!" Rikka's hand went to the knife at her belt. "Ugly little thing. Are they dangerous?"

"Some people train them to fight, but most Imps are carrion-eaters."

Blaize loosed his sword in its sheath. "You'd better get up front, warn Snow and the others."

"And what am I going to tell them?" Rikka wanted to know. "The Imps are coming?"

"The Imps are expecting to feed," Blaize said impatiently, his eyes scanning the trees and their back trail. "That means there's something a lot worse stalking us."

Chapter 13

Blaize's stomach tightened with unease when the pack train stopped shortly after Rikka set off for the front of the column.

"What are we stopping for if she told them something was after us?" Mikarl demanded.

A naked sword wavered in his hand as his eyes darted about even more nervously than usual.

Jon, the silent bowman, sat at ease in his saddle, reins looped around one wrist as he held his crossbow ready.

Only Blaize hadn't drawn a weapon. But the hand that didn't hold his reins hovered close to the hilt of his sword. "We don't know the danger is coming from behind," he said tightly.

The Imps had followed them through the trees like a bunch of playful, jeering children. Their happy noise only seemed to increase the strain felt by the men on the road below.

"They're laughing at us while they wait for dinner!" Mikarl snarled, turning to Jon. "Why don't you send a bolt at those vermin?"

"Waste of a shot," the crossbowman replied laconically.

Blaize silently agreed. Trying to hit the well-hidden Imps would take luck as well as aim. It might also distract Jon when the real attack came.

Besides, the ugly little winged things could prove useful. They'd probably go quiet when the real predator arrived, afraid to draw attention to themselves.

Word came back to them about the cause of the delay. "There's a river to ford," one of the drovers called.

Blaize nodded his thanks. The closer they got to the Roa Vizorr, the wider the tributaries feeding into the great river became.

"They say there's some sort of dam that busted," the Northerner went on. "Whole place is flooded out."

When they started forward again, Blaize saw the situation for himself.

The road disappeared into what looked like a large, mud-brown lake, reappearing on the far shore. Luckily, the flooded area wasn't all that deep, coming up to about the bellies of the load-beasts. But they had to swim as they actually crossed the river.

Off to one side, between the tree trunks, Blaize could see a bare stretch of mire that had probably been an irrigated field. Beyond was an earthen dam that had held a reservoir of sorts.

No more. The center of the wall had crumbled away, inundating the field and the ford into a marshy mess. All that escaping water must have created a nasty flood. Several of the ancient roadside trees had been uprooted, their branches broken off. Some stuck in the mud, others floated in water holes.

"I hope this place is in the charge of that fool who screamed at us back on the road," Mikarl said. "The one who wouldn't let us use his water."

"Seems he lost a lot of it here," Jon offered.

Blaize didn't speak, his eyes flicking around to spot possible avenues of attack.

He didn't like this. Getting across the swollen current divided their little force, leaving each group vulnerable to attack on either bank—especially when they had to slog through the marshy borders.

When there were only a couple of packhorses, Jon, Mikarl, and Blaize left, he allowed himself a sigh of relief.

"One good thing about this," Mikarl said as he sheathed

his sword. "With everything knocked down, we can see all around."

That was when the muck-covered figure erupted from under the water, brandishing one of those floating branches. With one inhumanly quick blow, it brained one of the load-beasts.

Blaize brought his pony around, clawing out his sword. It took him a moment to recognize the attacking creature under its coat of goo. As more of them surfaced, he managed to identify them.

"Lizard-men!" he yelled at the top of his voice.

Jon took the prudent course, backing his horse away to get more range.

Farther out, another packhorse shrieked in terror as one of the scaled Mage Spawn simply dragged it under the water. There had to be five other Lizard-men in the water. Now they all headed for the shore, driving the remaining loaded horses toward the three humans making up the rear guard.

Mikarl dithered in the face of the onslaught, his sword caught in the scabbard, losing the reins when his horse bolted at the monsters appearing from the water.

The nearest Lizard-man brought his tree-branch club back to his shoulder and swung it in a horizontal arc. It made a sickening sound, catching Mikarl in the chest, crushing ribs and breastbone.

Blaize was glad he couldn't see the Khamsin's face.

Jon's crossbow twanged, the bolt penetrating the scaly shoulder of the nearest Lizard-man. The Mage Spawn hissed in pain, but made a speedy rush for the crossbowman.

Blaize charged, hoping to give Jon at least the chance to reload. The short sword in the guardsman's hand would probably affect the oversized lizard about as much as a splinter.

Ride past and see if you can get in a slash, he told himself, trying to direct his pony with knees and reins.

The creature was fast, terribly fast in the water. In a second it was much closer than Blaize wanted it to be.

Blaize's pony tried to skitter to the side—and something

gave beneath its hooves on the boggy bottom. Momentum nearly flung Blaize over the pony's head and into the Lizard-man's arms.

The sickening crack of the pony's leg bone blended with the animal's shrill cry of pain. Then it was going down—and over. Blaize tried to get loose, to kick free of his stirrups.

Instead he was flung into two feet of mucky water, with the dead weight of the pony pinning one leg.

Blaize clung to his sword, although it seemed a useless gesture.

What are you going to do, stab the lizard in the foot? Try to hamstring him while he crushes you with that branch?

The club did come down—but on Blaize's still-kicking horse. His trapped leg felt the impact even through the pony's body.

His mount shuddered, voiding into the water, then lay still, a dead weight still holding Blaize in place for the Lizard-man's pleasure.

Another crossbow bolt slammed into the creature's body, but that scaly skin was tough. Blaize could see only a thin trail of blood leaking from the shoulder wound. Jon's second shot caught the creature in the belly, but it didn't seem to be slowing it down.

Blaize pushed himself as far up as he could, his submerged hand sinking into the mud. His other hand brought up his sword while the Lizard-man leaned back for a direct overhead blow.

If Blaize had heard the oncoming splashes, he'd have dismissed them as the threshing of another doomed packhorse, or perhaps the approach of another Lizard-man demanding half of a human meal.

He was completely unprepared to see Snow and his tall, rangy horse wallowing their way into the water. The grim-faced Rebel leader was standing in his stirrups, his axe raised high behind him.

The metal axehead described a gleaming arc, landing just to the right of the crest on the Lizard-man's skull.

It clove through the creature's head like a melon.

Even without guidance from a brain rent in two, the huge body somehow managed to remain standing. Then the overbalanced Lizard-man corpse began to topple backward.

Snow had his mount smartly sidestepping while he plucked the tree branch from the Lizard-man's dead fingers. The Rebel twisted, hurling the erstwhile club into the face of another of the advancing Mage Spawn. Yet another one floated facedown in the river, dispatched while Snow was still crossing.

That left five of the creatures still in the fight, advancing on them.

Blaize doubled up his free leg and kicked as hard as he could at the barrel of his defunct mount. He couldn't budge it. Snow vaulted from his horse and grabbed hold of the dead pony's saddle.

"Together," he said, "on the count of three."

The dead weight pinning him shifted, and Blaize pushed with all his might, squelching loose through gluey mud. His trapped leg came free, leaving his boot behind.

Blaize managed somehow to get to his feet, staggering back until he was only in mucky water up to his ankles. He still maintained a death-grip on his sword—which is what it indeed might turn out to be. The remaining Lizard-men were almost out of the water, too.

But now they were under fire from the far side of the morass. Everyone in the party who had a crossbow was trying to put a bolt into the Mage Spawn.

Not all the archers were expert—shots missed the beasts, and one errant bolt almost spitted Blaize. But enough of the missiles struck home to give the Lizard-men something else to think about.

Hissing with pain and anger, they tore loose the packs encumbering the horses they'd already killed, then vanished into the water with enough meat to satisfy them for a while.

It took everything Blaize had not to drop to his knees in exhaustion and relief. He turned to Snow. "Marway must have addled your wits to try that stunt," he said.

At least his voice didn't tremble.

Snow simply raised one enormous shoulder in a shrug. "I had the biggest horse," he said. "And they had their backs to me, busy concentrating on their next meal—or maybe on your gallant, last-ditch defense."

Blaize shot him a look. "Well, you saved my life. So you know what that means."

Snow responded with a guarded frown. "What?"

"You have to help move that pony's carcass so I can find my boot."

Snow allowed his grim expression to relax a little. The whole pack train was now across the river. They'd even managed to recover most of the cargo the Lizard-men had torn loose, although that effort had initially been slow until the riders finally realized they wouldn't become Mage Spawn provender.

One of the lost packhorses had been carrying food, but the caravan still had sufficient rations to make it to Caero. The sealed barrels of black power had actually floated, so they'd been easy enough to salvage.

Regarding the muddy water, Snow shook his head. *If we'd had black powder weapons out and ready, we could have torn those spawn to pieces without even having to get close to them,* he thought.

Then he sighed. Sarah had insisted that the first shot fired in public would be in Atlantis. And he and Sigwold had gone along, at the cost of three packhorses, one mount, and one rider.

They'd managed to catch Mikarl's horse, which had been cut off by the crowd of Imps that had given the first warning of trouble. A couple of shots from Jon Bowman had driven the little creatures from their prospective meal. Blaize now rode the dead Khamsin rider's pony. He'd also taken Mikarl's long horseman's sword.

They'd left the dead pony and the two Lizard-men for the Imps and the surviving Mage Spawn. Mikarl had been wrapped in a tarp and placed on a nervous packhorse. They would bury him in an unmarked grave as soon as they found drier land.

Snow gave the signal to move out, as glad as the rest of the party to leave the site of the ambush. He rode up to the head of the little column, to find that Rikka had Blaize up there again.

Probably to keep an eye on him before he has another adventure, Snow thought with an inward grin.

Whatever had prompted the Caeronn to lag behind, Snow considered it a lucky chance. At least they'd been on their guard when they arrived at the river. Otherwise . . .

Snow pushed away the possible losses in manpower and matériel. Eginhard and Sigwold were arguing over whether they should report the attacking Lizard-men.

"They're a deadly danger," Sigwold said. "We were lucky to get off as lightly as we did."

"And that was only thanks to Blaize," Rikka put in, not improving Eginhard's mood.

"What about other travelers?" Sigwold pressed his point.

"They'll have to take their chances, just as we did," Eginhard replied. "What would you have us do? Go to the nearest set of Imperials and say, 'Please, Master Oppressor, we were attacked by Lizard-men and they nearly got—'" He broke off, glancing at Blaize. "'—everything we were carrying?'"

"Eginhard is right," Snow said. "This is no time to be calling attention to ourselves. We'll have to give Mikarl a quiet burial and go on as if nothing had happened."

"What I don't understand is *how* it happened," Rikka said. "Blaize has told me about fighting Mage Spawn in the empty places out west, and I've heard that creatures sometimes make their way out of the Blasted Lands to wild places near Khamsin. But these things—" She gestured around at the maintained road, the trees, the seemingly peaceful fields around them. "They're living deep in the Empire, near a major city, where it's supposed to be civilized!"

"It's called depopulation," Sigwold said, "or so Sarah explained it to me. Back when this area was a patchwork of little farms, lots of people lived here. Now the farm-folk are gone, the villages are gone, and only a few hired hands live on the estates. In some places, the estate owners are changing to other kinds of farming—raising cattle, growing olives or vines—which need even fewer people on the land."

He shrugged. "When the number of humans in an area goes down, that leaves room for—other things."

Blaize spoke up, a frown on his face. "It was just outside of Caero that a caravan I was riding with got attacked by bandits—starveling types."

"Probably farmers pushed off their land and trying to find some way to stay in the area." Sigwold shook his head. "The Imperials would call them brigands, but that's a pretty broad term." He looked around with a crooked grin. "The Imperials would probably call *us* brigands, too."

"Only if they catch us," Snow replied.

When they were almost within sight of the city, Blaize was surprised to see the pack train turn off the Luxor-Caero road, heading instead south and east toward the canyon city of Venetia.

Was this another ruse on the part of the leaders, telling the caravaneers that the destination was Caero when it was really Venetia?

It made a certain sort of sense—Venetia was known throughout the Land for intrigue. Not to mention corruption, crime, and ruthlessness.

If this turns out to be another test . . . Blaize silently grumbled.

But long before they reached the flooded gorges and grottos cut by quarrymen centuries before, Snow detoured them off the road.

The ground had grown rocky and started rising into a series of low hills. Blaize could see places where the ancient Kosian workmen must have attempted to cut some of the stone for the great building projects of Caero, but these outcrops must have been too far from the river for easy transport.

And the stones were just too large, Blaize decided. They detoured around roughly carved cubes that were still taller than his head, even while he was on horseback.

The ancients had tried to move the blocks, though. A track of sorts had been scratched across the stony landscape.

Snow led the way toward the highest prominence, which obviously had been partially quarried. A slit had been hacked into the top of the hill, with several shattered blocks flanking it.

I think I can see why they gave up on this particular project, Blaize thought, looking at the ruined stone.

Beyond the slit entrance, though, the quarry opened up, offering more than enough space to stable the packhorses. There was even a cavelike section cut into the rock.

"We don't want some Imperial tax assessor pawing through the merchandise," Snow said. "So Sigwold and I will camp out here with the goods. Most of the rest of you can go home. From here on, a large group of Northerners and Khamsins might trigger a little too much interest from suspicious Imperial minds. Better to have this look like a Caeronn pack train with a few outlander guards."

He looked over the assembled group. "I want to keep four men on besides Eginhard and Rikka. Tulwar has shown himself good on the trail. Jon Bowman's shooting is a definite plus. Harolt has been running the pack train from Varsfield, and I want to keep him."

Then Snow glanced over at Blaize. "For our fourth, Blaize has shown himself to be useful. And as a Caeronn, he'll blend in with the new additions."

Blaize silently blessed all those tests he'd been put through.

Snow went on. "So off with you after we finish here. Those going to Caero should arrive by early tomorrow. Filter into the traffic entering the city—"

"No more than two in a group. I'll make sure one in each team knows the rendezvous." Eginhard's voice grew emphatic. "Rikka and I will go in together."

Rikka sat in her saddle with her mouth hanging open, looking from her father to Blaize.

Snow just shrugged. Obviously, he wasn't getting into the middle of this. "Fine," he agreed. "For the rest, find yourselves a partner—after we've unloaded the horses and stowed the cargo."

They packed the barrels into the farthest recess of the man-made cave. Then Tulwar led off a party to get fodder for the horses. Blaize went along, working up a good sweat as he attempted to chop grass for the packhorses using a sword.

"What we need is a sickle," he told Tulwar. "Maybe that curved thing on your hip—"

But the Galeshi shook his head, laughing. "It's sharpened on the wrong side, Caeronn." He watched Blaize mangle his way through the grass. "Just as well you went off to the army. You'd have starved to death as a farmer."

Riding with a heavy load of cut grass, Blaize took his time riding back to the cave. He stopped beside one of the wrecked blocks, and took a moment to scan the horizon. Reaching the abandoned quarry had been a higher climb than he'd first realized. The hilltop gave a view all the way to Caero.

It looked like a toy city, gleaming walls penning in a thick horseshoe of dun mud-brick houses and buildings. Closer to the river and the Port Gate, larger boxy edifices rose—Temples to the ancestors of the city's leading families. Beyond that stretched the great bridge across the Roa Vizorr.

But what really caught the eye was the quartet of pyramids rising up beyond the city walls. Each more massive than the last, the huge structures shone a dazzling white in the late-afternoon sunlight.

On his way north to Khamsin, Blaize had spent several days in Caero. He'd diligently worked at acquainting himself with his fictitious hometown, including a visit to the pyramids. Thus he knew the gleam came from an outer coating of white limestone over a body of red granite. These stone innards showed like a huge red wound in the smallest pyramid, which had enormous scaffolding erected along one side. Blaize had thought repairs were under way. But no, it had turned out to be a not-so-subtle reminder of Imperial hegemony. Lord Tackett, the garrison commander, had ordered his engineers to steal dressed stone so they could enlarge the local temple to Tezla.

"Amazing, isn't it?" Rikka asked, coming up from behind him. "I thought Khamsin was a big city." She shook her head. "But those pyramids make Khamita Castle look tiny."

"The Kosians of old must have had considerable time on their hands," Blaize said. "Not to mention a multitude of slaves."

She laughed, then stopped, looking embarrassed. "I didn't know my father was going to do what he did before. And I can't imagine why—"

"I can," Blaize said lightly enough. "Nor do I blame him. He doesn't know me, he sees us together a lot . . . well, maybe he'll come to know me better as we continue the journey. As I'll meet more of your comrades in Caero."

In spite of his tone, Blaize didn't think that would be as jolly an experience as he was suggesting. Looking down at the city reminded him that he was returning to civilization. And much as he'd come to like his companions—Rikka most of all—he had to face his responsibilities as an Imperial Altem.

Blaize had already made one decision. He wouldn't attempt to contact the local Atlantean authorities until after he'd met this new set of Rebels. Hints he'd gleaned from conversation suggested that several important leaders would join them.

So I'll continue as I have and see what I can learn. But the thought worried Blaize. He'd probably face more tests from the Rebels, not to mention a threat he really dreaded. Would he suddenly find himself walking helplessly off to follow Karrudan's will?

The pendant tucked in his shirt no longer encircled his neck.

But it seemed to have an even greater weight than ever before.

Chapter 14

THE breeze came from the north, a warm, arid wind that had moved for miles over wasteland, lifting a fine, sandy grit to bring along as a gift.

For about the thirtieth time, Blaize spat, trying to get the stuff out of his mouth.

"Welcome home, Blaize," Tulwar said ironically. "This Tezla-be-damned dustwind will probably blow all the time we're here."

Blaize had heard about the dustwinds of Caero. They might not be as blinding as the sandstorms of the Galeshi's homeland, but they had been known to lay a hot, droning presence over cities and towns as far south as Atlantis. The hollow sound of the wind had something of the tomb in it. And no matter how tightly the shutters were closed, the caustic, abrasive grit found its way into homes—and mouths.

He'd heard that the murder rate rose in Down Town whenever the dustwinds blew. How much worse would it be closer to the source?

He faced the others with the cheerful insolence of a man in his hometown. "This little breeze? You should be here in the height of summer, when the dustwinds *really* get going!"

Their group created a little eddy in the gathering river of humanity making its way into the mouth of the Port Gate.

Eginhard had led the reduced group of riders from the stone cave yesterday, pushing the pace against the declining sunlight. They'd even picked their way for two hours in full darkness before the Dwarf finally gave up.

His grim insistence on speed had kept conversation to a

minimum. Blaize was glad he'd had the chance to talk with Rikka before they left. By the time they set up a fireless camp, the riders were too tired to think of anything but sleep, except for the rotation of guards Eginhard established.

He was up again before dawn, leading them through murky grayness along the road to the Roa Vizorr.

By sunrise, they were in sight of Caero's walls. They also found themselves in the midst of a motley collection of people waiting to get through the gates. Caravans with pack trains or wagons, small merchants or farmers with high-piled carts pulled by amazingly small donkeys, travelers on horseback, even peddlers afoot with sacks over their shoulders stood waiting for the Port Gate to open. The growing crowd probably had representatives of every tribe within the Empire. Caero traded with all; she was the enemy of none.

Eginhard and Rikka pushed into the mob scene, quickly disappearing.

"We're to give them a few minutes," Harolt the Northerner said. "But then who goes in?"

Deprived of even waybread this morning, Blaize's belly let out a loud rumble.

"That's it, partner, speak up." Tulwar grinned.

"We could draw lots," John Bowman suggested.

"No one has dice?" Blaize rubbed his hands together. "We could put on some side bets—make things interesting."

"Typical Caeronn." Tulwar shook his head at the city's famed gambling mania. He lowered his voice. "I don't think Sigwold provided that purse to stake you to a game."

The Rebel leaders had proven remarkably thorough. They'd even given Blaize a little road-silver to show the gate guards he had the wherewithal for a week's stay at a local inn.

In the end, they played a finger game, and Blaize and Tulwar lost.

"This is your fault," Blaize accused while they waited after their friends were swallowed up in the throng. "You ruined our luck."

"If I depended on your luck in a dice game, we would both end up naked in the slave market," Tulwar retorted.

The squabble helped to pass the time. When they joined the line, true dawn had arrived.

And the dustwinds began blowing in earnest.

When they arrived at the gate, they found several squads of Imperial guardsmen. Most were searching incoming vehicles and pack trains, assessing taxes—or as Tulwar colorfully put it, "Taking the Empire's cut."

Only one squad dealt with individual travelers. An Altem Guardsman ran a disdainful eye over Blaize and Tulwar. "Vagabonds," he said, "dust on the road."

"Caravaneer," Tulwar corrected, "in search of a caravan."

"You have enough to pay your keep while you look?" the Imperial asked.

Both showed the contents of their purses.

"Best get lucky very soon," the Altem said. "Failure to meet obligations will send you to the slave blocks."

He passed them, though, and they walked their horses down Caero's Ceremonial Way, the widest, longest street in the city. Centuries ago, Kosian Priest-Kings had marched this pavement in solemn procession, blessing the city. Statues of the Ancestors were still taken out on parades.

"This is no place for us," Tulwar said, looking at the spacious pavement. He was the one entrusted with the route to the rendezvous.

"I thought you'd like to see the temple of my family's ancestors," Blaize replied.

"Your family has ancestors here?" Tulwar gave him a disbelieving look.

Frankly, Blaize had no idea, so he responded with a shrug. "So my Pap said."

He'd dreaded this part of the masquerade, the expectation that he should have an intimate knowledge of his supposed home.

But Tulwar had no intention of having Blaize serve as tour guide. They quickly left the wide-open streets of aristocratic Caero for a city of tight, twisting alleys. The walls around them were blank adobe, few windows, all stoutly shuttered, and even stouter plank doors.

Tulwar took them through the maze of a shopping district, where merchants literally sat on the windows of their stores, using removed shutters as seats and counters. Some of the merchandise was familiar, some—like the cult-items of various factions and religions—utterly strange.

"Third street from the red door," the Galeshi muttered aloud, turning a corner. "Find the house of herbs."

They found themselves facing a nondescript shop with bundles and dried greenery spread on the shutter. The owner was a wizened old Caeronn, his face wrinkled, the linen of his kilt yellowing. A pair of eyes like damp black pebbles peered at them between slit lids.

Tulwar bowed formally. "Tell me, Oldfather," he said, "have you something in your shop that does not grow in the Empire?"

If this was the man they sought, that sentence would identify them.

The old shopkeeper gave him a big smile, creating deep parentheses at either end of his toothless mouth. "For such a prize, the price is high," he said, giving the countersign. He raised his right hand to tug on his ear—another token. "My servant can help you," the old man said.

Blaize felt a presence behind him. Turning, he faced a tall figure in a hooded cloak.

"This way," a toneless voice said.

Tulwar and Blaize followed the shadowed figure to a door standing ajar in the expanse of the opposite wall.

Stepping through the entry, they found themselves in a fairly large kitchen. The smells of cooking reminded Blaize that breakfast this morning had been on the scanty side.

"Everyone is in the common room." Their guide threw back the cloak's hood, revealing a thin, aquiline face, pale skin, and a mane of even paler hair, pulled back and tied with a leather strap.

Even the man's eyes were pale—not washed out, but a nearly colorless gray. He smiled, and Blaize suddenly found himself under the scrutiny of a potent personality. He'd had encounters like this before, usually with veteran Altems or officers who'd spent years leading men into desperate situations. But never had the air of command struck him so forcibly.

Meeting the stranger's regard, it took Blaize a moment before he noticed the ears.

The pointed ears.

"You're an Elf," he said, brilliantly pointing out the obvious.

The elf's thin lips stretched in a wider smile. Something happened in those odd eyes. And suddenly what had seemed like a friendly expression looked more like a wolf's baring of teeth—the moment before blood would be drawn.

"Valerian," the Elf said in a stony voice. "Formerly of the Wylden Elves, now in the service of Sarah Ythlim. You have some sort of problem with my ears?"

Blaize shrugged. "Sometimes I've got a problem with *my* ears. Valerian, you say? I'm Blaize, formerly of the Imperial Army, now in service to . . . Feshku knows."

Valerian's smile became a bit more genuine. "Honest, at least. Come."

In the common room, they found Jon, Harolt, Rikka, and Eginhard seated around the ruins of a generous meal. Two strangers were also at the table. One was a woman, aristocratically good-looking, though past her first youth. Already, she had two deeply graved wrinkles between her brows. Lines that usually marked a thinker. Careless waves of gray hair tumbled to her shoulders, except for a black blaze at the front. Sharp, blue eyes seemed to leap from her tanned face, taking the newcomers in.

Even surrounded by breakfast dishes, the woman had a presence that left the man at the table in the shade. He was a fat Caeronn, his body straining expensive linen robes. With his shaven head, bulging cheeks, and pop-eyes, he reminded Blaize of a bullfrog.

"Sarah," Valerian said to the woman, "the last of our wanderers." He turned to the two newcomers. "Sarah Ythlim, and our host, Affrem. I believe you can tell who is who."

Tulwar flashed a bright grin. Blaize found himself bowing. He hadn't meant to. But that feeling of command he'd gotten from Valerian seemed to radiate tenfold from Sarah Ythlim. Blaize had heard of it, that some military leaders had it, but he'd never served under any. In his brush with Imperial power, Karrudan, he'd been looked upon like a piece of meat. Sarah made him intensely aware of himself as a person.

She smiled. "If you're anything like our friends here, you must be half-starved. Sit, eat. Did you see anything out of the ordinary on your trip through the city?"

Tulwar dug into the remains of the feast. Blaize found himself left to answer the question. "The gate guards seemed no more numerous than the last time I came into the city," he said. "And we saw few Imperial patrols. But then, they keep to the wider streets, and we were taking alleyways."

"As I reported." Eginhard's voice was suspicious as he glared around the room. "Do you expect some sort of betrayal?"

"Caero might be neutral, but the city is full of Imperial soldiers," Sarah replied. "It doesn't hurt to be careful."

"Not at all," Valerian agreed, his smile again feral.

Sarah turned to all of Eginhard's group around the table. "Affrem has arranged for us to be the only guests at this inn. The rest of our party will meet here two hours before the gates close. We'll mount up, ride out, and join our friends."

Sarah gestured around. "Until then, the inn is yours. There's a bathhouse in the courtyard. You can wash off the trail dust—"

"Until Brother Wind deposits a new coating on you." Valerian stood by a shuttered window, drawing a finger through the growing film of dust on the sill.

Sarah gave him a look, and he subsided. "Or you can rest until it's time to get ready," she finished.

"How many tubs?" Eginhard asked.

"Two," Affrem the Caeronn answered.

"Rikka will have the first bath," the Dwarf announced. "Beyond that, we'll decide."

They drew lots this time to establish the bathing schedule. Blaize came in dead last, with Tulwar winning the slot before him.

Blaize didn't care, though. There was still ample food on the table, and a feeling of considerable emptiness in his gut. While the others checked the accommodations, he enjoyed a mug of herb tea and ate.

Sarah, Valerian, and Affrem moved off to a table across the room, speaking in low tones. Blaize made no attempt to overhear. But he couldn't miss the interplay. Sarah was definitely the commanding officer here. But she was that rarest of marvels, a beloved commander. There was no stiffness, as there would be with an Imperial Warlord. She even laughed and joked with the Elf and the Caeronn.

The feeling was of veterans who'd fought long together, knowing one another's strengths and weaknesses.

Loyalty, Blaize thought. *And yet she still treads softly in case of betrayal.*

When his time at the bathhouse came, Blaize found Tulwar still lolling in the other tub while one of the female bath attendants whipped up a good lather in a mug.

"Friend Blaize!" the Galeshi greeted him. "The beauteous Roudi here assures me she is an accomplished barber. Do you wish that ugly stubble removed from your ugly self?"

Blaize ran a hand through the bristly growth on his chin and head, casting a dubious look at the girl.

Tulwar laughed. "Surely a man who faced Valerian the Smiling Devil wouldn't fear a little razor in the hands of a lass."

"Who?"

The Galeshi stared. "Maybe you know of him as Valerian Woodsbane."

That was an epithet Blaize had heard of. "He was a commander among the Elementals, wasn't he? Till they exiled him."

"Valerian was their best scout leader," Tulwar said. "Till

the day he spotted an Imperial column crossing the Roa Sanguine. They came into the Wylden from bonesucker territory. The Sect even provided guides to help the Imperials attack several Sanctuaries." He leaned over the side of the tub and spat.

"Only Valerian and his handful of rangers stood in the way—far too few. And he knew no troops could be gathered in time. Yet he stopped the invasion."

Now Blaize began to remember the story. "He set the woods afire."

"Roasting the Imperials and their Sect Elf 'friends,'" Tulwar said. "But he laid waste to leagues of forest."

"So he became known as 'Woodsbane.'" Blaize frowned. "No wonder he was exiled."

"Not exiled—hunted," Tulwar corrected. "The tree-lovers might have tolerated such a sin if it had been ordered by the Tree Golem."

Blaize nodded. The Elementals' Tezla-avatar was revered throughout the Wylden. But Valerian was no avatar. The Elemental League would have wanted his blood.

"But Valerian outdid his Wylden brothers in woodcraft, escaping them across the heart of their own territory. Then he crossed the Empire, where there was a price on his head, to offer his sword to Sarah in Varsfield."

Tulwar looked hard at Blaize. "And you had no idea what a dangerous character you were chaffing with? The Smiling Devil would cut a man's throat as soon as he'd eat breakfast." The Galeshi shook his head. "You may lose at every game you play, but you surely have Feshku's own luck."

After that, Blaize certainly couldn't reject the bath-girl's barbering services.

It was actually a pleasure, hot bathwater unknotting his muscles, gentle hands carefully drawing the razor over his head. Roudi was also something of a leech. She examined the knot at the back of Blaize's head and pronounced it nearly cured.

Blaize lay back in the tub, eyes closed, just enjoying, while Roudi tended to Tulwar. "If you drew no blood from his great dome, you must be a skillful barber," the Galeshi told her.

A certain amount of giggling and splashing accompanied Tulwar's shave. Blaize kept his eyes shut.

When they were finished, the attendants wrapped great towels around the men. Their clothes were being beaten and aired in the courtyard, and it was only a short walk to their rooms. Blaize went to put the medallion into his money pouch.

"There is a man not so far away who could fix that chain," Roudi offered.

"I thought the Street of Jewelers was across the city," Blaize said. *In the richer section of town,* he added silently.

"Wensu had a shop there," the girl replied. "But his son died . . . and he grew old. He plies a simpler trade now."

"Later, perhaps." Blaize yawned and stretched. "For now—sleep!"

Tulwar gave an elaborate shrug, slipping an arm around Roudi's waist. "Each to his own. Since you monopolize the fair Rikka, I'll seek solace elsewhere."

It was the first time Blaize had lain in a bed since Khamsin, but he didn't sleep. He lay alone in the upstairs room, considering the next part of their journey.

Whatever the mysterious cargo might be, it represented something very important to the Rebels, drawing their most important leaders here.

Sarah Ythlim—according to Sigwold, she was the creator of a machine that could come to rival the Empire.

If it's allowed to grow and prosper, Blaize reminded himself.

But despite all their precautions, a spy had joined them in their enterprise—Blaize. And if he took the way of the spy, he could betray them all right now.

But from what I saw of the shipment, it seemed . . . incomplete, Blaize thought. *There were two pack trains that came together outside Khamsin. What if there are other caravans making their separate ways to Atlantis?*

Easy enough to create fantasies of what-if, to put off an unpleasant duty. Whatever other strings the Rebels might have to their bow, this one was important enough to bring Sarah Ythlim into the game. The spy's way was clear—give them all up to the local authorities. Blaize could ignore the potent personal magnetism of Sarah or Valerian. Clever Sigwold, irascible Eginhard, and taciturn Harolt would be caught in the net—so would Jon Bowman, who'd fought beside Blaize; Tulwar, who'd rescued him from the mines; Snow, who'd killed to save him. Above all, Rikka would go into the maw of the Imperial machine . . .

Blaize frowned in the dimness.

Perhaps there was another approach to the problem—the soldier's way. He couldn't count the number of battles he'd seen where enemy fighters' will had collapsed after their commander died.

Remove Sarah Ythlim, and the money and direction behind the plot vanished. If he managed the deed and escaped, the Rebels would have to give up and escape, certain he would betray them.

Even if Blaize succeeded and died for it, Valerian would have to believe the effort compromised.

Either way, Rikka would hate me forever, he thought. *But she'd live.*

Easier to kill a comparative stranger than to betray comrades. Any soldier would understand that.

It will have to wait for tonight, Blaize told himself.

Having made his decision, he closed his eyes and rested a while.

Blaize rose with all the fatalism of a soldier before the battle. In the common room, he found a satisfied-looking Tulwar. Affrem had managed to get Eginhard, Jon, and Harolt into some sort of game.

Valerian sat off to the side, watching them with an ironic smile.

"Is Roudi about?" Blaize asked Tulwar. "I've decided I want to get that chain fixed after all."

Live hard, fight well, and leave a tidy corpse.

"Chain?" Valerian asked.

"It's for a medallion of mine," Blaize said. "The chain broke on the way here." He hoped the Elf wouldn't show any more interest. The last thing in the world he wanted was Valerian looking at Karrudan's handiwork.

The Smiling Devil gave a lazy flip of his hand. "Ask the girl," he said.

Then he turned his eyes on Tulwar. "You can stretch your legs and accompany your friend. If you didn't put your back out with the afternoon's entertainment."

Tulwar went red, and for an instant Blaize thought the Galeshi would go for his sword. Then Tulwar remembered who it was he'd be drawing on.

"We'll go find her," he said.

Tulwar didn't glance back until they were in the kitchen. "There's a strange one," he said in a low voice. "I'm not sure I like the way he amuses himself."

"I believe it was you who recently said, 'Each to his own,'" Blaize replied.

Roudi happily gave them directions. Blaize suspected Wensu was some distant relative of hers.

The route wasn't that complicated, taking them to a nearby neighborhood. Getting there took them out of the alleyways and across one of the wider streets.

The display on Wensu's shutter-counter ran to cheap brass objects—candlesnuffers and cookware. But beside the man sat a tiny dancing female figure. It wasn't even as tall as Blaize's thumb, but it was a perfect miniature.

He reached for the silver figure, but the old man shook his head. "Not for sale," he said. "It's a reminder of the work I once could do."

Wensu tried to keep his hands cupped together, but even so, his fingers twitched and jittered. Obviously it would be impossible for him to attempt such detail anymore.

Blaize took out his chain and medallion and explained what he needed. Wensu examined them.

"Nicely done," he said, glancing up at Blaize. "Delphane work?"

"Couldn't say," Blaize said with complete honesty. "I got it in Atlantis."

They haggled a bit. In the end, to spare Blaize's purse, the craftsman agreed to take one link from the chain for repairing it. Using a pair of snips, he removed his payment. Then he stirred up the heat in a small brazier, inserting a couple of irons. Turning back to the chain, he opened another link, slipped the medallion in place, then caught both ends of the length of silver together. Some work with small pliers had the link roughly back together. Then came the irons and some solder.

Wensu blew on the finished work and handed it back.

"Good as new," Blaize said, slipping the chain around his neck. He made sure the medallion came nowhere near his forehead as he put it under his shirt.

For a brief second, he froze, afraid that the replacement of Karrudan's talisman might somehow trigger the other spell implanted by the Prophet-Magus.

Nothing.

With a sigh of relief, Blaize went to move away.

"A moment," Wensu the silversmith said.

Blaize turned back, to find the old man extending a shaking palm with a piece of a silver coin.

"A bit of change." Wensu smiled. "The silver in that chain is of higher quality than I thought."

Blaize nodded and put the scruple in his purse.

Odd, he thought. *When the old man worked, his hands were rock steady.*

There was little enough to see in the neighborhood, so Blaize and Tulwar decided to return to the inn.

A squad of Imperials came marching up just as Blaize and Tulwar crossed the wider thoroughfare. Behind them, matching the soldiers step for step, came the hulking form of a Golem.

Blaize was a little surprised. Street patrols generally chose the strength and agility of a Brass Golem. The construct accompanying these troopers was an Incendiary Golem. The thing stood two heads taller than a human, fuel tanks swelling the shoulders into huge, bulbous shapes that dwarfed its head. The shoulders were brass, and so were the Golem's forearms and hands, outsized monstrosities with three spatulate fingers flanking the flamecaster set in the palm. Its legs seemed ridiculously short given the massive upper body, and they were thick to bear the weight. The feet thundering on the pavement were as large as a human torso.

Hard on traffic, Blaize thought, *and far too dangerous in a tinderbox city like this.*

The guardsmen stopped before a row of shops.

"By order of the chief magistrate," the Altem in command cried out, stepping back.

The Golem lifted its huge right hand, and flames vomited forth into the open windows.

Chapter 15

For one stunned second, the only sound was the screaming of the burning merchants and their customers. Then, as the Golem moved on to the next row of buildings, uproar engulfed the street.

Bawling in terror, people began running, abandoning the relatively wide street for the back alleys. The thick afternoon crowds had no idea what to do; their surge was just a mass attempt to escape the fire, the soldiers, the Golem.

And that's the plan, Blaize realized as he and Tulwar were dragged along in the panicked stream of people. The Golem moved on, firing its flamecaster. Now all the buildings on the far side of the street were ablaze.

A wall of flame barred the way to the rest of the city

Too bad for us if the inn were beyond there, Blaize thought.

But it might be worse that both the inn and Sarah Ythlim were on this side of the fiery cordon. Even for the Empire, this was high-handed behavior. The garrison commander wouldn't send his troops on such an attempt unless he believed there would be a large reward.

Blaize and Tulwar fought their way to the front of the torrent of runners. Then they were ahead, making their way through the alleys where the fleeing mob dispersed.

They reached the inn ahead of any of the refugees, bursting into the common room. Instantly, they faced a phalanx of suddenly drawn weapons.

"Imperial Golems are setting fires just six blocks away," Blaize reported. "They're backed up by patrols of soldiers."

"Looked like out-of-the-ordinary behavior to us," Tulwar added.

Affrem tried to leap to his feet—but failed. Valerian's foot pinned the Caeronn's robe to the floor. "How unlucky you weren't able to leave earlier, as you planned."

The fat frog-face, beaded with sweat, all but shouted confirmation of Valerian's subtle accusation. "The tax collector—Ramosi—was going to ruin me. I had to give the government something!"

"From the way the Imperials are acting, you didn't give them our exact location." Valerian's smile had gone completely feral. "Probably because you feared being cheated of a reward. Well, I have a reward for you, traitor."

Valerian seized Affrem's head, moving so quickly, Blaize only got a hint of movement. An instant later, the Caeronn lolled in his chair, a red gorget of blood spreading across his robe from a slit throat.

Wiping a knife on the dead man's linen, Valerian headed for the stairs. "I'll get Sarah—and your daughter, Eginhard. Get your possessions together, everyone. We leave immediately."

One thing Blaize had to give Sarah Ythlim—her actual practice matched her legend. The instant she got the news, Sarah was coming down the stairs, pulling a nondescript gray cape around herself. Valerian had also donned the floor-length hooded cloak he'd worn when Blaize first met him.

Blaize could smell the first traces of smoke in the air as the group exited the inn. "Which direction is the fire?" Sarah asked.

Blaize pointed.

Eginhard raised his face to the sky. "That's the same direction the wind is coming from," he said grimly. "They want it to drive us before it."

"A clever enough plan," Valerian allowed. "But I wonder if the Imperials realize how strong the dustwinds grow toward evening?"

Apparently, they didn't. Along with smoke, flaming debris were already flying on the breeze, landing all over the neighborhood, setting new fires. Cries of alarm rang out as people's homes went up.

"Is the idea to capture us or cremate us?" Tulwar asked.

"Either, I think," Blaize said. The adobe walls ahead seemed to come even closer together, and the cramped space between them was filling with smoke. As the fugitives negotiated a kink in the narrow alleyway road, they finally saw why.

A three-story house was well ablaze, thick smoke rising from the roof. No bucket brigade could stop the fire's progress.

Despairing wails came from the third floor as well. The window shutters had been thrown open, and a woman stood in the opening, holding two babies in her arms. Flames already flickered behind her.

"Please!" The mother's voice was raw from smoke, screaming, and emotion. "Someone—please—the children! Ancestors, help us!"

Sarah Ythlim stopped dead in the passageway, Valerian crashing into her from behind.

"Sarah." His voice was tight. "We can't—"

"We can't leave without helping them," Sarah finished for him.

A crowd of neighbors milled in the doorway, advancing, then recoiling. "The stairs are already alight," one of the Caeronns cried, her voice hopeless.

Rikka turned to Blaize. "Can you do your wall-climbing thing?" she asked.

He shook his head. "That's for stonework, where there are crevices between the blocks." He ran a hand over the adobe wall. The mud-bricks had been covered with a layer of clay. There was nothing to grab on to.

Then Blaize's eyes went from the flat wall to the five other males in the group. "But maybe we can build a ladder."

"No time!" Valerian said impatiently.

But Blaize was already moving, resting his hands against the wall, leaning against it. "Tulwar!" he called from his semi-crouched position. "Rest your hands against my shoulders. Do as I do."

Valerian stared, then realized what was going on. "Harolt! You do the same. Push against Tulwar. Hold tight, now!"

He swarmed onto Harolt's bent back, crawling onward across Tulwar until he knelt on Blaize's back. Then, raising his left foot, Valerian placed it on Blaize's left shoulder and pushed up and forward. His palms hit the wall, and now he rested one foot on either side of Blaize's head. "Jon, up behind me—then Eginhard, you go on top."

Valerian glanced down at Sarah. "It will be up to you and Rikka then."

Blaize groaned as Eginhard's weight joined Valerian's on his shoulders. But his stance against the wall let him maintain his position in spite of the load.

More pressure pushed down on him as Sarah and Rikka climbed the human ladder.

"We're up to the window," Rikka called down.

"One baby," Sarah said. "And here's the other. Can you stand the weight of the mother, too?"

"As long . . . as you . . . start getting down," Blaize grunted.

The weight against his aching shoulders increased, decreased, then increased again.

I don't know how long we'll be able to hold together, he thought, gasping for breath in the thick air. His arms were beginning to quiver.

But they lasted long enough for the trapped family to make their escape.

The desperate construction came apart from the top down. Finally Blaize could stagger away from the wall. He nearly fell flat when he tried to bring himself upright.

"We did it!" Rikka flung her arms around him in exuberance. The physical contact was a definite pleasure. But Blaize was just happy for the help in standing up.

Karrudan would have left those people to burn. The realization ran through him the same way the fire was spreading through the tightly packed neighborhood. *So would Portarr. Even Scarbro would have considered himself and his mis-*

sion more important than these dust-people. Sarah is definitely different.

Valerian, however, had an eye for the priorities. "Well done," he said. "Now let's get out of here." He pulled up the hood on his cloak, gesturing for Sarah to do the same. She was too noticeable among the dark-haired Caeronns. Rikka followed suit in her brown homespun as they left the weeping woman to the care of her neighbors.

But the Rebels' flight was short-lived. They hardly got a block away down the alley before they ran straight into an Imperial patrol.

The guardsmen stood five abreast behind a hedge of spear points.

"Hold!" the Altem in charge bellowed—an unnecessary order, considering the way his men blocked the street.

This was no arson squad. These guardsmen had been set out to plug this escape route. They were searching for something.

Or someone, Blaize thought.

"There's fire behind us!" Harolt's voice was a little too high with fear for it to be an act.

"And you'll stay here until we're satisfied, so don't waste our time," the Altem responded. He looked at Rikka and Sarah, both bundled in their cloaks. "Remember," he said to his men, "we're looking for a non-Caeronn woman with white hair."

Two guardsmen came forward to pull the females aside, grabbing their hoods. Sarah's face and hair were revealed. The one who'd gone for Rikka stepped back, gurgling.

Seizing the opportunity, Blaize tore his sword free and charged the line of spears. He dropped to bring himself under the shafts, rolled up to the guardsmen's legs, and began slashing.

"Tezla's—" The blasphemous exclamation abruptly cut off; Blaize guessed that the guardsman who'd gone for Sarah had met the business end of someone's blade. Running footsteps told that the others were in motion.

Blaize, however, didn't watch. He was intent on getting through the line and at the Altem.

Blaize knew what he would do in a situation like this if he were the Altem.

But Blaize was a second too late. The Altem got off one good blast on his brass whistle before Blaize's blade punctured a lung.

Returning whistles came from the distance—other patrols on their way. Blaize pulled his sword loose and ran.

In staying to deal with the Altem, he'd put himself at the rear of the pack of Rebels who'd burst through the gap he'd created.

As the battle-rush cleared away, Blaize suddenly realized what he'd done. Instead of quietly standing by and letting the Rebels be captured, he'd lashed out, opening the avenue of escape—*through* fellow guardsmen! Instant response had been drilled into him by his trainers, with their tales of warriors who'd hesitated and died.

But his instinctive reaction had been for his companions and against his Imperial comrades. *What was I thinking?* The question chattered through his brain.

He had no time to stop and contemplate. Blaize was hard-pressed to keep up with the tail end of the fugitives as Valerian led them on a wildly jinking course through the webwork of alleys.

All around them, though, the running Rebels could still hear the whistles. The sound even came from behind them.

Tezla blast it, Blaize swore to himself. *How often do you find a Utem using his head—not to mention a dead Altem's whistle?*

Smoke grew thick in the constricted passage, and he could see the redness of flames up ahead. Had they gotten turned around threading their way through the maze?

Blaize realized he had no idea where they were. He could only hope Valerian's forest-trained Elemental senses were doing a good job of guiding them.

A shout rang out behind them. Blaize risked a quick look back. More Imperials came clattering in pursuit—a fresh patrol by the look of it. They had a live Altem directing the chase.

From ahead came a *fwoomph!* and the sound of a collapsing roof.

Just better and better, Blaize thought.

He glanced over at Eginhard, who now ran beside him.

"Dwarves aren't built for this skitter-scatter." Eginhard's big chest heaved like a bellows with each breath, but he doggedly moved his short legs as quickly as he could, his battle-axe gripped in one hand.

They followed Valerian through another set of zigzags, in the hopes of briefly setting back the pursuers. The alley they ended up in swerved through an almost right-angle turn. When Blaize and Eginhard came round, they found a pair of absolutely blank walls, smoke, and the rest of their party preparing to make a stand.

Harolt, Tulwar, and Jon formed a rank across the passage. The drover looked scared, Tulwar looked eager, and Jon looked a little dubious. He'd had to give up his crossbow, leaving him with only a sword.

Eginhard grinned wolfishly as he took his place in the line. When Blaize gently tried to push in along, the Dwarf nearly took the human's hand off.

"You think to keep me from the fray?" Eginhard's voice went guttural.

Blaize shook his head. "I think you're a leader and should be with the leaders. Not to mention your daughter."

He pointed to where Valerian and Sarah stood, close together, arguing. Rikka stood miserably aside.

If he could follow his own wishes, Blaize would have gone to her, if only to say good-bye. Valerian hadn't chosen the most promising battle site.

The building providing the blank wall on their right was apparently the one that had lost its roof. Now it seemed to act as a giant chimney, sending a pillar of smoke and flame into the sky.

"What is that?" he asked, gesturing with his thumb.

"Warehouse." Tulwar never turned from the bend in the

alley, like a hunting dog on point. His sword was out, resting easily in his right hand.

Harolt stood beyond him, holding the left flank. He looked to be gripping his sword hilt far too tightly. But then, Blaize couldn't fault him for that. He switched his own sword to his left hand so he could work the sore muscles in his right before they got a cramp.

Jon Bowman would have been happier skewering the enemy from long range with crossbow bolts. But he stood his ground and held his sword with the same quiet competence he'd shown throughout the journey.

Blaize took his place at the far flank against the right-hand wall. He ran a palm against the dingy adobe, then snatched it back. The heat reminded him of Bruna's ovens.

What was fueling the fire in there? Casks of oil? Winter wine? Blaize wondered. He had a sick feeling that one more explosion in there might send the wall cascading down upon them.

"Does Valerian have some clever trick in mind?" he asked Tulwar.

The Galeshi shook his head. "Simple surprise. Let them come around, bloody their noses, push them back, and then run as if the Pit itself was opening behind you."

Which it might well be. But Blaize saw no benefit in sharing that thought with the others.

They waited long minutes. Blaize's concern began to grow. Valerian's attempted evasion couldn't have taken this long for the Imperials to figure out.

Either the search parties are consolidating their strength, or they're trying to establish a new cordon around us . . . or both.

None of those possibilities was comforting. Blaize glanced over his shoulder to see what the others were up to. On the left, Valerian spoke with Eginhard, bringing something out from under his long cloak and putting it in the Dwarf's arms. In a swirl of black wool, Valerian then joined the women—or so Blaize figured. He could barely make out Sarah's gray cloak in the distance.

Blaize could understand that.

This was the sort of predicament where Atlantean generals, even mage-officers, would be clearing out while leaving a rear guard to distract the enemy.

So what would their adversaries be up to? Blaize tried to think like an Altem. How would he handle this situation?

Our patrols should be converging on this area. I'd send out single scouts rather than patrols, gathering the rest of my searchers so we can strike decisively once we're certain where the enemy is—

His thoughts were interrupted as a single Imperial leaped around the corner, appearing right in front of Harolt. The Prieskan jumped back, not striking.

Neither did the Imperial, who vanished round the bend again even as Tulwar hacked at him.

The Galeshi's scimitar clashed off armor, and then the scout was gone.

Blaize reached past Jon Bowman to keep Tulwar from going in pursuit.

"They know we're here now," Blaize called over his shoulder, expecting to hear Valerian call off the ambush. Instead, the leaders silently kept their places.

Tezla's knob! Blaize silently swore. *What did they do, leave dummies behind for us to defend?*

From around the corner came the sounds of a sizable mass of men organizing for an attack.

The four men blocking the alleyway looked nervously at one another. The only good thing was that they were reasonably safe from any sort of Technomantic attack. A magical blast or even a Golem's heavy tread would bring the burning warehouse's walls down.

"Start pulling back." Eginhard's voice was soft and strained behind them. From the front, the sounds of advancing men became louder. Blaize heard a muttered command.

There's more here than we can hold. The realization chilled him as he retreated. He and the others were less than a forlorn hope. What was Valerian up to?

They reached Eginhard, Harolt stumbling as he backed into him.

"Turn and run!" Eginhard ordered.

Now Blaize could see what the Dwarf held cradled. A lightning gun! That was a weapon for the pride of the Imperial Army. What was it doing in the hands of a Rebel?

Blaize had no time—and no one—to ask. Harolt was already past, breaking into a run. So was Jon Bowman—prudence in this case obviously being the better course than valor.

Blaize and Tulwar still faced the bend in the alley as a host of Imperials came roaring round, Altems in the front rank. They stumbled a little when they didn't encounter the resistance they'd expected.

"Run, Marway singe you!" Eginhard grated.

Blaize wasn't sure whether the words were directed at him or the enemy. Either way, Eginhard triggered the weapon.

A spark of blue-white energy sizzled from the lightning gun, striking the wall Blaize had been standing beside moments ago.

It wasn't a full charge. But even so, it was enough to fill the narrow alleyway with the stink of ozone—and to fill Blaize's eyes with dancing afterimages.

He didn't see the wall start to crack, but he heard and felt the shift. A rush of rubble and flame surged into the alley as, half blind, he hauled himself away.

Eginhard pushed Blaize and Tulwar ahead of him. They were coming up on another intersection. Rikka and Valerian darted right into a cross-alley. Sarah, her pale hair streaming behind her, went straight.

Still blinking, Blaize pounded after her, suddenly very aware of the sword in his hand.

Catch up, cut her down. The wild thought burst upon him. *Complete surprise. Eginhard and Tulwar can't stop it. They might not even delay their escape to deal with you. When the Imperials circle round the blockage behind, you'll have the dead Rebel leader to show them—and Karrudan's sign on your brow.*

This wasn't the Prophet-Magus' voice commanding him, seizing control of his muscles. No, his usually calm battle-sense was urging him to take advantage of a momentary opportunity.

He was ahead of Tulwar and Eginhard and could strike without interference. Hoping they'd just run past was sheer wishful thinking. But the lightning gun *was* exhausted. Besides, it couldn't be used in such close quarters. Did Eginhard still have his axe?

Tulwar certainly had his scimitar.

A soldier's solution, Blaize thought, his feet pounding as he came closer to the white-haired figure ahead of him.

It would spare the Empire rebellion and sorrow, maybe even save the Prophet-Magus . . .

He was a bare step behind the gray-cloaked figure now.

I'm sorry, Rikka.

Blaize was bringing up his blade when the figure before him glanced over its shoulder, revealing the face hidden by that flowing mane of white.

The face of Valerian the Smiling Devil.

Chapter 16

SHOCK threw Blaize into a misstep, which nearly landed him facedown on the pavement.

"Careful with that." Valerian batted away Blaize's wavering blade with the back of his hand. His eyes were pensive, but his smile almost seemed to convey true amusement. "If I can surprise you, I think we managed to convince our Imperial friends."

Blaize now realized the gray cloak was a bit short on the Elf's tall, rangy figure. But a quick glimpse after being dazzled by the lightning discharge had been enough to convince him he pursued Sarah. As amazement drained away, Blaize faced new surprise, finding himself relieved—even *glad* that his wild plan had gone awry.

What is happening to me? he asked himself. *Attacking fellow Imperials—happy that I didn't kill the rebels' leader . . .*

Valerian's words penetrated his confusion. "The survivors of that first patrol we encountered must have passed on their description of Sarah," he said. "White hair, gray cloak. I realized that without the thong holding my hair back I might pass for Sarah in a pinch—if I was seen briefly from a distance. So we switched cloaks, waited for the Imperials to appear, and played our little charade."

His voice held a note of satisfaction. "They'll believe their quarry is heading north. Meanwhile, Sarah is heading south to join Snow."

While we play hare for the Imperial hounds, Blaize thought, *running right into the wind that's pushing the fire our way.*

He hesitated as Tulwar and Eginhard joined them. "Ah, isn't there a wall of fire waiting for us in that direction?"

Valerian Woodsbane nodded, his smile undisturbed. "Some might consider that a proper irony." He continued leading them north, apparently unconcerned.

"Have you got another lightning gun hidden under that cloak?" Blaize asked.

The Elf shook his head. "Regrettably, no. I was hoping the captured one I gave Eginhard had more of a charge. At least it was sufficient."

The smoke grew thicker as they continued on their way. Blaize could hear noises through the thickening murk—muttered curses, and then a crash.

"Good work," Valerian said as they came up on Jon and Harolt standing beside the door they'd just forced open. "There are two more doors on the other side of the alley. See if you can break them down as well."

With five of them, breaking in was easier. They tore down the door that had been opened and used it as a ram on the other.

Valerian had vanished through the first doorway. He emerged just as they finished. The Elf was tearing a piece of sacking into strips. "There's a water trough in the courtyard here. Soak these, then wrap them around your faces. They'll help with the smoke."

While the others did as he said, the Elf searched the area until finally he stopped in front of a statue. He pushed against it, and the base suddenly pivoted, revealing the black maw of a hole.

"Ho, ho," Eginhard said. "Caero has its Warrens as well."

"Not exactly," Valerian replied. "But the city does have smugglers, and they use tunnels."

Wrapping a wet rag around his own face, the Elf then felt around in the blackness beneath them. "There are iron rungs set into the wall," he told them in a muffled voice. "Eginhard, you go last. See if you can rebalance the statue over us."

With that, Valerian swung himself around and began descending. Blaize found himself third, after Harolt. As he clambered downward, he could hear the sounds of flint striking steel. Then light blossomed below.

He glanced down to see Valerian holding a torch. "Very well prepared, these smugglers."

That same organization showed in the construction of the smugglers' secret passageway. The walls were masonry, with large stone lintels every ten paces or so.

"Sturdy," Jon Bowman said.

It had better be, Blaize added silently. *We're betting our lives this will get us under the barrier of flame.*

The tunnel ran straight ahead. Blaize simply had to follow Valerian's torch.

As they proceeded, the air began getting warmer and thicker.

Smoke must be coming in from the other side, Blaize realized.

Still they continued. Blaize became glad of his improvised mask. It did seem to keep the worst effects of the smoke at bay. But now it was definitely getting hotter.

"Like a forge," Harolt said nervously.

It wasn't the happiest comparison—setting off thoughts of melting metal and searing flesh.

"Heat rises," Valerian said tersely. "We're below."

But even the bottom of a firepit grows hot enough to burn. Blaize suddenly remembered Bruna's bakeshop, where he'd cleaned cinders out from under the ovens. The stone was still scorching enough to blister unwary hands.

"How much farther?" he asked, his voice getting hoarse. The smoke was definitely thicker, and the heat was now stifling. His soaked face mask got a new source of moisture—sweat.

"I'm—not sure," Valerian admitted.

They continued on, Blaize now silently counting paces. Fifty . . . seventy-five . . .

Their light began to fade—the flame of the torch was guttering.

That can't be a good sign, Blaize thought. Flame needs air to breathe, even as we do.

Harolt stumbled, reaching to catch himself against the wall. He recoiled from the stone like a scalded cat.

"You're going to get us killed!" Hysteria quivered in the Northerner's voice. He was gasping like a fish out of water.

"If you have a better plan, Harolt, I wish you hadn't kept it to yourself." Valerian's voice sounded easy, but it had the impact of a whiplash.

Harolt sobbed, but continued onward.

Eginhard was the next to trip, falling all the way to the floor.

"You know," he said in surprise, "I think the air is a little bit better down here."

They made the last third of their journey on hands and knees, faces as close to the floor as they could bring them. Somewhere along the way, the heat began to decrease. They had made it beneath the raging fires.

Blaize's mind leaped ahead to the next problem. Would they reach the end of the tunnel only to find a charred building collapsed on the exit?

Everyone in the group was coughing now, a thick, disgusting mucus emerging to clog the masks they wore.

Blaize began to wonder if they'd even make it to the far end.

Valerian snuffed out the torch. They groped along in blackness until the Elf finally croaked, "A ladder!"

"Where?" Blaize could hear the sounds of Harolt blundering forward, then climbing, pushing . . . slamming. "Trapdoor on top. It won't open!" the raw-voiced reported.

A growl came from the rear of the group. "Let me at it," Eginhard said.

He crawled forward. Blaize heard the confused sounds of a short, sharp struggle in the darkness. Then from ahead and above came the sound of a deep breath, a grunt—and the crack of splintering wood.

The next few moments passed in agonizing slowness as the Dwarf struggled overhead. Then he subsided. "Got part of it open, but we need someone skinnier than I am."

A rustle of cloth—Valerian was shedding his cloak. "I'll try," the Elf said.

Blaize heard more confused noise as the pair changed places.

"All right." The sound of Valerian's voice had changed. It seemed farther away and had an echo.

He's up! Blaize realized.

Muffled grunts and sounds of strain came down to them. Then a welcome crash signified the trapdoor being thrown fully open.

They climbed up into a warehouse thick with smoke, but there seemed to be no flames anywhere near.

"Someone left the corner of a crate resting on the trap." Valerian was panting. "Let's see if we can't find fresher air."

Outdoors, the dustwind tasted like wine as Blaize pulled the wrappings away from his face. He suddenly doubled up, racked with a lung-twisting cough that hacked up thick wads of mucus to be spat out. The others suffered the same ill effects.

Valerian staggered over to a nearby horse trough, sluicing his face with a double handful of water. Blaize joined him, handing over the cloak he'd picked up from the tunnel floor. "Thought you might still need this," he said. Then he cupped his hands and threw water on his own face.

The group walked through empty streets, disheveled, smoke-stained, and wild-eyed. Valerian had wrapped the cloak around himself, pulling up the hood to hide his telltale hair.

Shadows were slanting across the streets. The remorseless dustwinds continued to blow in Blaize's face. Besides grit, it brought new traces of smoke.

"More fires—ahead of us?" Blaize wheezed. "But the wind—"

"Embers and debris might have been tossed around," Eginhard suggested.

"Or perhaps a burning torch was used to settle an old grudge," Valerian said. "It's been known to happen in times like these."

They continued on through streets grown dull with fading sunlight and clouds of smoke. Warehouses gave way to tenements, and then, as they came to the first wide street, they suddenly found shining new mansions. One of them was afire, adding to the local smoke quota.

A crowd had gathered to watch the spectacle, and some were accepting work on a sketchy bucket brigade that was bringing water to the harried house servants.

"A silver a head if you help save Master Ramosi's house!" Firefighting had taken a toll on the usually immaculate upper servant. His pectoral necklace was awry, his linen kilt stained with smoke. He stood in front of the crowd, jingling a leather pouch and looking desperate.

The tax collector behind Affrem's betrayal, Blaize thought, *not to mention our adventure on the road. Couldn't happen to a nicer Caeronn.*

Valerian's eyes showed similar thoughts, but his attention was more on the squad of Imperial soldiers leaning against the wall around one of the other mansions, enjoying the show. "A quiet exit through the crowd might be indicated," the Elf murmured.

Anything else he might have said was drowned out by a crash and terrified neighing.

"The stables!" cried the majordomo, running through the gates.

"On the other hand, we need horses," Valerian said, shepherding his group after the steward.

A couple of grounds servants had abandoned the fight to save the house, running for the stables. One of the menials threw open the door and began to lead horses out.

"You get the tack," Valerian whispered to Blaize and Tulwar. "We'll get the mounts."

The interior of the stables was thick with smoke. The fire had leaped from the roof of the mansion to ignite the stable's hayloft, and flames were quickly spreading. Horses were beginning to scream and kick in their stalls.

Tulwar led the way to the far wall, grabbing saddles and bridles, passing some on to Blaize.

As they headed out, Blaize spotted Harolt leading two horses. Whatever he lacked in personal courage, he made up for in concern for the animals. They moved as gently as if they were taking an exercise round.

The horse Eginhard led, however, kept trying to bite him. It made enough of a struggle to catch the eye of the steward. "Who are you?" the Caeronn demanded.

Then he saw Blaize, Caeronn in looks, but his arms full of saddles and bridles. "What are you doing, fool?" he screeched. "The horses are more valuable!"

"Not to us," Valerian said, coming up behind him. He had a knife in his hand and applied the pommel in the hilt behind the servant's ear.

Blaize noticed that the other two servants were already laid out in the courtyard.

"Let's get them saddled up quickly before someone else comes along to supervise," the Elf said.

Blaize threw a saddle over a trembling mare and tightened the girth. Tulwar tossed his gear to Jon Bowman and took over gentling down the horse still trying to take a bite out of Eginhard. Harolt turned his two horses over to Valerian, then turned to run back into the burning building.

"We already have enough horses," the dumbfounded Elf called after him.

"Just a couple more left—you wouldn't want them to *burn*!"

All the horses they needed were saddled up when Harolt returned.

"I suppose we'll have to move the humans out of harm's way as well." Valerian sighed.

With that chore taken care of, they mounted up and charged for the mansion gates.

The crowd recognized immediately that the riders were not Ramosi's servants and burst out in cheers. The Imperials turned, stared, and began pushing off from the wall where they'd been lounging.

But before the troopers could block the way, the Rebels

were past them, riding like mad for the Ceremonial Way and the Northern Gate.

This time, there was no polite waiting in line. They pounded along the street, and anyone who got in the way risked being trampled.

From the dodging pedestrians, the gate guards would have to suspect something was up. Very few Caeronns left the city just before the gates closed. Why start a journey when darkness would strand you barely outside the city walls?

Blaize could see helmeted heads turning toward him and the other riders. Altems began shouting orders, and their squads started deploying.

"Halt, scum!" An Altem stalked forward, his hand upraised. The arrogant fool couldn't believe the riders wouldn't obey. Valerian purposely swerved his horse to knock the Altem down.

The other Imperials were caught flat-footed. They had neither blocked off the exit with troops nor closed the gates. Blaize drew his sword, ready to lash out at anyone foolish enough to try blocking them now.

It was too late for the Imperials. The Rebels galloped through the open gateway. Safely outside, Valerian skinned back his cloak's hood, letting the guards see that the white-haired Rebel they were supposed to be on the lookout for had escaped—northward.

Blaize reined in his mount to a more moderate pace. "How far do we have to go to convince them?" he asked Valerian.

"As far as the pyramids," the Elf replied. "They'll block us from the sight of the guards on the walls. Then they'll have no chance of catching us . . ."

His words died away as they came closer to the nearest of the gigantic structures—and saw the figures gathered at the base.

"Feshku's bleeding Pit!" Valerian swore. "What are *they* doing out here?"

Blaize shook his head. "Perhaps after setting the place

alight, Lord Tackett decided it was a good idea to get all his flamecasters out of town."

The troops had apparently been sent out to the Empire's stone-stealing project at the smallest pyramid. Clustered around the scaffolding that surrounded the cut into the pyramid stood a group of Golems—Incendiary Golems. The hulking constructs dwarfed the robed mages who controlled them and made the Amotep Incinerators in the group look even odder.

Antiflash armor worn by the human incendiaries always gave them a bulky look. Add in the large fuel tank worn across the shoulders and the thin, curved visor in the Incinerator's helmet, and Blaize always saw a grinning monkey's head atop a short, squat body.

The Incinerators might look comical, but they presented a serious problem. Their flamecasters had a considerable range—they could cover the road. And the Golems could pursue any quarry tirelessly, if slowly.

Disengaging and escaping would be a much longer, more difficult matter.

"Off the road!" Valerian ordered as Golem and human heads swung to stare at them. Such amenities as the Empire provided for overseers and workmen at the stone removal site were by the road. The Elf now led the group of riders for the edge of the pyramid farthest from the roadside.

That's the only thing he can do, Blaize thought. *But it will convince those Imperials that we're up to no good.*

Indeed, as soon as the Rebels left the road, the Imperial troops began deploying. Some moved to block the paved surface. Others formed a line to protect the mages. Several Golems began making their ponderous way to the far end of the pyramid.

Blaize spurred his horse back to a gallop. It was a question of time and distance. Could they get round the corner of the pyramid before the Golems got in range? The riders had the longer route to travel, but they could move faster than the Golems. Galloping horses. Running machines. The stony ground beneath them—necessary to support such titanic structures—allowed top speed.

The only variable—Blaize spat grit out of his mouth—*is that the wind is in our faces.*

It would be a close thing, but it looked as though the riders would win the race. Then another variable raised its monkey-head.

An Amotep Incinerator appeared, already at the end of the pyramid.

The jet of flame he sent at the riders set their horses snorting and plunging, refusing to go onward. The Golems, however, continued advancing at their thundering, jogging trot.

"Hold the reins!" That was Jon Bowman snarling the order. Blaize turned to see the crossbowman's feet thud onto the ground. An instant later, he had his bow ready, and fired.

The bolt caught the Amotep in the leg, bringing him down. Another jet of flame vomited out as the wounded man tried to fire back. Jon was just out of range. He pulled his bowstring back into position and set in another bolt. The Amotep was clawing his way erect with the help of one of the uprights for the scaffolding when Jon fired again. This time, the bolt entered the Imperial's shoulder, just outside his armor. The hand that had held the nozzle of the flame-caster hung uselessly as the Incinerator fell again.

"Go! Go! Go!" Valerian yelled.

The riders tore through the danger zone. Blaize hung back, sword out, in case the Amotep made another attempt.

Speed would be of the essence. Blaize glanced toward the Golems. They were coming very close . . .

"Blaize! Watch out!"

The Amotep tried to seize the opportunity from Blaize's inattention, wobbling up with the nozzle in his good hand.

Blaize went to stab, but was blocked as Tulwar brought his horse over the Imperial. A gout of flame rose up. The horse reared, screaming, then collapsed.

Tulwar flew from the saddle, his billowing Galeshi

costume afire. He lived up to his "Windfoot" epithet, landing lightly and rolling to douse the flames. His mount, however, lay where it had fallen, kicking and giving bubbling screams.

Scimitar in hand, Tulwar limped to the prone Amotep and administered the finishing stab. His handsome face was starting to blister as he glared up at Blaize. "Get out of here, fool!"

"Climb up behind me!" Blaize fought to control his panicking horse.

"Riding double, we'd never escape them." Tulwar pointed his sword at the oncoming Golems.

"This is no time to argue—come on."

Instead, Tulwar knelt to grab the dead Amotep's flame-casting nozzle. "Go on, you crazy Caeronn. Win a war for Sarah. Make Rikka happy." Tulwar grinned at him, a grotesque expression for his burned face. "Just stay away from the wine, all right? You won't have me around to save you."

He aimed the nozzle at the nearest Incendiary Golem. Flame poured forth to bathe the oncoming machine, searing Tulwar even as he fired. The construct raised its own huge flamecaster for a countershot . . . and suddenly began to shudder.

"Got you, you misbegotten mechanical." Tulwar laughed.

Realizing what was about to happen, Blaize urged his mount around the corner of the Pyramid.

He'd just reached safety behind the monumental masonry when the Golem's fuel tank blew up. Even so, the blast was enough to jar Blaize's horse into a stumble.

Tulwar was too close and unprotected, he thought, riding out the shock as his mount recovered. *At least he knocked the other Golems on their mechanical butts.*

The blast did more than that. From around the corner, Blaize heard the scream of overstressed wood and then a crash as at least part of the scaffolding fell. Then came the grinding of stone against stone, a rumble, and finally a roar as the stone the Imperials had intended to steal collapsed in a sort of landslide down the miniature mountain.

Maybe some of the Golems might survive that.

But by the time they got themselves unburied, Blaize and the others would be leagues away.

Chapter 17

If escape had been difficult, the swing around Caero was even worse. Valerian did his best to change their appearance—his most of all. He hacked off his long hair and used some sort of nut oil to color it brown. The distinctive gray cloak was left where the Rebels had stolen and sunk several boats. With luck, the Imperials might believe their quarry had crossed the river and concentrate the search there.

Even so, they had to go well west of the city to avoid enemy patrols. "I'd say we managed to get the stick right in the middle of the hornets' nest." Valerian actually stood on his saddle, using the height of his horse to give him a better view of the surrounding country.

Blaize would never try that trick, even with a horse he'd ridden for months. Attempting it on an animal of less than a day's acquaintance seemed like an excellent way to get thrown on one's head.

But Valerian's mount submitted meekly. Maybe the Wylden Elf had some special way with animals. Or maybe the Smiling Devil had already scared any defiance out of his horse.

Valerian leaped from the saddle to the ground and began leading the way through the stubble of a recently harvested field. "No one in sight," he said. "And if anyone turns up, we'll tell them we're manuring for the next planting."

"I'm sure the Imperials will believe that," Blaize said.

"Perhaps not," the Elf admitted. "But I saw a path going through that unharvested grain yonder. The stalks are high enough to block anyone from seeing us."

Their circuitous route had some advantages. The depopulated countryside meant there were no villagers to see them pass. But it meant staying on guard for additional dangers besides Imperial patrols. Visions of hungry Lizard-men kept rising in Blaize's mind when they had to ford a river.

At last they reached the stony quarry region, and Blaize began to recognize landmarks. When they came to the vantage point on the side of the hill, he reined in for a look.

The scene below was much altered. Blaize had estimated perhaps a quarter of the city had suffered from the fires started by the Imperials. From here, though, it seemed a good half of the dun-colored adobe buildings had disappeared in a huge blackened swath. The dustwinds had blown the flames right into the temple district, although the stone buildings had fared better. Otherwise, the fire might have extended right to the Port Gate.

"The Empire rules with a heavy hand," Valerian said, joining Blaize.

"I never saw anything as raw as this out west—or even in Down Town." Blaize could already see teams of tiny figures hauling away wreckage, even though funnels of smoke still rose from other parts of the devastated area.

"Oh, you wouldn't see it in Down Town," Valerian said. "Too many nobles and faction leaders own real estate thereabouts. Most of the land here is in local hands. That makes it expendable."

He shifted his gaze farther north, to the pyramids. The wound gouged into the smallest one had grown larger and more jagged. There was no trace of scaffolding to be seen. "Looks as though we've also delayed their stone-stealing operation."

"Yes," Blaize said. "I think our visit here will be long remembered."

"Though our next journey may be more memorable." Valerian's voice was barely audible as he looked out over the destruction. Then he twitched his horse's reins. "Come on. Let's join up with Snow and Sarah."

They'd gathered fresh fodder on the way up to the quarry.

But the packhorses inside were far too eager to get at the feed. Valerian frowned. "Those horses shouldn't be acting so hungry. And we should have been challenged by now. Let's get into that cave."

"Rikka? Sigwold? Sarah? Snow!" Eginhard burst into the lead, worry sounding in his shouts.

"Father?" Rikka appeared from behind a pile of rock fragments, a crossbow in her hands. "Where were you? We expected you by daybreak at the latest. I was afraid I'd have to—"

"Where are Snow and Sigwold?" Valerian interrupted.

"Sarah sent them on ahead. In case—" She paused, struggling to control herself. "In case you didn't come."

Valerian's voice grew sharp. "And she didn't go on herself?"

That didn't fit in with the Sarah Blaize knew, even on their short acquaintance.

"She couldn't. A building fell while we were getting away. Sarah was hurt."

With an exclamation, Valerian was past Rikka, ignoring the crossbow in her hands. Eginhard ran after the Elf. Blaize stayed to relieve Rikka of her weapon. She sagged against him, and he put an arm around her waist.

Rikka looked as if she'd had no time for sleep or even washing herself since they'd parted yesterday. Her red hair was a rat's nest, she smelled of smoke, sweat . . . and Rikka.

To Blaize, she seemed the most desirable woman in all the Land.

"At least all of you escaped," she said.

Blaize shook his head. "Not all."

Rikka raised her eyes to scrutinize the riders as they went past them into the cave. "Tulwar?"

Unwillingly, he told her the story of Tulwar's final fight.

"To the Pit with every Imperial!" Rikka swore. "And their Tezla-be-damned machines!"

Blaize didn't mention that she had mixed mythologies in her imprecations, or that she'd called upon the Atlantean deity to crush his own works.

Certainly, Blaize didn't mention that *he* was an Imperial.

Instead, he said to Rikka, "Tulwar told me to stay away from the wine."

That brought a sort of smile to her downcast, tearstained face.

"He also told me to make you happy."

Rikka looked up, her eyes going wide.

"I suspect Tulwar had some hopes along those lines for himself," Blaize said. "Not that I can blame him. He died as a true comrade—and his final thought was of you."

She met his eyes slowly. "And that wish?"

"Is something I'd undertake for myself, not to honor Tulwar," Blaize replied, his voice tight. This was considerably harder than leading a charge. "But I promise you, I'd do my best—for you and for Kennet."

"I believe you would," she said quietly. "And I hope we can do something about that, when this whole affair is finished."

Their hands reached for one another, touched . . .

Valerian emerged from the cave. "Get your rest, girl," he told Rikka. "Your father and I will tend Sarah tonight. Tomorrow, you'll have to be fresh. We'll skirt Venetia, but leave the two of you in the town of Ragusta. They have a healing priestess there. While she gets Sarah back on her feet, we'll go on with the rest of the cargo."

"How do you know about this priestess?" Rikka asked.

"My falling out with the Wylden leaders didn't sever all my connections," the Elf replied.

"He still has some friends among the tree-lovers," Blaize translated. "This priestess must be very dedicated, to continue healing when Elementalists are proscribed in Atlantean territory."

"When it comes to Venetia, Imperial commands aren't exactly followed to the letter," Valerian pointed out. "I'd wager Themyskis is the most benign lawbreaker in the area."

He focused on Blaize. "You'd better get some rest as well. We still have most of the pack train, and we're shorthanded without the Caeronns who were supposed to join us."

Valerian retained his smile, but it looked pretty ghastly. "All of us face a long, hard ride getting to Atlantis."

"You make it sound as if we're expected there by a certain day," Blaize said.

His only reply was another pensive look from Valerian, then the Elf strode off to plan. Eginhard appeared to shepherd his foster-daughter away.

Left alone, Blaize shook his head and began to laugh. *I think we have an understanding, Rikka and I,* he thought. *We'll just have to find out when all this is over.*

Snow's mount stood hanging its head in the rain. In the saddle, Snow hunched as well, watching water dribble from the hood of his cloak. He clung to the rope that tethered the lead packhorse. After more than almost two weeks of unremitting toil, Snow felt little better than a beast himself.

Sigwold rode back, leading a packhorse that had broken loose from the string. "All the harsh words I ever said about those northern drovers—I take them back," he said. "This has *not* been an easy job."

Snow responded with a tired smile. Moving the powder barrels from Varsfield, meeting the Orcs with their load, fighting Imperials and Mage Spawn had merely been hard work. Carrying on with just the two of them after the disaster in Caero—that had wrung them out. They'd only taken a few of the strongest horses, carrying as many powder barrels as possible. But keeping an eye out for external dangers, riding herd on the train, caring for the horses, sleeping in snatches had all taken their toll.

After the first four days, talk had diminished to short warnings, grunts, and nods. Sigwold's comment was his longest speech in a week. Considering his usual spate of conversation, that alone showed how exhausted he was.

To make things worse, for the last day and a half they'd traveled under leaden skies with frequent cloudbursts. The softer margins of the road had turned to quagmire, so they'd traveled to the syncopation of clopping hooves on paving stones. Horses, human, and Dwarf all moved with downcast heads, either dripping or sodden.

Snow had to force himself to rein in, raise his eyes, and scan the horizon. He frowned. What was that in the sky ahead? One of those black anvil clouds that promised lightning as well as rain?

He sat for several minutes in the saddle, trying to track whether the cloud was heading in their direction. Finally he realized it wasn't moving.

The dark shape in the sky was anchored in place—and it wasn't a cloud.

It was the Floating City, Atlantis-in-the-Sky!

"Sigwold!" he called, shocked out of his half stupor. "There it is!"

"There what is?" the Dwarf's grouchy voice wanted to know.

"The city—Atlantis."

Squinting upward, Sigwold quickly spotted the unmoving shape in the heavens. He made an indeterminate grunt. "It will take"—he squinted a little harder, doing some sort of mental calculation—"the better part of two days before we get close to Down Town."

"That long?" Snow demanded.

"The Floating City is five hundred feet up above us. Land around here is pretty flat. Atlantis has to be at least fifteen leagues off—maybe more."

At this discouraging news, Snow lowered his head from the tantalizing smudge in the sky. "Then we've got a lot farther to go before I let myself get excited about it," he grumbled.

Rain and clouds dogged them all the miserable miles to the outskirts of Down Town. Atlantis-in-the-Sky became a larger presence. But where was the soaring city of crystal spires the poets all sang about?

Maybe the thick overcast robbed the Floating City of its glory. It's hard for the finest crystal to shine without sunlight.

Or maybe the poets lied, Snow thought.

It was possible. The only poets Snow knew sang for their suppers. Their songs could be bought for gold. And the Atlanteans had plenty of gold.

For Snow, the mile-wide city suspended in the air looked more like a gigantic fist upraised over Down Town, an omnipresent threat looming against a sullen sky.

Arriving at the gates of Down Town was almost an anticlimax.

Of course, there was the small business of getting past the gate guards. Sigwold had the papers—they'd figured this was a job for diplomacy.

Several squads of soldiers were examining shipments coming into the city and levying taxes. There was a difference between Atlantis and Caero, however. Merchandise destined for nobles and mages passed in untaxed.

Sigwold handed a sheaf of papers to the nearest Altem. The manifest showed a load of paint pigment arriving for the mansion of a Lord Ferank. Ferank was a real lord, and he had ordered an actual shipment. It had already been moved into the city piecemeal by Rebel sympathizers.

The guards opened a barrel to reveal grainy black powder. "Black paint?" The Altem in charge of the gate shrugged. But instead of passing them on, he cast an appraising eye along the pack train. "Lot of horses for so few hands."

Sigwold straightened in his saddle, but Snow spoke up. "Had a third feller with us," he said in a thick up-country accent. "Big green thing come out the river—et him."

The Altem frowned. "And where did this happen?"

"North a ways—a day's journey," Snow replied. "Big green thing, with teeth and all."

If he'd situated the incident closer to the city, the Altem might have to investigate. Instead, the Imperial decided it wasn't his responsibility and dismissed Snow's report as just another traveler's tale.

"And you didn't hire on a new hand afterward?"

Snow looked shocked. "Pay good silver after we done most of the work ourselves?"

Shaking his head over countrymen's tightfistedness, the Altem waved them in.

The first thing Snow noticed about the big city was the richness and variety of its stinks. They passed a slaughterhouse, a tannery, and an ironmonger's yard. He blew out a deep breath and said, "I begin to see why the folk who run things might prefer to float so far away from all this."

Sigwold glanced speculatively up at the bulk of Atlantis-in-the-Sky, cutting off what little sunlight was available. "The brains may reside up there, but the sinews of the Empire are down here. Be interesting to see what happens when—"

He abruptly shut up. "Let's be on with our business."

They moved out of the industrial zone into a residential area, cheap tenements, then island-castles of a higher class. Next came a ring of public buildings around a deep, bowl-like depression in the ground. This was where the palace-complex of Throne had stood before Tezla levitated it to become the centerpiece of Atlantis-in-the-Sky. The result was commonly called Tezla's Pit, although it wasn't quite as dire as Feshku's place of punishment.

The lowest part had been turned into a much-needed reservoir for the city, with the sloping sides supposed to be park land. In actuality, though, the park was filled with crude half structures where the poorest Down Towners lived.

The planned route should have skirted the pit, but a rumbling line of wagons blocked the way. Squads of guardsmen forced traffic—including the pack train—into a detour.

At last, however, they found an unblocked major street that took them in the right direction. Soon they came to an area of warehouses and cheap inns, centered on an open square. At one end stood a building whose hanging sign was marked with two grindstones.

"The Mills of Circumstance," Sigwold said.

He caught the eye of a boy outside the inn and tossed him a bit of silver. "Get Perrin," he called.

Perrin was a stocky Prieskan with threads of silver showing in his dark hair and beard. The innkeeper ran a neutral eye over the road-worn pair with the small pack train. "Looking for lodgings?" He appeared ready to stipulate payment in advance.

Snow pulled a thong from around his neck. "A lady asked me to show you this."

Perrin's eyes sharpened when he saw the ring. "You'll want to get your cargo stowed. We've a small storehouse next door."

He even helped them unload their horses before turning the animals over to his hostler. Rather than taking his guests to the common room, Perrin led the way to a small private parlor.

"Let's see this ring," he said, after they were seated with a couple of tankards.

Snow slipped the thong from around his neck and handed the ring to the innkeeper.

Perrin manipulated the false bezel and looked hard at the seal it had hidden. Then he glanced at the little pile of black powder that had fallen when he opened the ring. "Is that—?"

Snow took the candle stub set on the table and brought the flame close to the powder. The small heap vanished in a hiss and a flash, leaving a scar on the wooden tabletop.

"I'd heard rumors, but never seen it." The Prieskan shook his head. Wonder faded from his face, replaced with a look of calculation. "You can't have carried much of this powder with such a small pack train. Weapons have been trickling into the city for months. Lead has all but disappeared from Down Town—everything we can get our hands on we've been turning into bullets with those molds you sent. But unless they only use a pinch of your stuff, the weapons we've hidden in this neighborhood alone will use up what you've brought."

"We were sent in advance," Snow said.

"Advance?" Perrin repeated, letting some anger show. "The summer solstice is in two days. It's not like we'll have another chance at this. The Prophet-Magus' Grand Audience is the first time he's appeared in public for weeks."

Snow could feel muscles tightening in his belly. "He knows something?"

"He's received bad omens, if the rumors are to be believed," Perrin replied.

"Let's hope we can make them come true," Sigwold said in a low voice.

"My people won't be doing much if they don't have powder for their weapons," Perrin told them bluntly. "I've worked for years setting up an organization. We have groups all over the city waiting for the signal to rise. But they're not going to take on Imperial guardsmen with clubs, staffs, and the occasional rusty sword."

"The rest of the supplies will be here," Snow responded, hoping he was telling the truth. "We encountered a hitch on the road." He hesitated. "The lady was hurt."

Perrin sat up very straight in his seat. "She's not going to be here?"

"She'll be delayed," Snow said.

"But—but this is her plan. She was going to—" Perrin broke off. Some things were best not discussed, even in a private parlor. "Who will do the deed?"

Snow took a deep breath."Who was sent with her token?" he asked in return.

Perrin shot him a look with considerably more respect.

Maybe it was the haze of exhaustion from a week in the saddle, but Snow felt strangely calm, as if this whole conversation were unreal. "You have a way to get me—?" He hoisted a thumb upward.

The innkeeper nodded. "That was our first concern since this all started." He cast an appraising eye over Snow. "In a way, this makes things a little easier."

Perrin leaned forward. "But I'll need whatever gear you're bringing. That will have to be packed to escape at least a cursory search by the Imperials."

Snow nodded, rising from the table. "I'll fetch—"

"No need," Sigwold interrupted, throwing off his cloak to reveal a cloth bandoleer running from his left shoulder to his right hip. He shrugged himself free of the long package wrapped in oilcloth that had hung across his back.

"You carried that all the way?" Snow demanded.

The Dwarf nodded. "Muzzle-down—a good idea in all this rain." He smiled. "You can hide a surprising amount of stuff under a good, roomy cloak."

Setting his package on the table, Sigwold drew a knife and opened some of the stitching. First came a plugged cow's horn.

"Powder," the Dwarf said. "Check that the moisture hasn't gotten to it."

Next came a flat box. "Cartridges and extra ball."

Finally, he drew out a familiar weapon. It wasn't the Dwarven fuser rifle Snow favored, but the lighter weapon he'd tested back in Varsfield.

Snow ran a finger along the metal dragon that formed the trigger guard. "I remember this," he said.

"I didn't tell you at the time, but Sarah had it specially made. She intended to use it for . . . this enterprise."

Remembering how it had outshot his weapon of choice, Snow slowly nodded. "The proper tool for the proper job," he said.

Then he turned to Perrin. "How soon will it take to get it—and me—into place?"

"Tomorrow, I hope." Perrin paused, apparently choosing his words. "Our connection can be a bit . . . whimsical."

Snow gave the innkeeper a hard look. "Then why use him?"

"I suspect he thinks he's using us," Perrin replied. "And whimsy or not, it's our surest route to . . . up there." He shrugged. "You seem to have a pretty thick hide. I suspect you'll need it."

After a quick bath, Snow headed for the common room in search of food. Sigwold was already there, working on a bowl of stew. Snow ordered the same, with a tankard of ale.

"Do you think I have a thick hide?" he asked the Dwarf.

Sigwold shrugged. "I would have said a hard nose." He

looked at his human friend. "Or maybe just a good front. You sounded very positive with Perrin. But I think you're worried about Sarah . . . at the very least."

"We left her all but alone." Snow lowered his voice. "Who knows if the others got loose? I know Rikka is resourceful, but how could she move Sarah if she had to do it on her own?"

"With all the packhorses and crates, she could build a litter if she had to," Sigwold said. "But that's not all, is it?"

"I hate not knowing," Snow admitted. "All this past week, I kept expecting Valerian and the rest to catch up to us. At least they could have sent an outrider with a message. Tulwar could have ridden ahead. Even Blaize."

"They're shorthanded, too," Sigwold pointed out. "And they probably lost time making sure Sarah got to safety. Valerian would have made sure of that."

Snow surprised himself by laughing. "I guess he would, just like he took care of those two Necro assassins before he even met the lady."

"A good advertisement for his services," Sigwold said dryly, "especially since he was coming to her essentially as a sword for hire."

Snow frowned. "I'd say he's more than that now."

His Dwarven friend nodded. "Sarah has that effect on people. I remember this big farm boy who managed to escape from a Magestone mine."

"More muscles than brains?" Snow grinned, but that faded as he went on. "Without the Rebels, I'd probably be up in the mountains, ambushing travelers for a palmful of roadsilver. It was Sarah who brought us together, gave us a cause."

"And recognized that you had brains, as well as a cursed good eye with a fuser rifle," Sigwold added. "The same way she took a jeweler who made fripperies and offered me real work to do." He took a long draught from his own tankard. "Her belief in all of us has taken the plan to this step."

"A cursed large step," Snow muttered. As he came closer to accomplishing what he'd been dispatched to do, the enormity of it all threatened to overwhelm him. Perhaps the daughter of merchant-princes could plan and carry out this assassination. But for a raw lad who'd spent most of his life on a farm or in a mine pit to set his sights on such an eminent target . . .

Sigwold leaned forward. "You ken that Sarah is a good judge of folk. Things she's asked of me may have been challenges, but they've never been beyond me. If she feels you're the man to finish this business, that means you can do it."

Snow looked down at the congealing grease floating atop his stew, not sure what to say.

When he finally met the Dwarf's eyes, he merely got a bantering smile. The moment had passed.

"And where will you take that oversized thick hide after you finish stuffing it?" Sigwold asked.

"Upstairs to a soft bed," Snow answered immediately. "And if it rains tonight, I made sure I got the room that *doesn't* leak."

Chapter 18

VALERIAN spent the two weeks' ride from Caero to Atlantis cursing lost time—and lost riders. He kept the pack train moving with solicitous concern for the load-beasts . . . and absolute relentlessness toward his amateur drovers.

They had enough horses to give twenty men a full day's work. With only four companions, Blaize's world quickly shrank to loading and unloading casks, heading off strays, watching for robbers and Mage Spawn, and tumbling into sleep whenever he wasn't tapped for night-watch.

Oddly enough, this hellish trip was Harolt's time to shine. The Varsfielder might have been the weak link during the fighting and escape from Caero, but he made up for that on the weeks southward. Without his knowledge of load-beasts and how to shift them with only a small crew, they'd have lost days. Even Valerian deferred to him.

Blaize lost track of the date as he slogged through damp grayness. He could hear the noise of the Roa Vizorr, but the river was hidden behind a perpetual wall of fog. Tezla only knew what could be moving behind that. The only sign of passing time was that Valerian's habitual smile grew thinner, until it disappeared.

"Mother Earth swallow those bastards for getting Tulwar," the Elf muttered one day, blaspheming against his Elementalist beliefs.

"We could use another pair of hands," Blaize agreed in a spiritless voice.

"To the pit with that," Valerian said. "We could have sent him on ahead with word that we're coming."

He swore again, tugging on his reins to cut off a packhorse that had pulled away from the string.

Rain began to spatter more heavily as the Elf returned. "And Tulwar could have ridden back to help us out—maybe even brought reinforcements."

Their arrival at Down Town didn't feel like a homecoming for Blaize. The Floating City looked grim rather than majestic up there in the sky. Was it just the weather, or had Blaize's experiences in the outlands tarnished his whole view of the Empire?

The line made its way briskly enough toward the guardsmen at the gates. They were going over the merchandise of a caravan, the Altem assessing taxes. Just ahead of the pack train was a rustic wagon, crudely pegged together, resting on two solid roundels rather than spoked wheels. A tired-looking ox was yoked in front, led by an equally weary peasant. The cart was piled high with cabbages, atop which perched a young woman—the peasant's wife—who nervously twisted the ends of her kerchief.

"Payder," she begged her husband, "we could still go to one of the up-country fairs."

"We can sell the crop for a higher price here," Payder replied. "And we need the silver." He led the ox forward to a trio of Utems.

"What have we here?" one of the Imperials said. "A pair of dirt-grubbers with a cartload of disgusting Troll scat."

"Doesn't all look disgusting." One of the other guardsmen reached up, running a hand under the peasant woman's skirt.

She cried out, and her husband whirled. He got one step before a spear butt took him in the pit of the stomach, courtesy of the third Utem.

"You know, resistance to Imperial authority is punishable by death," the first guardsman told the peasants. "Unless you can offer some reason why we shouldn't." The second soldier continued his depredations.

The farmwife whimpered.

Blaize began to urge his horse forward, his hand drifting toward the hilt of his sword.

Valerian's mount suddenly blocked the way. For once the Elf wasn't smiling. His colorless eyes burned into Blaize's, conveying a silent message: *We're fighting a larger battle than stopping a single injustice.*

So Blaize stayed in place as the Utems amused themselves with Payder and his wife. The guards even dumped most of the cabbages under pretense of searching for contraband.

Blaize shut his eyes and tried to blot out the heartbroken cries ahead of him—and the coarse laughter. The irony made his head spin. As an Altem, he could stop this abuse of Imperial power. But it was just one instance of the rot in the Empire—again, the rebels were fighting a larger battle. They hoped to offer a decent alternative, which Blaize could destroy by giving them away to the guardsmen here. Yet that was something he now found he couldn't do.

This was, in its way, even more frightening than Karrudan's geas, because this compulsion came from Blaize's own heart. He suddenly felt cast adrift, from his family, his home, his army comrades. So much of what he'd believed in seemed *wrong*. But what seemed right? An uprising doomed to failure? If the Rebels had a ghost of a chance . . .

He moved along like a sleepwalker as the pack train reached the gate. At least they got a different team of guardsmen, who passed them through with only a desultory search. They had no interest in paint supplies supposedly destined for Lord Quintaine's real-estate holdings.

Blaize still felt numb as they entered the city. The only blessing as they moved through the streets of Down Town was that the rains had at least cleaned the pavements. Rubbish and ordure collected quickly in the public ways, in the poor sections especially. It was one of the hazards of walking patrol in Down Town.

But if the streets were cleaner, Blaize had to notice that the guardsmen were much more numerous, not to mention more arrogant. Every few blocks seemed to bring an encounter with a new patrol. And when they passed Tezla's Pit, Blaize saw the heavy stone walls surrounding the reservoir were thick with guards. The shantytown in the park had disappeared, replaced with a tent city in military ranks.

Scarbro doesn't want to waste time ferrying troops down if there's trouble, Blaize thought. *He has most of the garrison already in place down here.*

And it was all his fault—or rather, the fault of that first mage-writ he'd sent when he'd first arrived in Khamsin.

Blaize glanced at Valerian, who took in the military buildup with enigmatic eyes.

Maybe this will change their minds. An uprising against prepared troops would be slaughter.

Pushing his guilty thoughts away, Blaize busied himself riding herd on the pack animals as they followed the Elf. Soon enough, they were in the square facing the Mills of Circumstance. A small figure who'd been lounging in front of the inn leaped up—Sigwold.

The Dwarf disappeared inside, to return a moment later with Snow and a graying, thickset man who introduced himself as Perrin, the innkeeper. He was obviously more than that, Blaize suspected, as a group of young, tough-looking men joined them to help unload the packhorses.

After the travelers had cleaned up, they joined Snow, Sigwold, and Perrin for dinner in the inn's common room. Blaize noticed the rest of the place was full of hard young men eating almost silently.

Like troops on the eve of battle, he thought.

"Spirits be praised that you arrived," Perrin said, smiling through his thick beard.

Blaize caught the Prieskan's use of the old backcountry divinities instead of the official Atlantean religion.

But then, one couldn't go asking for Tezla's divine blessing while attempting to overthrow his Empire.

"We brought the whole load through," Valerian said, poking suspiciously at his stew.

Snow gave an impatient nod. "I'd expect no less from you. Tell us more about Sarah."

"She was well enough when we left her, though in pain." Valerian's usual hard smile softened slightly. "Well enough to show me the rough side of her tongue. Our Sarah intended to ride on with us as soon as my friend Themyskis had her sufficiently repaired to stay in a saddle. Feshku's Pit, she'd have ridden in a sledge!"

Snow smiled at this reassuring show of spirit. "But?" he asked.

"Themyskis isn't the kind to do a quick patching job. She said Sarah would have to stay until she was sure her healing had taken. There was some rather loud healer–patient discussion."

Blaize smothered a laugh. That was a mild description for the clash of wills between the two determined women.

"And Sarah lost?" Sigwold said in disbelief.

"Themyskis put her to sleep, and the rest of us ran like cowards," Valerian admitted. "I'm afraid Sarah will have some harsh words for me when next we meet."

"Which will probably be sooner rather than later, if I know the lady," Eginhard rumbled. "Riding alone, she and Rikka will be able to make better time than we did leading a bunch of burdened horses."

"And she'll be setting off stronger and more healed," Valerian agreed.

"Sarah would hate missing tomorrow's . . . festivities," Snow said slowly.

"Especially since she's been planning the event for years." Sigwold turned to Valerian. "But she'd never forgive herself if she was forced to be late with the party favors."

"Well, we'll have plenty of folk eager to use what you brought," Perrin said. "And more."

Eginhard cast a professional's eye around the room. "If they're all like the lads you have here, we should be able to give the Imperials a royal black eye."

Perrin nodded. "If we keep to the plan."

"Sarah would expect no less, whether she was here or not," Snow said. "And since my part of the plan begins before dawn, I think I'll leave you now."

His face was somber as he rose from his place and headed upstairs.

"There goes a brave man," Perrin said quietly.

Sigwold nodded. "Sarah handed him a heavier responsibility than he's ever carried before." The Dwarf smiled. "But he has the shoulders to manage it."

Perrin, Sigwold, Valerian, and Eginhard all exchanged grim, knowing looks. Harolt looked puzzled, while Jon Bowman maintained his usual imperturbable mask.

Blaize hoped his face didn't show the frustration he felt. He'd all but decided to throw in his lot with these oddly assorted adventurers. He just wished he knew what they were talking about.

The great day came with a watery but clearing sunrise. Whether it was an oddity of the weather or some potent Technomancy, Blaize had no idea.

Certainly, the masters of the Atlantis Guild wouldn't want rain showers marring the program for the Grand Audience. All the great and powerful would be gathered to celebrate the Empire's glory, as concentrated in the person of the Prophet-Magus. Karrudan would come forth to receive petitions, offer the words of Tezla's Avatar, and accept the ovations of the ruling elite and as many common folk as could fit in Temple Palace Square.

Meanwhile, the downtrodden folk below the Floating City will express their own opinions about the Empire—and probably get killed for them. Blaize poured water from a pitcher into the basin in his room, sluicing the tepid liquid onto his face.

The closer it came to the time to act, the more this whole uprising seemed like a mad, hopeless undertaking.

His silver medallion clanked against the heavy pottery bowl, reminding him of another alternative.

No. That would merely open the door to another bloodbath, where the victims wouldn't even have the chance to fight back.

Blaize was suddenly glad that Rikka was off with Sarah,

wherever that might be. At least she wouldn't be in Atlantis when this maelstrom began.

The door burst open, and Blaize pivoted to grab his sword. He had it half out of its sheath before he recognized Sigwold, his face almost crimson.

"Sarah's here!" the excited Dwarf announced, then raced on to the next room.

Blaize slammed the blade back in place.

So much for that hope.

Pain had sharpened Sarah Ythlim's aristocratic features into even higher relief. She might be tired, but she stood straight as she conferred with her chief subordinates. Blaize lurked at the fringe of the group, listening with only half an ear, given Rikka's presence.

She gave him a brief smile, but mostly devoted herself to the business of rebellion.

"We're all glad to see you, Sarah," Perrin said. "I know Snow would have been gladdest, but he's already set off. By now, he may well be in place. Your cargo has already been distributed. We only await the signal."

"You've all done well." Sarah glanced at Valerian. "Even you, you conniving Elf." She placed a delicate hand on her side. "The burns are gone, but the bone is still knitting. Themyskis held me as long as she could, still dubious whether I was fit enough to ride . . . but I was determined to be here."

"You rode hard enough to arrive in time," Rikka said. She, too, looked travel-worn, the skin of her face tight over her bones.

But then, she had the task of ensuring that Sarah arrived whole and well. *Such responsibility would be enough to exhaust anyone,* Blaize thought.

"Even if I can't have the place I wanted, I won't miss the fight," Sarah said emphatically. "When does Karrudan come forth?"

"It will be late in the ceremony," Perrin said. "Three o'clock, our people say."

"Then I have some time to rest, build up my strength," Sarah said. "Do you have a room for me?"

"Prepared as soon as you arrived," Perrin said. "Right at the top of the stairs."

"Then all I need is someone to help me get there." Sarah glanced around the group. "Blaize, would you mind?"

"Me?" Blaize hoped he wasn't gaping. "No. Of course I'll help."

Sarah took his arm and rested against it as she made her way up the stairs. Blaize noticed how carefully she moved. How could she have handled all those hours in the saddle?

He opened the door to the upstairs room and helped her inside. Sarah sighed as she sank onto the bed. "Kindly close the door."

Blaize was halfway out, swinging the door behind him, when Sarah called, "With you still inside, please."

He reentered the room and shut the door.

"Valerian and I had a brief conversation about you while we were in Ragusta," Sarah said, "about how you saved me one moment, then rushed after my gray cloak with an upraised sword. He told me I should either make sure of your loyalty or kill you."

Blaize felt his hands tighten into fists. "And have you decided?"

Sarah nodded. "I'm going to trust you, even if there are strong reasons not to," she said decisively. "You're a very competent fighter, who turned up . . . most fortuitously."

He nodded, feeling beads of sweat appear on his forehead.

"Everything you've done—getting into Khamita Castle, the cavalry skirmish, discovering the Imps, and fighting the Lizard-men—all of that was very professional—more the work of an Altem Guardsman than a lowly Utem."

She looked at him thoughtully. "The only uncharacteristic thing about you was your episode of drunkenness after being asked to join the journey south. Perhaps you were upset, and the wine truly went to your head. Or you may have set out to denounce us."

Blaize opened his mouth to protest, but Sarah waved that away. "I have no doubt you were sent to seek us out. Perhaps you were dispatched by Karrudan, or maybe by one of the other Imperial factions who take the prophecies more seriously than he does."

"Both," he croaked out, glad of the chance to confess at last. "I'm an Altem of the Atlantis garrison—"

"And as such, a remorseless servant of the Empire," Sarah finished. She smiled. "But it seems we infected you with, at least, doubts about that service, doesn't it? You had your chances to betray us and risked your life to help us instead. You leaped to attack the patrol that had us in Caero. And Valerian told me how you responded to an incident here at the gates. Instinctively, you wanted to do the right thing. Our Elven friend is a great one for instincts."

Her lips pursed. "And then there's the question of Rikka."

Blaize tried to show nothing, but Sarah's head-shake told him he'd failed. "Your eyes give you away," she said. "Do you love her?"

"Ye—" His voice came out as a squeak. "Yes."

"Can you see a life for her and her son in the Empire?"

Blaize shook his head.

"So you can understand our cause, even if you think it's hopeless."

That got his attention.

"Suppose, though, we had a better chance of success than you believe?" Sarah asked.

"But how?" Blaize asked.

"You haven't seen our weapons, but you have seen our methods," Sarah replied. "Small groups have been working for years, laying the groundwork for rebellion. We won't topple the Empire overnight; we don't expect to. But with the word of Karrudan's assassination, we'll light a blaze that the Imperials will never quench."

"Assassination? Is that the business Snow has gone off on?" Blaize asked.

Sarah nodded. "He'll accomplish it, too. And when he does, Down Town will go up. We'll beat the garrison, in spite of the reinforcements." Her quiet confidence was more convincing than any bluster or speechifying.

"You sound so sure." Blaize faltered. "But the whole idea seems—"

"Mad?" Sarah finished for him.

And you want me to be loyal to this? Blaize wondered.

"I do have one concern, though," Sarah went on. "If the Down Town garrison is on such an alert, the guardsmen above must be pressed to even greater vigilance. I know Snow will get in . . . "

Then Blaize understood.

"But he'll have trouble getting out, unless he has help," he finished. He frowned. "Snow saved my life. What can I do to help?"

"You could become a guardsman again . . . for a little while," Sarah said.

"Long enough to get Snow out of Atlantis-in-the-Sky." Blaize thought for a moment. "I believe I can swing getting back to duty. Beyond that"—he shrugged—"I'll just have to improvise. Where would I find Snow?"

Sarah named a building on the far end of Temple Palace Square from the portico where the Prophet-Magus would appear. Blaize looked dubious. "What is Snow going to be able to do from there? Call a curse down on Karrudan?"

"You'll see when you get there." Her enigmatic smile turned to a look of concern. "When will you go?"

"Right now," he replied. "If people want reports and things, that may take some time."

"Good luck, Blaize," Sarah said as he went through the door.

Rikka stood waiting on the other side. Blaize pulled up short, then shut the door behind him.

"What did Sarah want?" she asked quietly.

"I'm going up to help Snow," Blaize said.

Her eyes went wide in disbelief. "What? How are you expected to do that?"

Blaize took a deep breath. "I'll be able to do it because the Imperials still believe I'm an Altem Guard. I was sent off on detached duty to find Rebels. What I found—was you."

Rikka snatched for a knife hilt, her face a cold, chiseled

mask. "You're an *Imperial*?" Although her blade didn't come out, her tone couldn't have cut Blaize any deeper.

"I was—*was,*" he repeated in an agony of confession. What good would a new life be if he lost Rikka?

"Sarah and Valerian figured out what I was. That's why Sarah wanted to talk to me. I've joined—they're giving me a chance to prove myself." *You're babbling,* he thought. *Slow down.*

Rikka was not impressed. "The more fools they," she said. "You lied to them, to all of us—to me. Are you even a Caeronn?"

"I grew up in Atlantis-in-the-Sky," he admitted. "The face of the Empire is different up there. It wasn't until I was with you . . . you opened my eyes."

Her face was still closed and angry.

"I was doing my duty," he said uncomfortably, hoping she would understand. "What I thought was the right thing to do."

"And why are you telling me now?" Rikka demanded.

"Because now I'm free to. Comrades don't lie to comrades," Blaize said simply. He hesitated. "And I thought—hoped—we were more than comrades."

He gazed into her eyes, hoping for acceptance and, perhaps, forgiveness. "I did wrong, and I'm sorry for that. I've renounced the Empire, I'm leaving that whole life behind me. Sarah's offered me a chance to do the right thing. I'm not lying about this—I want a new life with you if I come back. And if I fail—" He paused for a second. "—I wanted our last words together to be the truth."

They stood in silence for a moment, then Rikka spoke. "I suppose I should be glad you told me," she said in a small voice. "It's just—we're trying to shift the world. So many large things are going on—"

"What's between us is no small thing," he said.

Rikka nodded, making a determined effort to pull herself together. "If I get a vote, I hope that you succeed. I . . . I want you to come back, Blaize."

"And I want to come back to you, Rikka." He opened his arms, hoping she didn't see them shaking.

They moved together, holding tight, and kissed.

Rikka stirred in his embrace, brushing at her travel-stained clothes. "Why is it that whenever we get close, I'm always such a mess?"

He smiled. "Just lucky, I guess?"

Her laugh choked a little. "I hope you stay that way."

The sun wasn't yet up when Snow arrived for the rendezvous with whoever was going to get him into Upper Atlantis. Perrin had provided him with rough, worn workmen's clothing, a set of passwords, and the useful information that he'd be meeting an Elf.

Snow had some choice words about Prieskans and their national sense of humor as he walked through the predawn streets. He'd expected to meet his contact near a liftgate. Instead, he was directed to a wharf on the Roa Vizorr.

The ungodly hour wasn't that bad. Snow had grown up on a farm. He knew what it was like to start working early. Seeing the fisher folk returning home as the sun rose, however, that was really strange.

"Are your aspirations upward?" a voice asked from behind him.

Snow spun—and found himself looking up at a face that would have been more at home on an idealized statue.

It was an Elf, all right—one who made Valerian look coarse.

The tall, regal figure looked down at Snow as if he'd just detected something unpleasant stuck to the sole of his boot.

"Must I repeat myself?" the Elf demanded.

"Ah—no. My fate is in the skies," Snow said lamely.

"I am Lord Daraton." The Elf sounded as if he were conferring a great honor by giving his name.

Knights Immortal. The words seemed to leap into Snow's head. He decided to act on his hunch. "You're a long way from the snowcapped Rivvenheim, my lord."

The just-stepped-in-something expression on Daraton's

face seemed to curdle at the mention of his mountain homeland. "I serve Prince Hamund with his embassage to the rulers here."

"Then why are you doing a favor for us?" Snow asked curiously. "Obviously you don't like—"

"I serve Prince Hamund," the Elf interrupted tonelessly.

Snow suddenly remembered Perrin's last comment. "We're a royal whim?"

The barest hint of a frosty smile twitched Daraton's lips. "Perhaps the prince has difficulty discerning one tribe of humans from another."

Calling the Empire a tribe—that was pure High Elf arrogance.

Daraton demonstrated more, snapping his fingers and beckoning. "Let us be on with it."

Fuming, Snow silently followed the Elf to another wharf, where a string of humans awaited with various boxes and bundles.

Porters, Snow realized.

Daraton pointed. "*That* is for you."

The square crate was half as tall as Snow, and heavy as he hefted it. "Does it have to be—"

"You cannot handle the load, human?"

Ignoring the Elf, Snow turned to the porters. "Anyone have some rope?"

They proceeded through the streets, Snow nearly bent double under the weight of the crate. A loop of rope ran from his forehead to the top rear of the box, helping him hold his burden in place.

Daraton seemed in no rush to reach the nearest liftgate plaza. But then, hurry probably played no part in the High Elf image. Sweat beaded on Snow's face and stained his jerkin while Daraton spoke with the guards. Then the Elf and his porters stepped into the three concentric circles of dull stone that marked the actual gate.

Snow had heard them described, though he'd never actually seen one before. When the whole group was in place, the inner stone circle suddenly turned a brilliant emerald green. Beneath his feet, Snow knew that buried Magestone was charging to send them upward.

The brilliance shifted to the next stone ring, then the outermost ring ignited in emerald fire. Suddenly, the whole group was impelled into the air on the circle of stone.

A soft moan went through most of the porters, who directed their eyes upward. Daraton watched Snow, who, thanks to his posture, was looking almost straight down. Their movement wasn't all that noticeable, except for Snow's peripheral view of the ground steadily receding beyond the edge of the circle. A new rush of sweat drenched his jerkin, and it had nothing to do with the strain of his burden.

"Interesting, in an ostentatious sort of way," Daraton commented, watching the shimmer of magic.

Snow wondered how much of the crate he might force up the supercilious Elf's nose. Or still better, he could use the rope to tie Daraton to the oversized box and send both of them tumbling back to the ground.

They arrived at their destination, a circular opening in the immense flying shield that was Atlantis. Lambent green light flashed around them in three expanding circles. Then the fire died, to reveal pavement as solid as if it stood on the ground so far below.

"Set those loads aside," a voice ordered. "They'll have to be searched."

Daraton glared at the young mage-officer. "As I explained to the Altem below—"

"All incoming items must be searched, by order of Lord Scarbro."

"Including those going to our embassy?" the Elf demanded. "Prince Hamund is giving a feast tonight in honor of this Grand Audience. If anything spoils . . ."

The young mage seemed caught between two dangers, a lord and a prince.

"If you must muck about, why not choose a large parcel?" Daraton smacked the crate that Snow carried. "This one, perhaps."

Three guardsmen moved to shift the oversized box. Snow straightened, trying to keep the strain from his face. What was Daraton up to? Or was this another Elvish eccentricity?

An Altem levered up the wooden top, then swore under his breath as he uncovered—ice.

"Well, dig in, man," Daraton ordered.

A guardsman began inserting the point of his sword.

"Carefully! You don't want to destroy any of them!"

Gritting his teeth, the Altem dug in with his fingers and unearthed a large, openmouthed fish.

"Faugh!" the guardsman cried, dropping the scaly creature and wringing his hands.

"Do you want to try the flame-melons next?" Daraton inquired. "We also have several crocks of honeyed jerboas."

The mage-officer had had enough. "Pass on," he said shortly.

Snow repaired his box and lumbered off. He was wheezing gently when they finally stood in the embassy courtyard, outside the kitchens. The other porters were gone by the time Snow got free of his encumbrance.

Straightening himself by degrees, he haltingly asked Daraton where he could find tools to reopen the crate.

"I wouldn't do that," the Elf said. "Chef will be annoyed enough to discover his fish have been tampered with."

"Then . . . where—?" Snow still fought to catch his breath.

Daraton pointed to a burlap-wrapped cross-pole one of the porters had used to carry sacks of vegetables. Snow removed the burdens and then the sacking, revealing a familiar oilcloth bundle.

The Elf made a dismissing gesture. "Farewell, human."

Snow walked off, wishing he could risk practicing his marksmanship before completing his job.

He had a wonderful target in mind.

CHAPTER 19

AFTER a stiff walk, Blaize arrived at the nearest liftgate plaza to find it thronged with people. Most entrances to the plaza were blocked, and a line snaked down a side street as guardsmen examined those trying to get to the upper city.

Blaize strolled down the street until he could see the head of the line. A troupe of musicians set to play for a nobleman's feast showed a letter of passage and entered. A shabby-looking juggler got the truncheon ends of several guardsmen's spears and was hurled at Blaize's feet.

"Probably hoping to steal purses in the crowds," growled the Altem in charge. He gave Blaize a long, skeptical look, pausing to take in the short sword hanging from its baldric. "And what's your business here, vagabond?" Blaize leaped to attention, snapping a crisp salute.

"Altem Blaize Audrick's son, on detached duty for Lord Scarbro, returning to report," he said.

"This is not a day for foolery," the Altem said, his eyes growing harder.

"Lord Scarbro sent me on a special reconnaissance. I bring news from Caero—and beyond."

"Any city loafer knows how to salute and play soldier." The guardsman scowled uneasily.

"Send to the lord's office and see what orders return," Blaize replied.

Such confidence obviously unnerved his fellow Altem, who finally asked Blaize for his name again, sending off one of his Utems to confer with higher authority.

"If you are playing the fool, you'll end up envying that

one," the Altem said, pointing to the bruised, groaning juggler limping away.

A guardsman stood with one hand on Blaize's shoulder and the other on his sword hilt until the red-faced Utem came puffing back. "You're to bring him to the gate, sir—immediately."

Staring at Blaize as if he'd suddenly grown antlers and fangs, the Altem sent two guardsmen ahead. Then he gestured for Blaize to precede him, maintaining a hold as if he wasn't sure whether he was escorting a person of importance or a prisoner.

They ignored murderous looks while bypassing folk who'd obviously been waiting a considerable time for their turn at the gate. Muttering began. And if the comments became too loud and pointed, the Utems responded freely with their spear butts.

A young mage-officer stood at the transport-circle—Emillon, Blaize's former company commander. "Back at last, eh? They're most eager to see you up above."

He added Blaize to the latest batch of traffic, and in moments Blaize found himself standing on the golden pavement of the Imperial city.

Another squad of guardsmen surrounded him, marching him to Scarbro's office.

The commander of the Atlantis garrison was strapping on full armor as Blaize entered. Scarbro dismissed everyone else from the room. "Did I miss a mage-writ or two, Altem?" the older man demanded. "The last word we got was from Khamsin, a good four weeks ago if not more. What have you been doing?"

Blaize stood at attention and gave his report, a bare but honest recitation of the facts—as far as Caero.

"The burning of the city took most of the Rebel leaders and their pack train," he said. "A few guards and drovers were arrested, while a bare handful escaped, running northward. I spent several days trying to make any sort of contact and failed. It seems whatever organization the Rebels might have had, it was destroyed. I then reported to the governor.

Since whatever plot might have been afoot was obviously wrecked, he ordered me to Atlantis to report."

"And the mage-writ?" Scarbro said.

Blaize did his best to keep his face blank—just like a subordinate having to comment on a political rather than military situation. "Since he apparently regarded it as a dead issue, perhaps Lord Tackett didn't consider such a report worth the expense." He sighed. "And then . . . the fires got out of control, burning down a very large section of the city."

"An embarrassment for Chief Magistrate Khiza. Nor would Tackett want to admit his part in such a failure," Scarbro said, leaping to the conclusion Blaize had hoped he would. "Even so, it's very unusual for him to flout Karrudan's will."

Blaize just maintained his brace and his blank expression.

Scarbro stepped from behind his desk and began to pace the office. "What did you make of the mood in Down Town?"

"Little enough, sir—I didn't loiter to talk to anyone. Although I did notice the expanded patrols."

The commander shook his head, frowning. "Whatever we may have crushed up north, there's still deviltry afoot in the city." He tapped the armor he'd put on. "Your message arrived just as I was about to go down and take personal command." Scarbro's gaze grew speculative as he looked at Blaize. "I've seconded my best security people to Lord Jethren—"

Blaize knew the name—Jethren commanded the bodyguard detachment protecting the Prophet-Magus. He held his breath. What if he were detailed there?

"So I could use some people around me whom I can trust," Scarbro finished. "Draw full kit, armor, and weapons. You'll report at my command center by the reservoir."

Blaize snapped a salute. "Request permission for a brief visit to my family, sir. I'd like to let them know I'm back in Atlantis. Also—" he allowed himself a slight grin—"I have a uniform that fits stored in their place."

"You may get that nice uniform dirty if the dust-folk

rise." Scarbro smiled back, then he nodded. "Go. Just keep the visit brief. Dismissed."

Blaize saluted and made his escape. There was much he had to accomplish and not much time, especially if Scarbro should send a mage-writ to Caero to check on the report he'd just received.

Walking up the stairs in the island-castle to his parents' apartment, Blaize had a moment of apprehension. What if Father had decided to stay home today? The Grand Audience was a celebration of politics and Imperial glory rather than a religious holiday. Audrick had never interrupted his work for a festival before.

But Father's not as young as he used to be, Blaize reminded himself. *He might have decided to avoid the crowded streets and take an easy day at home.*

Blaize hoped not. What he had to do would be hard enough without his father's presence.

When he knocked on the apartment door, his worry turned out to be for nothing. Laure answered, looking at him in surprise. "Blaize! Are you back in Atlantis? Your father will be pleased—he's in his offices right now. Can you stay for a meal? It won't be anything exciting. The markets are a madhouse, and I'm afraid all the eateries will be crowded for the festival."

"I'm afraid I can't stay, Mother. I just came to get my uniform."

Her welcoming smile grew more fragile. "They're putting you right into duty? Will you be posted up here in the city?" She paused. "Or in Down Town?"

Blaize tried a gently teasing voice as they went to his former room. "How would you know anything about Down Town?" he said. "You haven't been near a liftgate in years."

"Your father and I used to go down below fairly often, visiting his colleagues in their country villas. It was pleasant to go forth among the greenery." Laure's reminiscent smile faded. "Traveling out there, though, we had to pass through Down Town. Audrick got so he wouldn't set foot down there.

He said it was dangerous, that the people living there were like animals."

Her lips set in a straight line. "Treat people like animals, and you shouldn't be surprised if they respond in kind. How they must hate us, looking down at them."

She gave Blaize a very direct look. "It will be bad down there, won't it? Worse than just riots?"

He stopped trying to tease her along. "What makes you think that?"

"They've all but stripped the city of soldiers up here," Laure said somberly. "That can't be a good sign."

"I'm afraid there'll be fighting, maybe for a long time." Blaize pulled a fat purse from his satchel, half the savings he'd withdrawn from the army bank. "Things may be seriously disrupted—food could get very expensive . . ."

"You won't be back." Laure's gaze was very steady as she spoke.

"I don't know when I'll get back," Blaize said carefully.

"Because you won't be fighting for the Empire."

Whatever soothing words Blaize might have uttered seemed to freeze in his chest.

"I think you're right." Laure shook her head. "Your father loves the Empire. He's blind to its faults. But somewhere, things began going wrong. Maybe it was when they enslaved the Dwarves, or when the Elementalists were banished. Or maybe it was before then. The Empire was supposed to use magic to protect the simple folk. Is that what's happening in Down Town? We might live pleasantly enough up here, but the smell still wafts our way. And I don't mean the Down Town stinks that people complain about. Something is rotten in the Empire. And if you're going to war, you can't defend that."

She gently kissed him on the cheek. "Fight for what's right, son, with your mother's blessing. And I'll pray to the gods that someday we'll see you again."

Blaize held her tightly for a long moment, made sure she took the purse, and set off back to the military zone.

He'd need armor and weapons for what came next.

. . .

Snow pushed against the trapdoor that led to the roof of the building. On normal days, the place housed administrative offices connected with the temple next door. Today, though, the place was empty. The people who usually manned the cramped desks and cubbyholes must be outside, helping to swell the crowd standing in the square.

Perrin had arranged for Snow to get into the place as a replacement on the janitorial staff. While cheers from the mob outside resounded through the building, Snow had pushed a broom, working his way upward toward the roof.

Now, standing under the open sky, he felt a sudden tremor of fear. Snow crouched, leery of exposing himself to view from the square below. He made his careful way to the frieze that edged the front of the structure, scanning the other rooftops before ducking down.

Some of the buildings closer to Throne Palace had guards on their roofs. Here on the far side of the square, such security had been dispensed with. The point where Snow knelt was four times beyond effective crossbow range from the planned site of Karrudan's appearance. A longbow might reach Throne Palace's portico, but the bowman would have to stand outlined against the sky to get his shot. That would make him a target for magical blasts and everyday crossbow bolts.

Shielded by his magic and his guards, Karrudan might count himself unassailable by mundane weapons.

Snow's only protection was a stone parapet, luck . . . and a weapon the Empire had never seen before. Kneeling, he unslung the oilcloth package from his back. He removed the fuser rifle and the box of cartridges. That was when the shakes overtook him.

The twists of paper filled with black powder charges and bullets flew loose, landing helter-skelter on the roof. Snow scrabbled to reclaim them, chagrined.

Maybe this job is just too big for a great lump of a plowboy, he thought. *Guarding barrels might be more fitting.*

Certainly, I managed that well enough from Varsfield to Khamsin—even to Caero.

But the new responsibility laid on him after the disaster in Caero—he'd spoken bravely enough that night. But here, in Atlantis, in the pitiless light of day . . .

It's the thinking on it, he realized. *Two weeks on the trail, I was too exhausted to consider the whys and wherefores.* And when it finally began to penetrate his thick head last night, Sigwold had been there with encouragement.

Now Snow stood alone. What recommended such a one as him for so vast a deed? His wide shoulders? His strength? His aim? To turn the Land on its head, create a world without precedent—

Then perhaps it's time to create a precedent. A blaze of defiance rose in the back of Snow's brain. *Everywhere else, even among the Elves and Draconum, the great of the Land decree and rest of the people are dragged along like thralls. Maybe the ones they treat like dust should express their will. What was it Rikka said that night in the quarry? About it being better to strike a blow for many folk than for one person's vengeance?*

Snow swung round, sitting with his back to the low parapet, replacing the gathered cartridges. His hands were skillful and steady as he began the ritual of loading. Grasping the tail of the dragon-figured trigger guard, he twisted. The threaded bolt moved easily, unscrewing to create a well leading to the breech of the weapon.

Setting his teeth in the paper of the cartridge, Snow tore it open. He dropped the bullet into the well, letting it roll forward to block the rifled barrel. Then he dribbled most of the black power into the breech as well.

A countertwist on the trigger guard set the bolt back in position. Finding a few crumbs of powder clinging to the metal top of the bolt, Snow brushed them away. The last of the powder in the cartridge went into the priming pan.

Rising up on one knee, Snow risked a view of the square. A sea of humanity jostled in the space below. People were packed so tightly that their heads formed a strange sort of shifting pavement that extended right up to the steps of Throne Palace. There a line of guardsmen and mages held them back.

The clouds of recent days had either subsided or been magically whisked away, leaving brilliant sunshine for the climax of this great day. Beams of light angled down to give the portico maximum illumination. That was probably why Karrudan had chosen this hour to appear.

Excited cries broke from the crowd as more guardsmen filed into place at the top of the stairs. The folk below began chanting in one huge voice, "Karrudan! *Karrudan!* KARRUDAN!"

Then that monster voice dissolved into confused hurrahs as the Prophet-Magus put in his appearance.

The front of the temple had been polished, the columns garlanded, the spaces between hung with exquisite tapestries. Some of these stitched works of art represented years of effort by Atlantean needleworkers. Others were spoils of war, seized from conquered cities. They made a brave display but merely served as background for the focal point, which Karrudan now occupied.

Like all members of the Atlantis Guild, he was clad in purple and gold. But Karrudan's sumptuous robes were grander than any mage's garb. The purple silk was embroidered in various iridescent hues, creating shimmering designs that caught the eye. The cloth of gold gleamed in the sunlight. So did the gloves of finest silver mesh that covered the Prophet-Magus' hands.

Walking forward into all this adoring noise, Karrudan gave his people an arrogant smile. He turned slightly, directing a sardonic comment to the guards officer at his side. Then he threw up his hands, palms outward, to quiet the mob.

Snow knew that the Prophet-Magus had a reputation for not speaking until all was hushed. And Tezla protect any unfortunate individual who spoke out when the head of the Atlantis Guild wanted silence!

As the crowd's noise died away, Snow lined up the sights of his fuser rifle on the Prophet-Magus' chest.

Karrudan opened his mouth. Snow never got to hear a word. He couldn't, not with his ears filled with the rushing of his own blood.

His heart pumped madly, as if tearing loose from its moorings inside his chest. But his hands were rock-steady as he squeezed the trigger.

The detonation of the weapon going off was like the thunder of some angry god. It penetrated the roaring in Snow's ears. He heard the sound of the blast echo off the stone fronts of the buildings lining the square.

Below, Karrudan seemed to move in preternaturally slow motion. He flinched, staggering back. One hand went to his chest. A bright red stain blossomed across the broad stripe of gold at his breast. Then the Prophet-Magus of the Atlantean Empire dropped without a word to the marble floor of the portico.

The echo of the shot was just dissipating as Snow replaced his gear in the oilcloth bandoleer, slinging it across his back.

A sickening, choked sound filled the square below—a multitude all struggling to draw breath together. Snow turned his back. Still crouched, he headed for the trapdoor in the roof.

Blaize kept his stride measured as he moved along the side street, passing a series of rear entrances much humbler than the gleaming fronts these buildings displayed on Throne Palace Square.

Don't run, he warned himself, *it only draws unwelcome attention.*

Most of the attention in this area right now was focused on the head of the square. Even through the buildings, he could feel the roar of what sounded like a single mighty voice chanting "Karrudan! *Karrudan!* KARRUDAN!"

The Prophet-Magus must have appeared, because the noise turned into a babble of individual cries. The noise died away just as Blaize reached his destination. He strained his ears, wondering if he'd catch any of Karrudan's speech.

Instead, he heard a great, rolling explosion. Even as it echoed, the sound was overtaken by a vast collective gasp from the hidden crowd. Then a terrible, terrified wail rose from thousands of throats up to the heavens.

Blaize faltered, the muscles in his trunk constricting as if a gigantic invisible hand were squeezing his guts to jelly. He fought to keep from collapsing in a retching heap.

The deed is done, he realized. *We face a new world now.*

He managed to stay upright, just reaching his destination as the rear door opened and Snow emerged. The big Northerner's face was pale, and he actually recoiled when he saw Blaize's uniform, one hand going for the knife in his belt.

Then he took in the familiar face and forced his hand away from the hilt. "Blaize?" he said in disbelief.

"Sarah sent me," Blaize replied crisply. "Get over here. I'm supposed to get you out, and we'll be seeing guardsmen in a moment."

No sooner had Snow made it to Blaize's side than they saw a flood of guardsmen come pouring around the corner.

"Sir," said an out-of-breath Utem, "have you seen anyone come out of that building?" He pointed to the door where Snow had just exited.

"No," Blaize said. "What was that noise we just heard?"

The soldier still seemed in the midst of a struggle to control his breathing. "The Prophet-Magus has been struck down. We've been ordered to seal off the area."

"Best put a guard on that door if you think there's an assassin inside," Blaize ordered. "My man and I will take the word to Lord Scarbro."

Now they had a reason to hurry. Blaize and Snow moved quickly out of sight.

In spite of their speed, though, word had preceded them to the nearest liftgate. A mage-officer barred their way, his authority backed by a line of spear-men. "By order of Lord Jethren, none are to leave," the mage said.

"We have urgent information for Lord Scarbro." Blaize let some of his frantic impatience show. "Events up here may have repercussions in Down Town."

The officer guarding the magic gateway looked as if he'd give much to hear exactly what events Blaize was talking about.

So, Blaize thought, *apparently the order has gone forth, but not the reason.*

Soon enough, though, Jethren or one of his subordinates would appear to question anyone trying to escape Atlantis-in-the-Sky. The Rebels might as well fling themselves into a five-hundred-foot fall as wait for that.

Blaize stood speechless as a slightly less desperate plan flared across his brain. One hand reached up to remove his Altem's helmet. The other went to his breast, tugging on a silver chain.

"Sir Mage," he said, "we travel on imperative business."

Blaize brought up the medallion and placed it by his brow.

The mage-officer's eyes nearly bulged out when he saw Karrudan's sigil. He turned to his men, snapping, "Clear a way."

All through their descent, Snow maintained a dazed silence, finally broken with fragments like "What—?" and "How—?"

Blaize shook his head. "Too long a story right now." To himself he said, *Even a dead Prophet-Magus beats a guard commander.*

CHAPTER 20

EVEN before they reached the ground, Blaize and Snow could hear shouts, cries, and sharp, barking explosions coming up from the streets below.

"It's started." Snow's grim expression lightened a bit. "I didn't know if they'd hear my shot in Down Town."

"But they obviously heard the outcry when Karrudan died," Blaize said. The folk in the square weren't the only ones to find the Prophet-Magus' death unthinkable. In the end, Karrudan himself hadn't been able to take the threat seriously, even with the prophecies.

They returned to solid earth to find an embattled Imperial company trying to improvise fortifications around the liftgate circles. "We tried to patrol the edges of the plaza," the mage-officer in charge said. "But Rebels with those little weapons fired at us from inside the buildings."

The mage-officer watched his men manhandling boxes, bales, barrels, and even wagons into some sort of rampart. "This way, they'll have to come into the open to get at us, and we'll be able to fire back with crossbows."

"You're acting as if you're completely isolated, sir," Blaize said.

The officer glanced to make sure his men weren't close enough to overhear as he spoke in a low voice. "For all practical purposes, we are. This uprising has spread all over the city. A number of patrols were overwhelmed. Lord Scarbro sent a messenger to the upper city asking for reinforcements. He also ordered mage-writs dispatched to all nearby garrisons, commanding them to march here at once."

Blaize found a sudden surge of sympathy for the commander. Such a direct admission of failure would probably wreck his career. But like a true warrior, his concern was stopping this rebellion rather than salvaging his reputation.

"Why did you come down here, Altem?" the mage asked. Blaize also caught his silent query—*Why isn't anyone else coming to help?*

"We bear messages for Lord Scarbro on the situation above," Blaize replied. He, too, lowered his voice. "The Prophet-Magus has been assassinated. All liftgates have been secured."

The mage-officer didn't seem to know which news was worse. "You want to get to the reservoir from here?" He looked at his troopers and at the guardsmen already laid on the pavement, wounded or dead. "I can't spare a detail."

Blaize had already made that calculation, and was glad. The last thing he or Snow needed was an escort to make sure they got to Scarbro. "Then we'll have to try and blend in." He stepped behind the thrown-together wall and removed his armor and helmet.

The last time I'll wear Atlantean battle regalia, he thought.

He was joined by the mage-officer. "Your most direct route would be from the western edge of the plaza," the Imperial said. "I'll take some men off to the east and create a diversion."

It was a brave offer, putting the officer in certain danger. Of course, until Blaize and Snow contacted the Rebels, they were in danger, too.

Blaize drew his sword, Snow his knife. The young mage took three crossbowmen and set off in the opposite direction. Immediately, sharp, popping sounds broke out, followed by the greater explosion of a magical blast.

The two Rebels broke into a run for the edge of the plaza, hoping they wouldn't be hit by fire from their own side. Reaching a street, they continued to pound along until they came to an intersection. They whipped round, and out of sight of the Imperials at last, Snow opened the oilcloth bundle slung across his back to remove his weapon.

"Fuser rifle," he identified it for Blaize. "Long barrel, long range. The little poppers you hear are called pistols. They're accurate to about crossbow range."

Projectile weapons, not polearms, Blaize thought, comparing Snow's weapon with the one he'd seen from a distance weeks ago.

"How far is that good for?" Blaize asked, gesturing to the long barrel.

"It was good enough to take Karrudan in the heart from the length of Throne Palace Square," Snow replied.

"You took Karrudan?" a voice blurted from behind them.

Blaize and Snow whirled round to discover a group of men emerging from the basement of a building. A couple were similar to the hard young types Blaize had seen at Perrin's inn. They carried the weapons Snow called pistols. But there were others, of all shapes and ages. A skinny lad flourished an axe that looked as if it was used to cut kindling—except now the blade bore bloodstains. A strapping young man, a blacksmith's apprentice from his build and leather apron, had chosen a heavy hammer as his weapon. A couple of shifty-looking types, probably professional cutpurses, had knives and well-worn cudgels. A half-starved older man carried a four-foot length of pipe. Others waved chair legs and other improvised weapons.

So many different sorts of people, but the same thing showed in their eyes. Blaize remembered his mother's lament. *How many of them hate us?*

"Nice popper you've got there," one of Perrin's pistol-wielders said. "That true, what you said about the great purple cheese up there?"

"It was my job," Snow replied matter-of-factly. "We wanted to show what our rifles could do—and what better symbol to start with than the head mage?"

He glanced around. "Now we have to report in to Perrin, Valerian, or Sarah. Any idea where they might be?"

"The Mills," the gunslinger said. "They're running everything from the inn."

Blaize stared, aghast. "You can't be serious. They're telling everyone where they are? Even people"—he gestured at the group—"in the field?"

The young man raised his pistol. "You have some problem with that?"

"No—but *they'll* have a problem if you get captured. I can't believe Valerian would let this happen. It's just a question of time before Scarbro knows where our commanders are."

"So?" the young fighter said. "We know where Scarbro is—down in Tezla's Pit, at the reservoir."

Blaize nodded. "And if you tried to attack him, you'd be up against most of the garrison-trained soldiers. Do you think you could get through them?"

The gunslinger opened his mouth to give an angry retort, then looked down. "Guess not, or we'd be trying it."

Blaize nodded grimly. "Now look at it the other way. Suppose these trained soldiers are heading for the place where our irreplaceable leaders are. Can you stop them?"

The young man's face went white. "We'd best be heading in with a warning."

They set off through the streets, Blaize and Snow in the lead, a long, trailing procession behind them as those who couldn't keep pace fell back. But before they'd gone even three blocks, they heard shouts—more like howls—rising from off to their right.

Following the sounds, they came upon the remains of an Imperial patrol surrounded by a furious mob. The uprising had apparently caught the soldiers in the midst of a ramshackle market square. The Imperials had gone to ground among some of the stalls and tables, with benches and crates piled upon them as a barricade, using their crossbows to keep the crowd at bay.

If the whole horde of people jostling in the streets attacked, their numbers could have overwhelmed the defenders. But they were rabble, not trained soldiers. No one wanted to lead the way and die for it. So paving stones and bottles flew one way, and the occasional crossbow bolt winged the other.

"Might as well do for them on our way," the young gunslinger said. He turned to the crowd. "What's the problem, you great lumps of Troll scat? You think you're going to live forever?"

The young man aimed his pistol, shot down a crossbowman, and charged. His group followed, and then the roaring crowd joined in. Blaize stood where he was. They could just as easily have bypassed these bedraggled Imperials. He saw no reason to make the mob's job easier. Snow, however, began manipulating his weapon, raising it to his shoulder.

Snow's long gun had a deeper, more bellowing roar than the pistols. His every shot was aimed, and each took down one of the enemy soldiers. The lighter popping of the pistols was more frequent, more hurried. Blaize noticed the young gunslingers often missed.

"I've had practice," Snow said. "These lads are learning while they fight."

Blaize watched while one of the young men broke open his pistol to load it, then staggered back, a crossbow bolt in his neck. Even as he fell, though, the crowd was over the hastily built defense wall like a wave striking a sand castle.

Shaking his head, Blaize moved forward to the stricken gunman. He looked much younger as he lay still on the ground, staining the pavement with his blood.

"Mama!" he cried, his voice bubbling. "Ma—" He shuddered, and lay still.

Blaize took the pistol from slack fingers.

"You'll want the bag hanging across his chest," Snow said, appearing beside Blaize. "That's where the lad kept his cartridges."

They left the mob to its butchery and ran on toward the Mills of Circumstance. As they came closer to the inn, they heard growing sounds of gunfire. Thick clouds of smoke obscured the sky.

"I can't believe all that is coming from our black powder," Snow said.

"Remember Caero?" Blaize shook his head, grim experience showing in his face. "Riots breed fires."

Sudden shooting broke out almost ahead of them. Blaize and Snow ran forward, to find a group of Rebels huddling behind heaps of furniture blocking the street.

They must have pulled this stuff out of the houses on either side, Blaize realized.

The few Rebels with pistols crouched behind what cover they could find, reloading and rising to pepper shots farther down the roadway.

About seventy paces away, a company of Imperials came forward at the double. The Utems' spears were useless at that range, and their shields offered no protection from the bullets. Men cried out and fell to the pavement. The Utem crossbowmen were doing their best to lay down a covering fire, but they were taking losses, too.

Blaize checked his own pistol and advanced to a firing position.

Open. Tear the cartridge. Pour the powder. Snap it closed again. He cocked the trigger, squeezed . . . and was rewarded with a hollow *snap!* instead of a *bang!*

"You've got to prime it," one of the pistoleers beside him called. "Put a little powder in the pan."

"Oh. Right." Blaize dribbled a little powder from another cartridge, cocked, and fired.

An Altem spun, clutching his shoulder.

"Back! Back!" someone began screaming. "They've got a mage!"

The center of the barricade vanished with the impact of a magical blast. Blaize was knocked flat. He was up on his knees, blindly trying to reload, when he spotted a flash of gold and purple well behind the advancing Imperial battle line.

Stepping to the side so he could better direct his next attack, the mage raised his arms. Blaize got to his feet, trying to aim his pistol, knowing the range was too great. The deep-throated blast of a rifle roared out from behind him.

A neat hole appeared where the Imperial officer's Magestone implant had been a moment before. The mage all but flipped into a somersault, revealing the red ruin the back of his head had become.

Even without the officer's help, however, the remnants of the company were too close, and that last blast had cleared a way through the Rebels' defenses.

"Get out of here! Get back!" a voice yelled in Blaize's ear. Even as he staggered in retreat, someone threw a burning torch onto one of the piles. It landed on a straw ticking, which promptly burst into flame.

The resulting smoke gave Blaize a racking cough, but covered him so that he could get out of there.

As he fell back along the street, Blaize found Rebels who didn't have the new weapons breaking into more houses, dragging out the makings of another barricade.

We can slow them, as long as we can give ground, the tactical side of his brain pointed out. *But we can't stop them. This company is just out protecting the flanks. Where is the main column heading?*

Trying to find out involved Blaize and Snow in a succession of swirling streetfights. Disorganized groups of Rebels tried and failed to stop the advance of Imperial flankers. Their defense line—if they ever had one—was being pushed back to the breaking point.

Somewhere in the confusion, Blaize got separated from Snow. He continued trying to reach the inn, sometimes getting involved in wild running combats over several blocks, sometimes managing to skirt the fighting.

He reached the square fronting the Mills of Circumstance just in time for the last-ditch resistance. One end of the open space was packed with Imperials. Scarbro must have committed the bulk of his force to this spearhead, hoping to decapitate the beast of rebellion before it could rear up in full strength.

Bereft of leadership from Sarah, Valerian, Eginhard, and Perrin, the uprising would undoubtedly degenerate into a simple riot. There would be plenty of damage; many would die. But the true danger to the Empire would be averted.

The little knot of Rebel commanders stood behind a horn-shaped earthen breastwork piled up before them. They also had a flag of sorts—a bedsheet painted with a crude symbol. It looked like a shield intersecting a larger, darker circle.

Blaize felt sick. The person holding the pole for this improvised banner was Rikka.

Attempting to shield her and the others from the gathering Imperial might was a thin line of defenders sheltering behind yet another street barricade.

At least the Rebels had been able to put some time and thought into this construction. They hadn't gotten their materials from five minutes of hasty pillaging. Large barrels and crates had been moved from nearby warehouses. Heavy wagons had been overturned. Maybe some of the big tuns had come from the inn's cellars. Blaize saw one group of defenders weakening their defense wall by broaching one of the huge barrels and drinking the contents.

They'd even dug up the paving stones and heaped earth on their rampart, creating a sort of ditch or moat before the wall. Even so, Blaize could tell that it wouldn't hold against the gathering force of professional soldiers. It couldn't.

Blaize had been an Imperial guardsman. He knew that the bronze-armored machine at the far end of the square would advance as implacably as any Golem, accepting losses, dealing out death, until it broke through.

Sarah and the others had to know it, too. So why were they hanging themselves out like some sort of sacrificial offering? Was it simple suicide because their plan hadn't worked? Did Sarah believe she'd attained her vengeance against Karrudan and now didn't need anything else?

This is going to get us all killed, Blaize thought.

He found an empty place on the wall and checked his pistol.

The battle array before them comprised a spear wall in the middle with clouds of crossbowmen at the flanks. Heavy bolts flew through the air as the flank parties tried to provide cover fire. The return volley from the Rebels was more ragged—but also more deadly. The bowmen had to stand to restring their weapons. The pistol-armed Rebels could remain crouched under cover, barely exposing themselves to fire.

They can reload faster, too, Blaize thought as he slammed his gun together, aimed, and brought down another crossbowman.

The space needed for ammunition was much smaller—a pouch versus a quiver.

If these weapons survive, they may truly change the course of warfare. After that, Blaize no longer had time for intellectual appreciation of the battle. His only calculation was how many enemies he could bring down before the Imperial line reached the barricade.

The hard answer was, not enough. They hurt the guardsmen, all but wiping out those with ranged weapons. Their galling fire slowed the spear line. The Rebels bloodied the advancing Imperials, creating gaps in the line. But those gaps were always filled by men from the rear ranks.

Occasional blasts of rifle fire kept the mages too far back to make themselves useful. So it was down to the superb discipline of the infantry. By the time they were close enough to hurl their spears, Blaize could read the faces on the oncoming soldiers. They were furious at suffering so horribly at the hands of the despised Down-Towner rabble.

As they unsheathed their swords, the Imperials were determined to use them for slaughter.

The popping of pistol fire grew even more rapid, more desperate. There was no longer a need to aim. They were facing a human wall mere yards away.

Blaize fired, managed to fire again . . .

The Imperials were in the trench. Blaize fired another shot. Beside him, a gunslinger howled as a blade swung blindly over the wall amputated both hand and pistol.

People were running now. Blaize fired point-blank into an Utem's contorted face as the guardsman came over the rampart.

A great noise came from the Imperials as they surmounted the wall—part victory cry, part animal snarl.

Blaize found himself alone.

Then someone was tugging at his arm. "Get back! Out of the way!"

It was Sigwold, armed with an axe and a torch. A hasty shove sent Blaize staggering back while the Dwarf hurled the axe, not at the enemy, but into the middle of the defenses. The blazing brand followed, landing on a pile of strangely familiar barrels. One had been stove open, leaking a trail of black powder . . .

There was a sudden hiss, and the world vanished in a sudden, brilliant glare.

Blaize seemed to be flying, but not with the steady ascent of a liftgate. He felt as if he'd been caught up by a giant wind and flung away.

Something soft suddenly impeded his progress. Then Blaize found himself tumbling along the pavement, finally coming to a stop just in front of the inn door.

Bruised and dazed, ears ringing, he managed to get himself up on his hands and knees.

Before him was a crater, blown deep into the surface of the earth. Around it staggered burned, blind, bleeding, and dismembered Imperials.

The Empire's war machine had abruptly run out of momentum.

And then a storm of lead sleeted into the face of the stunned warriors.

Blaize could make out the lighter barks of pistol fire, joined with the deeper blasts of fuser rifles. There were more guns at work now than he'd heard on the firing line of what he'd thought was the Rebellion's last-ditch defense.

Sarah and the others had indeed been holding themselves out—not as a sacrifice, but as bait to tempt Scarbro into committing his forces. The Rebel leaders had also been regathering all the gunslingers they'd sent out to spearhead the uprising.

Blaize couldn't tell how much firepower had been assembled. There were riflemen in the inn windows and on roofs of buildings overlooking the square. Young men with pistols were massing and moving forward, firing as they went.

The Imperial guardsmen, victory literally blasted out of their hands, tried to stand. They were the best-trained, steadiest human warriors in the Land. But human flesh can only take so much.

As the withering fire continued, the Imperial ranks wavered, then disintegrated.

Still firing into the running fugitives, the Rebels cheered a sight few had ever seen—an Imperial warhost in full retreat.

The gunfire slackened, but voices rose in harsh argument. Some of the more hotheaded Rebels screamed for pursuit, eager to settle some more scores with the fleeing guardsmen.

"Do that." Valerian's voice overrode them with surprising clarity. "Scarbro has reserves out there, and by now he'll have fixed positions of his own. They should cut you up handily." Blaize managed to focus his eyes enough to make out the Elf giving the dissidents his most demonic smile. "Just don't expect us to rush off to our deaths beside you."

"Then what's the good of it?" a frustrated voice demanded.

"What's the good of it?" Sarah Ythlim's voice rang out—from where, Blaize couldn't quite see. "We've removed the Empire's evil genius and beaten the Empire's army on its own ground. What more can you ask for from a day's work?"

"But the Imperial pigs are still out there!" another voice complained.

"Did you expect to change everything in a day?" Sarah strode into Blaize's view. "Yes, the Imperials are still out there, but they're on the defensive now. That gives us time. How you use that time will be up to you. I intend to head north. There's a Magestone mine nearby—I intend to liberate the slaves the Imperials are keeping there. And there are more mines, cities, towns . . . All your lives, the Empire has told you that you're mere dust, ground up by the Mills of Circumstance."

She pointed at the sign on the inn, now hanging askew from the blast. "But our dust—black powder—has changed all that. I'm a Black Powder Rebel, and I'll be fighting until everyone oppressed by the Empire is free. What about you?"

There were cheers for that, but Blaize didn't join in. It was enough of a job getting himself upright and into some sort of motion.

The blast that had stopped the Imperials had sent him plowing right through the earthworks defending the Rebel command post. He moved forward, stumbled over something, and looked down.

Blaize's heart lurched. He was standing on the Rebels' painted-bedsheet flag, torn and blackened from the explosion.

Rikka?

He broke into a shambling trot, his head down to look at bodies, afraid of what he'd see.

Then Blaize crashed into Eginhard, doing the same thing. The Dwarf looked singed and bloody . . . and his eyes were full of tears.

No, a chilled voice cried out in Blaize's skull. *No, no, no, no, no!*

"The lads who were supposed to set off the black powder barrels either fled or died," Eginhard said in a bleak voice. "Three of us went to finish the job. I ran into some Imperials who'd made it over the wall. Perrin . . . I didn't see what happened to him." Then anthracite eyes under shaggy brows looked pleadingly up at Blaize. "Have you seen my brother?"

"Yes—he got to the powder with a torch and stopped the Imperials," Blaize said. "He saved us all. That much I saw. But beyond that . . ."

The Dwarf's shoulders slumped as he turned away, resuming his search of the dead.

"Wait!" Blaize desperately called. "What about Rikka?"

"Blaize!" cried a voice he'd feared he'd never hear again. "Gods above! There you are!"

He turned, nearly falling under the impact of a slim, strong form that clung to him. And in spite of bruises and scrapes, Blaize embraced Rikka just as fiercely. Blaize rested his cheek on Rikka's red hair, which smelled strongly of black powder residue.

"Here we stand, arms around each other—filthy as usual," Rikka said.

Blaize found himself laughing even as he blinked away tears. "Well, I can stand it if you can."

She looked up at him. "As long as I can stand by you."

"We'll just have to get used to it," he said more somberly. "Sarah's right, you know. This won't be over today, or tomorrow, or any time soon."

"It will be a hard world for Kennet to grow up in." Rikka sighed.

We'll just have to fight to make it a better one, Blaize thought.

They remained clasped together, silently contemplating a most uncertain future.

At least they would face it together.

Rebel Thunder Scenario
Caero Is Burning
Black Powder Rebels vs. Atlantis Guild

Now that you've read *Mage Knight: Rebel Thunder,* play out the scene in which the Rebels escape from Caero, with your very own **Mage Knight™** figures, brought to you by WizKids games!

Mage Knight is a collectable miniatures game in which players take on the role of leaders commanding squads of fearsome warriors to victory! **Mage Knight:** *Unlimited* Starter Sets are available at most game and hobby stores. These Starter Sets contain everything a single player will need to play this scenario: rules, figures, a ruler, and dice.

For more information on the game, and the ever-growing **Mage Knight** world, visit our Web site at www.mageknight.com. If you want to get involved in the **Mage Knight** storyline, know that every month hundreds of stores all over the world participate in the **Mage Knight** Campaign series. Each victory in these Campaigns affects the course of the **Mage Knight** story! Each week's winner receives a special Limited Edition figure and a specially designed pin. Additionally, because WizKids is a strong proponent of sporting play, at the end of each night of Campaign play the participating players in each store vote for the player who was the most fair, helpful, and courteous—and that player gets a special figure and pin as well!

We hope you enjoyed *Mage Knight: Rebel Thunder,* and we hope that the following scenario intrigues you, whether you are an experienced **Mage Knight** fanatic or a player who's new to the scene!

Background

By setting fire to a section of Caero, the warriors and mages of the Atlantis Guild attempt to arrange the mass capture of as many Rebel spies as possible. The Black Powder Rebels must successfully escape the Atlantean trap or face imprisonment by the Empire!

Objective
This scenario is intended for two players. The Rebels player is attempting to rush past the Atlantean defenders, while the Atlantean player is trying to capture or eliminate as many Rebel figures as possible.

Army Size
Two-player game, with 200 points per player. Player 1 represents the Atlantis Guild. Player 2 represents the Black Powder Rebels.

Time Limit
50 minutes

Rules Set
Mage Knight: *Unlimited*

Preparing the Battlefield
Clear a 3´ x 3´ space for play, then set up terrain as shown on the Battlefield Map. Terrain pieces F, G, and H are considered to be blocking terrain. Terrain piece templates can be found on the WizKids Web site. If you don't have access to our Web site, you can use cans of soup, pepper shakers, or any other household object to represent the houses and shops in the district.

Special Rules
1. Caero is burning! At the beginning of each player's turn, that player rolls one die. If a player rolls a 4, 5, or 6, he or she chooses one building to set on fire. Note the burning building with a token (such as a penny). At the end of any player's turn, any figure with its center within 1″ of any burning building takes 1 click of damage.
2. The Rebels must escape! Any noncaptured Rebel figure that ends the game in the Atlantis Guild starting area is worth an extra 20 victory points.

Victory Conditions

Use standard **Mage Knight:** *Unlimited* victory conditions, and add the points as described in Special Rule 2.

Battlefield Map

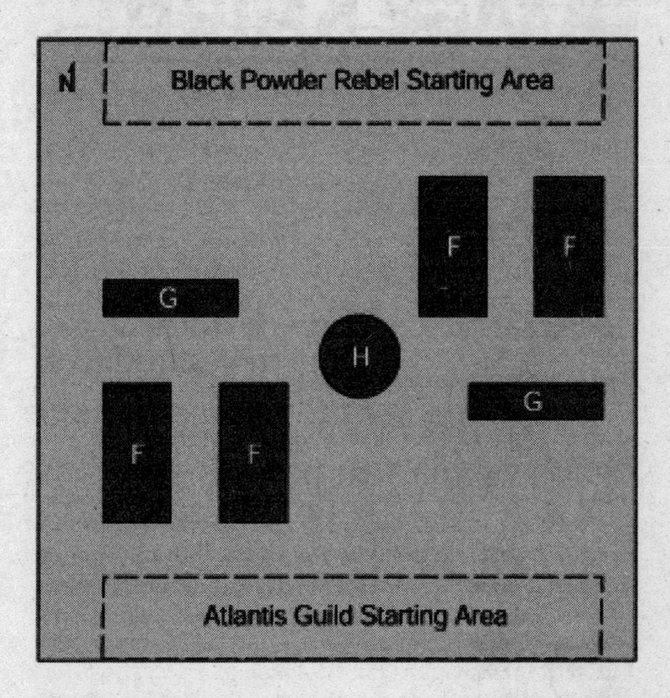